Stolen Hearts Series

MELODY J. WILLIAMS

For Callen. The boy who lived through the unimaginable. Your smile is magic. I'm so blessed to call you mine. Always and forever.

1

MACKENZIE

W ow. Today was really one for the books. You know . . . the kind of books you douse in an entire quart of lighter fluid, hold a match to them, and watch them ignite in an explosion of angry flames? Yeah. It was one of those days.

It all started when I arrived at work. Anything and everything went wrong—malfunctioning equipment, missing memory cards, coffee spills, overdue rush orders, printer jams, seething customers. If there were ever a day that would have finally convinced me to leave Ellwood Photography behind for good, this would have been it. Why didn't I quit the stressful job I hated? The answer was simple: I was good at my job, and I had no idea where I wanted to go from here.

When I lifted my time card and pulled it through the strike stick, swiping my way to freedom at last, a great release of tension washed over my body. It was like an anesthetic, temporarily numbing the last remaining bits of work-related stress plaguing my mind—for the weekend, anyway.

I secured my purse strap over my shoulder and walked toward the employee exit, pausing only to switch off the lights and set the alarm on the building.

The brisk night air prickled my skin as I stepped out into the hazy darkness—a bit unusual for the middle of April in Mesa, Arizona, but not unwelcome. The streetlight overhead flickered erratically, giving the abandoned parking lot an eerily pulsating glow and sending an unpleasant flutter of nerves to the pit of my stomach. *Stupid streetlight.* I lengthened my stride and crossed the parking lot to my Ford Ranger as quickly as my tired feet would allow.

An owl hooted mournfully from a nearby tree. I immediately glanced over my shoulder, fumbling to find the keyhole in the dark. I don't know why, but I just had this creepy feeling, like I was being watched. "That's it! No more *Unsolved Mysteries* before bed," I muttered into the darkness, appalled at the ball of nerves I had become.

My frustration increased as I continued to struggle with the door lock, forcing me to reach for my phone and open up the flashlight app. *Finally.* I slid my phone back in my pocket, swung open the door, plopped into the driver's seat, and set my purse down on the floor. I stuck the key into the ignition and turned. Nothing. Not even a hum or a sputter.

"No, no, no! Come on, Beasty! Don't die on me now!" I tried again. No click. Nothing. "Ugh!" The piece of trash battery was only two months old. I slammed my palm against the steering wheel. Hard. *Ow.* I shook out my hand to try to ease the throbbing.

Just perfect. I was a sitting duck. Alone. In the dark.

After locking the door, I removed my cell phone from my pants pocket, opened my contacts list, and scrolled down to Sydney Freeman. I rubbed my still stinging hand up and down my thigh as I waited for my roommate to answer the call.

"Hey, Kenz!" Sydney's melodic voice greeted me. "What's up? Are you finally on your way?"

The muffled rumble of conversation sounded through the speaker, reminding me that I was interrupting her game night. I felt terrible. My truck literally couldn't have picked a more inconvenient time to crap out on me. Well . . . maybe that wasn't exactly true. At least she wasn't on a date.

I inhaled a steadying breath. "My truck won't start. Can you please come get me?"

"You're kidding!"

"Unfortunately not," I said. "I'm so sorry, Syd. I know it's not the greatest timing."

"Don't worry," she assured me kindly. "I'll be right there."

"Thank you," I replied, ending the call and shoving the phone back into my pocket.

I tossed the keys into my purse with a sigh, then rested my head on the steering wheel and closed my eyes to block out the creepy scene surrounding me. Strobing streetlight. Abandoned parking lot. Yeah, that's totally not the perfect setting for a murder. I breathed in deeply, willing my irrational fears to calm. *Nobody is watching me. I am completely safe.*

Besides, it was only nine in the evening. Murderers didn't come out until midnight, right?

I mentally visualized how I was going to get my truck up and running before seven-thirty tomorrow morning; the dull ache of stress started to build at the back of my neck. *Autozone* was already closed for the night and wouldn't open again until seven. *Ugh!*

A little sooner than I expected, headlights flashed across my windshield. I slowly lifted my head, thinking I'd see Sydney's white Nissan Altima, but instead, I found a blue Chevy Silverado pulling up in front of me. *Who is that?*

My heart started working double-time when a tall man in a dark shirt hopped out of the driver's seat. He reached into his truck to retrieve something I couldn't see and tucked it into the brim of his jeans. *What's he doing?* I strained to focus on the stranger in the dim light, searching for something, anything familiar about him, to put my mind at ease. When he finally turned his gaze on me and started heading my way in long, determined strides, my stomach dropped to my feet. There was nothing—not one single glimmer of recognition. *What should I do?* My palms started sweating. *Remain . . . calm.*

A glint of shiny black metal captured my attention as he walked in front of the glowing headlights of his truck. My blood ran cold. That thing he tucked into his pants was a gun.

Oh . . . I'm dead, I'm dead. I'm dead!

My pulse raced, and my heart pounded in my head like a drum. I never should have put off taking those self-defense classes. With shaky hands, I grabbed my purse and reached for my pocket-sized taser, feeling totally unprepared for an altercation and yet completely resigned to zap the attacker as many times as necessary for my escape. *If only my stupid battery weren't dead, I could just drive away!*

Come on, Mackenzie! You're a problem solver. You can figure this out.

Headlights. Yes! He left the engine idling for a fast getaway. A crazy idea popped into my mind. *If I could just get into his truck . . .*

The clock was ticking. He was almost at my door. My mind scrambled to make sense of the ludicrous plan. Was it even possible? I could stay in the locked cabin of my Ranger and crouch to the floorboards . . . but was that really the safest option?

Ha! Who was I kidding? With a gun in the equation, the only "safe choice" was compliance.

I remembered the woman on TV who mysteriously vanished and was never seen or heard from again. *This guy could make me disappear.*

I wasn't going to let that happen.

Just as the guy lifted his hand to presumably tap on the window and lure me out, I unlocked the door and slammed it hard against his body, taking him by surprise and knocking him back a step or two. With adrenaline coursing through my veins, I held tight to my purse and sprinted from my Ranger toward his Silverado.

"Wait!" the assailant demanded, halting my progress as his hand enclosed around my stupid purse strap.

I screamed and tased his arm, causing his fingers to lock around the leather strap in an unbreakable grip. He growled and reached for my taser with his other hand. I panicked and dropped the weapon to the ground, then wrenched my purse free in the commotion, and dashed for his truck. I didn't dare look behind me, but his fast, scraping steps across the asphalt told me he wasn't far behind.

I yanked the door open and grabbed the steering wheel, pulling my body into the driver's seat and slammed the door just in time. I hit the lock a millisecond before he pulled on the handle. He banged on the window, effectively drowning out whatever profanities I imagined he was trying to yell at me through the glass. I ignored the fleeting impulse to listen to what the man had to say, and reached for the gearshift instead.

I drove like a madwoman out of the parking lot, tires squealing, laughing in disbelief that my plan had actually worked.

"I'm still alive!" I cried aloud, my pounding heart finally starting to calm as I drove farther away from the creep.

"Holy . . . I just stole a car!" The realization hit me like a ton of bricks. My stomach churned with a fresh wave of anxiety. How the heck was I supposed to explain myself to the police? Technically, my attacker hadn't laid one finger on me, because I never gave him the chance. The guy didn't even try to shoot me. Did I overreact? I rubbed at the worry lines on my forehead and groaned.

No. I reassured myself with a shake of my head. I acted out of fear for my life.

But would the police believe that?

They had to believe me. I was the victim. *He* was the criminal preying on innocent women, not me.

Safely a few blocks away, my mind began to clear.

Oh no. Sydney! She was coming to pick me up. I needed to call her ASAP and warn her to turn back. Then I would call the police.

Come on, Syd, pick up the phone!

On the last ring, she finally answered. "Kenz! Did Tanner help you solve your car problem?"

"Tanner? Who's Tanner?" I could hear voices laughing in the background. Sydney was still at the house. *Why hadn't she left yet?* I started getting this funny twisting feeling in my gut, as if I knew I was going to dread the next words out of her mouth.

"The guy who volunteered to go rescue you. He should've arrived by now."

No! I gasped as I pieced together the ugly truth. "Does he happen to drive a blue Silverado, by chance?" *Please say no. Please say no!*

"Yeah, that's him."

"Oh no . . ."

"What is it?" she asked, her voice a mix of confusion and amusement.

I hijacked my rescuer's truck! Mortified, I turned around at the first possible opportunity and raced back to the photography studio— while going the speed limit, of course.

"Kenz?"

I had forgotten Sydney was still on the line. "Why didn't you tell me some guy was coming to help me?" I demanded.

"I guess I forgot to text you." She chuckled. "Is everything okay?"

No, I freaking tased the guy and stole his truck! I wanted to yell into the phone, but I kept the embarrassing declaration to myself. *Ugh!* "Yeah, just peachy. I have to go now. Bye." I ended the call without waiting for a reply and dropped my phone into my purse with a growl of frustration. "I'm such an idiot!" I needed to deliver one incredibly big apology to a complete stranger, and I was quite certain that nothing I said or did would ever make this better. I wouldn't be surprised if this Tanner guy decided to rip me out of his truck and leave me behind without a second glance the very moment I arrived.

I slowly coasted into the parking lot and pulled up next to my Ranger. Tanner leaned against the driver's side of my truck with arms folded across his broad chest. I couldn't make out his expression in the dim light, but I was certain he must be plenty upset. If some crazy person stole my truck when I came to help them, I would be fuming mad.

He stood perfectly still as I got out of his car and sheepishly approached with my eyes trailing the ground beneath my feet. My head throbbed and my stomach toiled with nerves. I finally looked up to see an unmistakably gorgeous face, even in shadow, clearly annoyed by my very existence. *Oh, why does he have to be so good-looking? Worst night of my life!*

I swallowed and found my voice at last. "So you're a Chevy guy. I have to admit the Z71 Silverado is nicer than I expected. Drives like a dream. I like the way it looks with the all-terrain tires. Are they new?"

He lifted his brows in apparent disbelief and just stared at me in deafening silence.

Okay . . . small talk to take the edge off is definitely a bust. I cleared my throat and tried again. "Look, Sydney didn't tell me a guy was coming to rescue me. I thought you were a murderer trying to abduct me. I can't even express how sorry I am." Still, he stared at me without saying a single word, his expression unchanged, so I said, "If I had known who you were, I never would have tased you . . . or shoved you with the door . . . or hijacked your truck." My cheeks were burning with shame. "I promise I have never done anything like that before in my life. I am truly so sorry."

He blinked and exhaled slowly, his shoulders relaxing a fraction as his arms dropped to his sides. I internally debated whether or not I should offer to make him apology brownies. I doubted it would help any. I bit my lip and stared at his deliciously muscular arms instead. They weren't overly huge, like he was trying to brag about how much he could lift. They were a more ordinary size that looked trim but strong. I could hardly believe I had brutally assaulted one of those arms with ten thousand volts of electricity. I forced my eyes to meet his gaze with an extra rippling of remorse. "How's your arm?" I asked quietly.

He extended his right hand, palm up, to show me. A small discoloration of the skin marred his forearm. Although it was hard to tell in this lighting, I figured it was probably a burn mark.

I cringed with regret and nearly jumped when he finally spoke to me. "I'm going to need my keys back."

It wasn't the ferocious growl I had expected, but my heart still sank at the command. He was leaving me, and I didn't blame him. Not one little bit. I nodded solemnly and relinquished his keys without a word. He secured the red lanyard around his neck and stretched out his hand again. "Now yours."

My brows lowered in confusion. "What?"

"Give me your keys."

I immediately fished the keys from my purse and handed them over, too, not really sure why he wanted them. He opened the unlocked door of my Ranger and leaned over the driver's seat. After sticking the key in the ignition, he turned over the motor, and my truck roared to life.

"What? How did you? There's no way."

Tanner stepped away from my truck and mumbled out a gruff, "You're welcome," when he passed me by. I stared after him, completely speechless, as he revved his own engine to life and disappeared around the corner in seconds.

I inhaled a ragged breath, climbed into my truck, and slammed the door behind me. After buckling my seat belt, I shifted into drive and headed home in utter shame. I was never going to live this down. This was, without a doubt, the most humiliating night of my life.

2

TANNER

I sped away from Sydney's crazy roommate, exhaling with a loud groan. *So this is what it feels like to have your butt handed to you by a woman.* If the guys on my squad ever found out about this, they'd never let me forget it for the rest of my career.

I rubbed the back of my neck, wondering how I'd let things spiral so far out of control. It all started with that dumb game night. I never should have let Mom talk me into going in the first place. I moved back home to help her lift Hunter in and out of his wheelchair while Dad recovered from surgery—not to check out the gaggle of cackling women living across the street.

"Go spend some time with Sydney and her friends," Mom had said. *"It'll be fun,"* she'd said.

Ha! In the twenty minutes I'd spent in that house, I had learned everything I needed to know. Not one of those delicate spring flowers could handle the stress of being a police officer's wife, and no amount of love or undying devotion would ever be enough to change that. Trust me, I knew. All too well.

The second the opportunity to escape had arisen, I'd seized it without hesitation. Little did I know I was about to experience the biggest embarrassment of my adult life.

I had to hand it to Mackenzie—she had some serious survival instincts. Even though she'd tased me and stolen my truck, I couldn't help but admire the woman a little for her presence of mind in an intense situation. She wasn't like any woman I'd ever met before— gutsy enough to defend herself and steal my truck, and mature enough to come back and apologize when she realized her mistake. She knew a bit about my truck, too, which was unexpected, coming from a woman—not that women couldn't know cars; it was just, I hadn't ever met one who did.

While Mackenzie ran off with my truck, I'd popped the hood of her old Ranger to troubleshoot why her car wouldn't start. I was surprised by the lack of grease and gunk in the engine bay. At the time, I'd assumed she must have a very thorough mechanic, but now I was starting to wonder if she did her own maintenance. *A twenty-something woman fixing her own vehicle?* I scoffed and shook my head. *Not likely.* She wouldn't have needed my help tightening a loose battery connection if she did.

She probably just threw around her limited car knowledge to try to impress me. I hated that it'd almost worked. I sighed and loosened my grip on the steering wheel, mentally and physically exhausted from a long and trying day.

I flexed my right forearm, which still felt a little tender, and glanced down at the small red mark where the taser had made contact with my skin. It was nothing to get excited about. Probably wouldn't even leave a scar. I'm sure my experience with "riding the lightning" in the academy helped. Police-level taser guns hurt so much worse than the wussy pink thing Mackenzie carried.

Well . . . had carried, really. The poor excuse for a weapon was currently in my pocket. I had meant to give it back to her but was too distracted by the woman's incessant groveling to remember back at the studio. Okay, okay. She wasn't groveling; she was funny and sincere. And if I'm being completely honest with myself, her voice was annoyingly soothing. Somehow, she'd drained just about every last bit of irritation right out of my system. It was alarming, and so I did what I do best—I escaped.

I pulled up in front of my parents' house, parked on the street and killed the engine, waiting patiently for the ninja-thief to arrive. I didn't doubt the woman could take care of herself, but still, I wanted to make sure she got home safely. You never can trust those old Ford trucks.

Her black Ranger turned down Javelina Avenue and pulled up onto the driveway across the street from where I sat. I watched and waited, expecting her to exit the truck and disappear into the house right away, but she didn't seem to be in any hurry to go inside. She just sat there in her truck, staring at the house.

What is she waiting for?

I was about to give up on my brilliant plan to stay out of sight when the door of her Ranger swung open. Mackenzie stepped down, secured her purse over her shoulder, and shut the door gently, as if she didn't want to announce her arrival to anyone in the house. She crossed the corner of the grassy lawn, passed the front door, and stopped at the side gate.

What is the crazy woman doing now?

After sorting through her keys, she stood on tiptoes and hooked her arm over the top of the gate, probably searching for a padlock on the other side.

She's avoiding the game night, too. I didn't know why, but the thought made me smile.

Mackenzie brought her hand back over to her side of the fence and shook it out before reaching over the top again. Obviously, she was struggling to reach the padlock. *Must be tough being so short.* I chuckled to myself, almost glad to see her having such a hard time in a twisted sort of way.

Unbidden, I recalled the words Mom had ingrained into me when I was young. *"Never ignore a person in need."*

Dang conscience.

Did Mackenzie *really* need me, though?

After about thirty seconds of trying to talk myself out of going over there to help, I remembered the taser sitting in my pocket. *I should probably return that to her.*

Grudgingly, I got out of my truck and walked over. The lush winter grass muted the sound of my footsteps enough to escape her notice, so I hung back a few feet as I spoke. "Need any help?"

Mackenzie jumped and shrieked like a frightened cat, then spun around to face me with her hand now buried in her purse. Knowing exactly what she was searching for to defend herself, I dug her taser out of my pocket and held it up. "Looking for this?"

"Oh! It's just you!" She retracted her hand from her purse and placed it over her heart, then momentarily squeezed her eyes shut, probably trying to calm a wave of adrenaline coursing through her veins.

Given our short history together, I wasn't surprised by her jumpy reaction, but I still felt bad for startling her. "I didn't mean to scare you," I said, lowering my hand. "I saw you struggling and thought I'd help." It was the truth, more or less.

Her eyes snapped open, meeting my gaze with a spark of annoyance. "You made me drop my keys."

My eyes darted to the ground for a moment as if I would find her keys lying there in the grass. Why would she be annoyed with me for that? Then it hit me; she dropped them on the other side of the fence. Alright. I could see how that may have thrown a wrench in her plans. It was kind of funny, though.

Mackenzie reached for her taser, I lifted it high in the air just out of her grasp. "Can I trust you with this dangerous weapon?"

She rolled her eyes and placed her hands on her hips. "Yes." She extended her palm out to me expectantly, waiting for me to return what was rightfully hers.

"Good." A hint of amusement tugged at my mouth. This was a different side of the woman I hadn't expected to see. Gone was the girl trying to please. I handed over the taser and watched her stash it in her Mary Poppins bag of tricks. Now . . . on to solving the mystery of why she was trying to sneak in through the backyard. "Do you have something against using front doors?"

Judging by the narrowing of her eyes, Mackenzie didn't appreciate me finding humor in her predicament. "No." Her frown lines softened as she sighed and covered her face in her hands. "I thought you were inside," she admitted quietly.

All this was an attempt to avoid seeing . . . me? My smile slipped away as I considered what that meant. I guess I was guilty of doing the same thing. Only I hadn't just been hiding from *her*; I had been trying to avoid all the women in that house.

"Ugh," she groaned through her hands. "You're right. I'm being dumb. I'm going to go through the front door like I should have done in the first place."

After all the awkwardness I just put myself through, I wasn't going to let a perfectly good escape route go to waste. "No, you're not. You just stay right there," I said, springing into action. In three quick strides, I gripped the top of the six-foot block fence and launched my body over to the other side.

"What are you doing?" she called after me in disbelief.

"Helping." I bent over to retrieve her keys. "You do live here, right?" I couldn't pass up the opportunity to tease her a little more. "You're not trying to steal a house too?" I chuckled to myself as I tackled the lock.

If the silence on the other side of the fence was any indication, Mackenzie was not amused.

When I finished with the latch and swung open the gate, I wasn't surprised to see a scowl on her pretty face. "Too soon?" I asked innocently, as I held out the ASU Sun Devils keychain.

She snatched the keys from my hand. "Trevor or Tyler . . . whatever your name is—"

"Tanner," I provided, kind of amazed that she didn't remember my name—further proof that she wasn't just another girl setting her sights on me.

"Tanner," she corrected, folding her arms across her chest and meeting my gaze. "Thanks for coming to my rescue for the second time tonight." Her voice sounded more exhausted than annoyed. "Now, I hate to be rude, but I've literally had the worst day of my life —even before my truck wouldn't start, it was . . . I don't even want to talk about how bad it was." Her admission piqued my curiosity, but I remained silent as she continued. "So I'm going to go hide under a rock for the next five years and try to forget that any of this ever happened. Again, I'm sorry for what I did to you. If you're lucky, you'll never have to see me again."

Fat chance, considering we're neighbors. Maybe she wasn't aware of that little detail . . .

Before I could even respond, she was pushing me out of her backyard and closing the gate between us. Despite all the awkwardness and the embarrassment we had endured together thus far, I smiled. Mackenzie was definitely something else. And I had to admit, I wouldn't mind seeing her again—if only to see what crazy thing she'd do next.

3

MACKENZIE

Peaceful music pierced through the haze of my unconscious mind, slowly pulling me back to reality. The ceiling glowed with muted gray sunlight, seeping in from the blinds that covered the north-facing window in my room. *Morning already?*

I groaned and reached for my nightstand to silence the soft piano ballad still playing from my phone. Although this morning's alarm was a rendition of Claude Debussy's *Clair De Lune*, one of my favorites, I was in no mood to enjoy it; not after the restless night I'd endured.

I must have spent hours tossing and turning as I ran through a constant stream of scenarios in my head, wondering how I could have handled my interactions with Tanner differently or what exactly had possessed me to react the way I did. Yes, I had a bad day at work. And yes, I enjoyed watching a bit of *Real Crime* and *Unsolved Mysteries* now and again, but was that really cause to lose my freaking mind when I saw his gun?

No, it wasn't.

Apparently, in Arizona, anyone over the age of eighteen can pack some heat. That was an enlightening bit of information that I totally looked up before I went to bed last night. Being born and raised in California where openly carrying firearms in public was illegal, I'd foolishly jumped to conclusions. You know . . . the whole thinking Tanner was a murderer thing.

It was kind of Tanner's fault, though. If he hadn't volunteered to step in for Sydney, everything would've been perfectly fine. Yes, I would've had to deal with replacing a dead battery on my truck today, but I wouldn't have lost any sleep over it. Thanks to the combined efforts of my dad and my car-loving brother, I knew all about vehicle maintenance and how to tackle repairs when necessary. However, just because I knew how to use a few tools, it didn't mean that I liked getting grease under my fingernails.

I guess I should be grateful Tanner somehow fixed my Ranger when I was off making my debut as a car thief, but I didn't quite understand how he had brought the battery back to life without jumper cables. As far as I knew, it couldn't be done with an automatic transmission. So at this point I really didn't know if I should be impressed by his feat or concerned for my safety.

I had other important questions I wanted answered. Like, *why* did he fix my Ranger after I had tased him and took off in his Silverado? Why did he jump in to help me with the lock on the gate? And why the heck did the guy feel it necessary to carry a gun on his hip when coming to help a defenseless woman? Well . . . I guess I'd more than proved I was not as defenseless as some might expect. *That's right. I totally saved myself like a boss!*

But that didn't change the fact that, had he left the gun in his truck, I probably wouldn't have jumped headfirst into full-blown survival mode.

Wondering about the "whys" and the "what ifs" was pointless. It's not like I would ever see him again. And that was fine by me. In fact, more than fine. Without Tanner around to remind me of the most humiliating day of my life, I could pretend the whole thing never happened.

And that was just what I was going to do.

I pushed back my warm cocoon of blankets, flung my legs over the side of the bed, and sat up with determination. Today was a new day, a blank slate, a chance to move on from my mistakes and let go of the last . . . say . . . twenty-four hours? I firmly planted my bare feet onto the cream shaggy carpet, summoned the strength to stand, and began my morning ritual with purpose.

After showering and throwing on some old clothes I wouldn't mind getting stained with paint, I put in my contacts and ran a brush through my long, stick-straight hair. I gathered three small sections of hair at the crown of my head and weaved my thick chocolate mane into a simple French braid to keep it out of my face. Next, I brushed my teeth and applied minimal makeup, grateful I didn't have any stubborn blemishes to cover up today. With little time to spare, I grabbed my purse and sailed down the hall with my keys in hand, trying not to think about the growling of my hungry stomach as I passed the kitchen. *Sorry, body. Don't hate me. I really needed a shower more than food today.*

I stepped out into the cool, spring morning air, locked the door behind me, and turned toward my Ranger in the driveway, wishing the weather would stay this pleasant all day. A Mourning Dove cooed and pulled my gaze from the concrete path to the Ponderosa Pine on the far side of our yard, where the brownish-gray bird nested high in the branches. I smiled softly, picturing an attentive mother waiting for her chicks to hatch.

My smile slipped as something alarmingly familiar appeared in my peripheral vision. I turned and gasped, my jaw falling slack. Tanner's bright blue Silverado was parked across the street, haunting me like an unsightly ghost from my past.

No, no, no! Why? Why does the universe hate me?

I climbed into my vehicle scowling, my mind running a million miles per hour. What was that truck still doing here?

Okay. Best-case scenario: Tanner ironically ended up having car problems of his own and had to get a ride home? It was a stretch, but what else could explain why his truck was still parked there as if it hadn't moved all night?

Worst-case scenario: he came back here . . . to what? To have a morning chat with the psycho that treated him like garbage? Yeah, right. Like he would ever want to see me again. Tanner was more likely to come back for one of my roommates than anything else. Plus, I couldn't see the guy anywhere so . . .

Sydney's car was missing.

That's it! The two of them must have gone somewhere together. With how drop-dead gorgeous Sydney was, I shouldn't be surprised that Tanner had fallen under her spell so quickly. It happened to the best of them.

I wasn't too concerned by this development, because Sydney never held onto their hearts for long. It had something to do with a boy-next-door fantasy that she'd been harboring since the third grade. Apparently, no guy could ever hold a candle to whoever that boy was. I'd give Tanner a week before she lost interest.

That was good, though, wasn't it? Once Sydney kicked Tanner to the curb, I would never have to see him again.

Breathing a little easier now, I turned my key in the ignition, firing my engine to life. *Yes! Tanner really did fix my truck.*

My eyes darted to the rearview mirror as I carefully backed out of the driveway. The garage of my neighbor's house slowly lifted, revealing Mr. Hansen emerging from the darkness. I hadn't ever spoken to the middle-aged man before, but he seemed a good sort, always quick to offer a friendly smile and a wave in passing.

I shifted gears from reverse to drive, straightened out the steering wheel, then pressed on the gas pedal. Anticipating Mr. Hansen's usual greeting, my gaze drifted out the window to acknowledge him as I drove by his house. *Whoa, whoa, wait. That is NOT Mr. Hansen!*

I slammed on the brakes to a tire-skidding halt and gaped over my shoulder in disbelief. Tanner stared back at me with an irritating smirk, offering a little wave of his own before opening the driver's side door of his Silverado. Just perfect. The guy freaking lived across the street.

Or did he? It was possible he was just visiting.

Judging by the way Tanner walked out of the garage like he

owned the place, he had to be related to Mr. and Mrs. Hansen—their son, perhaps?

Not good. I sped away with an unsettling feeling in my gut. My grip tightened on the steering wheel. I didn't know what to think. My mind was caught between the hope that he wouldn't come back and the worry that he would. A girl can take only so much humiliation. I hadn't meant to embarrass myself in front of Tanner again, but it would seem that was all I knew how to do when he was around.

If I had any luck at all, he wouldn't come back to the neighborhood for a nice long while. *Please, Tanner.* Don't. Come. Back.

Within minutes, I pulled up in front of my aunt's house. I stepped down from my truck, grabbed my purse off the passenger seat, and made my way around the desert themed yard, landscaped with a variety of cactus, shrubs, and crushed granite.

Arriving at the welcome mat, I extended a finger to ring the doorbell. I had just enough time to drop my residual scowl when my aunt swung the door wide, ushering me inside.

"Kenzie!" Aunt Crystal said, pulling me into a hug. "It's so great to see you! How are you?" She stepped back to meet my gaze with an infectious smile, her hazel eyes crinkling at the corners.

I immediately responded to her cheerfulness with a smile of my own. "I'm good," I answered automatically. Honestly, with the events of the last twelve hours alone, I was anything but good right now, but I didn't want to trouble her with my problems.

Fake it till you make it, right?

"That's great!" Aunt Crystal reached behind her neck and tightened her low chestnut ponytail. "Thank you so much for coming to help."

"I wouldn't miss it," I said with complete sincerity. Ever since Aunt Crystal's husband died four years ago, I've been trying really hard to be there for her and my cousins. Especially since they'd been such a big support to me when I moved to Arizona five years ago.

"Jess and Drew are almost done taping down the baseboards," Aunt Crystal explained as she led me down the hall. "Do you think you can help me lay down the plastic to protect the floor?"

"Sure," I replied.

I entered the living room and seventeen-year-old Jess glanced over her shoulder from her position on the floor to my left. "Kenzie!" She hopped up to greet me with a quick hug and a glowing smile.

"Jess! Hey!" I replied, wrapping my arms around her slender frame for a beat before stepping back. "How's it going?"

"Ben asked me to the prom!" she gushed, her voice rising in pitch from her excitement.

I couldn't help grinning at her enthusiasm. "Really? Oh, that's so great, Jess!" She'd been telling me about this particular crush for months, so I was glad he finally got the hint and asked her out. Oh, to be in high school again when life was simple, and all your girlish-dreams could be fulfilled by going to one silly dance on the arm of the guy you liked.

"We've already been to three different stores, trying to find the perfect dress," Aunt Crystal added with a sigh of exasperation, her sparkling eyes betraying her delight.

"Yeah, and they keep dragging me along," Drew complained from the other side of the room, his back still turned to us as his steady hands worked.

Before I could even utter so much as a "hello" to my grumbling cousin, Jess protested with a perfect pout on her lips. "You have to help me pick, Drew! How else am I supposed to know what Ben will like best?"

Drew paused and turned to face his twin sister with annoyance. "He's a guy. He won't care what you wear!"

"That's so not true! If I showed up in a potato sack, he'd never talk to me again!"

"Then don't wear a potato sack. Problem solved," Drew replied with a decisive nod.

Jess shook her head vehemently. "I can't do this without you! You know Dad's not here to give me manly opinions."

"Really, Jess? You're pulling the Dad card?" Drew's fists tightened in frustration. I felt for him; it had to be tough being the man of the house when you're still practically a kid.

"Please?" she added with a hopeful smile.

Drew rolled his eyes. "Here's an idea," he retorted. "Why don't you leave me out of it and just ask Ben to go with you instead?"

"But I—"

"Okay you two," their mother cut in with her hands propped on her hips. "We can continue this conversation later. Let's focus on painting now or we'll be at this all day."

Drew immediately turned back to taping the baseboards in silence, while Jess reclaimed her spot on the floor and set to work with a little huff of injustice.

I bit back a smile and disappeared into the next room, setting my purse on the kitchen counter—where it would be safe from splatters of paint. I swiftly returned to my aunt's side, picked up one end of the long sheet of see-through plastic she had just finished unrolling, and pulled it taut across the tiled floor. Jess and Drew helped us tape it down, making our prep-work in the living room complete.

"Drew, will you please go out to the shed and grab the ladder?" Aunt Crystal asked.

He nodded once and retreated from the room to do his mother's bidding like a dutiful son.

When the doorbell rang, Aunt Crystal turned to her daughter with a sense of urgency in her voice. "Oh, that's probably Peg! Will you please gather all the paint brushes, rollers and trays? They should be in the garage."

"Yeah," Jess replied, her auburn ponytail swishing back and forth as she retreated from the room.

My aunt rushed to follow her, but paused and turned back to ask, "Oh! Kenzie? Would you mind grabbing a couple cans of paint out of the garage?"

"Not at all," I assured her.

"Thank you! Jess can show you which ones," she called over her shoulder as she disappeared down the hall to answer the door.

When I returned to the living room with a can of Misty Gray paint in each hand, my aunt waved me over to introduce me to her friend.

"Peg, this is my niece, Mackenzie," Aunt Crystal said with a maternal gleam in her eyes.

A middle-aged woman with comfortable curves and short, glossy black hair flashed a friendly smile. "It's so nice to meet you, Mackenzie. Do you live nearby?"

I bent at the waist to carefully lower the cans of paint to the floor and replied, "Yes. Just a few miles from here."

"How nice."

Drew returned with the ladder. Jess soon followed with the rest of the painting supplies. Aunt Crystal rubbed her hands together with an eager smile. "Alright! Let's get started!"

I worked alongside my cousins with a roller in hand, applying a layer of light gray paint to the living room while Aunt Crystal and Peg prepped the dining room.

Jess paused to shake out and stretch her arms when the doorbell sounded through the house. "I hope that's reinforcements," she complained. "My hand is starting to cramp."

"Come on, Jess. Tough it out. We've only been at this for like ten minutes," Drew quipped.

I chuckled when Jess let out a long, enduring sigh in response.

Aunt Crystal's voice drifted into the living room, explaining to the newcomer that his height would come in handy since none of us were tall enough to reach up to the ceiling without traveling around the room with a ladder.

"Happy to help," his deep voice rumbled in reply.

"Drew, honey, this is Tanner. Can you put him to work for me?"

I froze, my arm mid stroke. *Did she just say Tanner?* It couldn't possibly be the same guy, could it? My body flooded with nervousness as I strained to focus on the words being spoken on the other side of the room.

"Why don't you help my cousin over there?" Drew suggested.

"Sounds good," the voice replied.

Don't turn around. Don't you dare turn around, I internally demanded, for fear of what I might find. I knew it was silly. It's not like I could blend into the wall if I held perfectly still. Speaking of holding still . . . my white-knuckled grip on the handle of my roller was so tight, a painful tingling started radiating up my arm. I forced myself to relax and mentally braced myself for the moment of truth.

"Hey, neighbor. I thought I recognized your truck out front."

No, no, no. This cannot be happening!

4

TANNER

Mackenzie turned around with a look of horror on her face. Clearly, she wasn't happy to see me pop up in her life again so soon; which, honestly, made me strangely glad to be there—not that I enjoyed torturing the woman—she just . . . well . . . I didn't exactly know why I liked it. *Huh.*

"Hey." Mackenzie's voice was calm and serene—a stark contrast from what her face had conveyed only seconds before. "What are you doing here?" she asked, her rigid posture giving way to her discomfort.

I lifted up the paint roller Drew gave me to show her the obvious. "Helping."

She tilted her head and arched a brow, as if my answer didn't satisfy her. "How do you know my aunt?"

"I don't." Not personally, anyway. Mom was the one with the connection.

She narrowed her eyes at me in suspicion, causing one side of my mouth to twitch. "Did you follow me here?"

I choked back a sudden laugh that threatened to surface and shook my head. "No. My mom is one of your aunt's clients. She saw something that Crystal posted on social media asking for volunteers and sent me over." I lifted my brows for emphasis and added, "I had no idea you would be here."

"Oh, she's your mom's hair stylist," Mackenzie stated with understanding, the accusatory glare finally leaving her warm, brown eyes. "Small world." Her tone was almost welcoming. Almost.

"Yeah," I agreed, steadily holding her gaze, my mouth slowly curving upward.

After an awkward moment of staring at each other in silence, Mackenzie blinked and turned away as if suddenly remembering why we were there. "Could you cover the top half of the wall while I do the bottom?" She bent over to coat her roller in fresh paint from the tray on the floor.

"Ten-four," I responded, beginning part one of the fail-proof test I'd devised to see if she could be a potential candidate for *Mrs. Tanner Hansen*—not that my mind jumped straight to marriage with Mackenzie specifically; I just liked to vet a woman before I got too close. Sort of like an insurance policy that protects me from falling for the wrong kind of girl. Maybe it sounded a little dumb, but after having my heart ripped out by someone who waited until a week before our wedding to tell me that she wanted me to change careers —something I was definitely not willing to do—it was a necessary precaution.

"What?" Mackenzie turned to give me a questioning look.

"It's police code," I explained, bracing myself for her reaction as I dipped my roller into paint. "It means 'okay.'"

"Oh." Her lips pulled into a smirk as she returned her focus back to the wall. "Do you listen to police scanners in your free time?"

My brows lowered in confusion. I had a feeling that we weren't exactly on the same page here. "Free time? No. On my shift? Yes," I clarified, while finally putting my roller to good use.

Her arms stilled. "You're a police officer?"

"Yep." I listened carefully to get a read on her body language while I casually rolled paint up and down my five-foot section of the wall.

After a few seconds, I heard the sticky sound of paint smearing onto the wall near my feet once again, and I knew she had resumed painting. "Wow," she stated in a frustratingly bland voice.

Was that a good wow or a bad wow? I briefly glanced her way, finding her face devoid of expression as her arms pushed through the strokes. *That doesn't help me.* "Not what you expected?" I watched her closely, waiting to see which way the scales were going to tip.

Mackenzie turned away to reapply paint to her roller. "Uh . . . yeah," she answered hesitantly, her curious eyes darting my way as she pivoted back to the wall. "I've never met a cop before. Aren't they supposed to have mustaches and an unhealthy appreciation of donuts?" Her gaze flicked to my midsection briefly.

A full on grin split across my face, and my shoulders shook in silent laughter. Her stereotypical jab was unexpected, but that wasn't why I was laughing. I was laughing because—

"What's so funny?" she asked, her lips curving cautiously.

It took me a moment to inhale a calming breath and find my voice. "I brought a box of donuts to share. That's why I was late."

"Of course you did!" She burst into a laugh of her own. The sound was utterly attractive; not anything close to resembling a hyena, which I thoroughly appreciated.

So what did this mean for part one of my test? Mackenzie didn't fail, but she didn't exactly pass, either. I guess I was going to have to dig a little deeper with my questioning if I wanted to know how she truly felt about my line of work.

I bent down to dip my roller in the paint tray and chanced another glance her way. Mackenzie's smile had been replaced with a look of alarm. "Is something wrong?"

"You're a cop," she blurted, then covered her mouth as if she hadn't meant to say that aloud.

Here we go. True colors always shine through. What was it about my line of work that people found so repulsive? I'm a first responder; I serve and protect! How was that a bad thing? I narrowed my eyes and asked defensively, "Do you have something against law enforcement?"

She cringed and shook her head. "Nope."

That wasn't convincing at all. "Then what?"

Exhaling slowly, she glanced over her shoulder at her cousins before responding in a hushed voice, "You aren't planning on arresting me, are you?"

Ah, so that's what this is about. I released the breath I had been holding and smirked. *I could have some real fun with this.* "Aggravated assault is a pretty serious offense; class two felony," I informed, carefully matching her soft volume to keep the twins from overhearing. Turning to face her, I rubbed my jaw as if I were considering it. "Another arrest would boost my numbers."

Her eyes widened. "Please tell me you're kidding."

I shook my head, holding back a smile, and slipped out a set of handcuffs from my pocket. "Put your hands behind your back."

Her jaw fell slack and her cheeks instantly drained of color.

My serious expression finally cracked, a hearty laugh breaking free. Mackenzie's worried look eventually soured into a glare. Yeah, that was a pretty jerk move on my part. I shook my head, regaining control of myself. "I'm sorry. I couldn't help it." I offered her a warm, reassuring smile and put the handcuffs back in my pocket. "In all seriousness, you have nothing to fear from me. I'm not going to arrest you."

"You're such a jerk!" Mackenzie lightly smacked my arm with the back of her hand. "Why do you carry handcuffs and a gun around with you, anyway?"

My eyebrows lifted, impressed that she noticed the gun. Most people were usually pretty oblivious. "It's better to have it and not need it than to need it and not have it."

"I guess that's true," she agreed, dropping her arms to her sides, grazing the side of her right pant leg in the process with her roller— which she didn't seem to be aware of in the least. "Look,"—She tucked a loose strand of hair behind her ear—"I'm really sorry about last night."

"Don't worry about it. It could've happened to anyone." I was just glad she didn't wreck my truck.

"So I don't need to bring you apology brownies, then?" she asked, still unsure.

Well . . . I wouldn't complain if she did. I smiled and shook my head. "No, you don't owe me anything."

Mackenzie's mouth curved until her entire face glowed with radiance. *Wow. She's beautiful.* I felt an annoying little twinge of manly satisfaction, knowing that I had been the one to put that smile there. *Snap out of it. She hasn't exactly passed the test yet.*

When she turned back to the wall, looking as though a weight had been lifted from her shoulders, I scrambled to find the right words to pose my next question. Working side by side as we were, I couldn't waste this opportunity to get to know her more. But all I could think to say was, "Were you really going to bring me apology brownies?"

She shrugged. "Maybe. Would it have helped?"

"That depends," I said, my gaze fixed on the wall as I pushed the roller back and forth.

"On what?" she asked, curiosity lacing her voice.

"On how good they taste." *Obviously.*

Our eyes met, and she shook her head, a devilish gleam dancing in those alluring brown eyes. "I'll try to remember that the next time I feel like borrowing your truck without asking."

My brows lowered involuntarily. *Um . . . she's just pulling my leg, right?*

"Your face!" Mackenzie chuckled, her eyes crinkling with amusement. She touched my forearm briefly, which left a singe of warmth in its wake. "Tanner, I'm kidding!"

Look at that, she remembered my name.

"That's too bad." My smile veered toward downright malicious. "I was really hoping I could break in these new handcuffs." I patted my pocket with the shiny silver cuffs inside.

With little effort, she instantly smoothed away her smile and said in a serious voice, "That's not funny."

The sudden change in her demeanor was so comical, I burst out laughing. In turn, her tight lips curved slowly upward, revealing her true feelings before that adorable laugh of hers rang out strong. Man, with her beautiful smile and quick wit, the woman was thoroughly distracting. More so than any woman I've met in a while. *Test. Focus on the test.*

Before I could form my jumbled thoughts into words, she asked a question of her own. "So do you live with your parents? Or are you just visiting for the weekend?" Her expression held no judgment; no condescension, only curiosity.

"I moved in yesterday, actually," I revealed, dipping my roller in paint again. "I'll be there until my dad recovers."

"Recovers?" Her smile fell away as her dark brows lifted in concern. "Is he sick?"

I shook my head. "No, he broke his collarbone," I explained. "He just had surgery to help everything heal properly. It's most likely going to be a long road to recovery, so—"

"You moved home to help out," she supplied, an odd expression on her face that I couldn't quite decipher if it stemmed more from admiration or disbelief.

"Yeah." I scratched the back of my head as I turned my attention back to the wall.

"How did you fix my Ranger last night?" she suddenly asked, squatting to paint the section just above the floorboards. "I could've sworn I'd be buying a new battery today."

I was impressed she knew it was an issue with the battery. Did she have a bit of experience working with cars, after all? Eh, I'd doubt it. Her truck was kind of a beater, so I imagined any "experience" she had was more along the lines of being rescued by suckers like me when the thing broke down. I mean, come on. When you're driving an old Ford . . . *what else can you expect?* "It was the battery," I began, "only it wasn't dead. The connection was loose."

"You're kidding!" She groaned. "If only I had just popped the hood, then we could have avoided . . . all that unpleasantness last night."

So she does know something about fixing cars. Interesting.

"I don't know," I responded, not really knowing why I felt the need to tease her more. "I thought it was kind of fun." *Careful now. That's getting dangerously close to flirting . . . if I haven't crossed into those muddy waters already.*

"Fun?" She scoffed, then lowered her voice to a near whisper. "Yeah, I'm sure getting tased by a woman and then watching her drive away in your truck is every man's dream."

I couldn't help but laugh.

With a donut in hand, Drew called out from the doorway to the kitchen, putting a quick stop to my laughter. "When you two love-birds are done flirting in there, can you help us out in the dining room?"

Mackenzie turned toward her cousin, looking a little embarrassed. "Yeah, sorry! We're almost done."

"With the painting," I clarified in a voice loud enough to carry across the room. "Not the flirting." Yeah. I was knee deep in that muddy water now. *No turning back.*

Honestly, it was satisfying—letting my more playful side come out unchecked after a long, three-year hiatus. It was like rediscovering a part of myself that I hadn't even realized I'd lost.

"Tanner!" Mackenzie hissed, her cheeks instantly flushing a deep red.

I grinned, practically giving her permission to retaliate.

When she moved to swat my arm, I backed out of her reach, catching the side of the paint-tray with my foot, spilling a wave of light gray paint all over my black and white high-tops before it puddled onto the floor. *Dang. That's what I get for flirting.*

Mackenzie was laughing so hard at my misstep that I had to share some of the love. I may or may not have swung my foot in her direction to purposely fling a little paint her way. *Direct hit! Paint has sprayed the kneecaps. I repeat, paint has sprayed the kneecaps.*

She gasped, now brandishing her roller like a weapon with a mischievous bit of fire in her eyes. "You did not!"

I laughed, holding up my left hand between us, trying to call a truce. "Come on, I've got a little paint on me . . . you've got a little paint on you. We're even."

She shook her head with an impish smile and went in for the plunge, rolling sticky paint up and down my outstretched hand. "Now, we are even," she stated triumphantly.

Yeah. I definitely deserved that. But since my hand was now covered in wet paint, it was awfully tempting to wipe it off on the nearest dry surface I could find. "You know I'm going to have to put this perfectly good paint somewhere, right?" I made a show of roaming her person, looking for the best spot to make my mark.

Her lips parted and taunted, "You wouldn't dare."

"Oh really?" My eyes locked with hers as I stepped forward, grinning wickedly, prompting her to take two steps back.

She extended her roller between us like a shield, her brows forming a stern line. "Tanner? Seriously, don't. We need to finish the wall!"

I shrugged and let my left hand hang at my side in a show of compliance. Turning towards the wall, I stepped forward and pushed my roller across the textured surface, patiently waiting for her to let her guard down.

Cautiously, Mackenzie returned her focus to the wall and resumed painting a foot further away from me than she had before. *Smart woman.*

Biding my time, I waited until we finished covering the rest of the wall before making my move. It didn't take long. My hand was still plenty wet. "All done?" I asked, turning to face her as she rose from a crouch to stand beside me.

"Yep."

"Great! We make a good team," I said, strategically placing my left hand on her shoulder with a reassuring squeeze and a playful smile.

Her eyes widened as she twisted her neck to stare at my messy hand on her shoulder. Yeah, she never even saw it coming.

When her gaze snapped back to mine, there seemed to be a dangerous gleam in those rich amber eyes. The look vanished as her focus shifted to my cheek. "You've got a little something on your face there, Tanny." She tapped her left cheek, showing me right where the offending spot was.

Tanny? A little caught off guard by the ridiculous nickname, I lifted my hand from her shoulder to wipe at my cheek with my wrist.

She smiled, biting her lip in the cutest way. "No, you missed it." She lifted a hand to touch my face. "Here, let me get it for you," she offered innocently.

And like a fool I let her, because the sweetness of her voice and the curve of her perfect, smiling lips had me frozen in place.

When I felt something wet trail along my cheek with the light pressure of her finger, I knew I had been duped by the little brown-haired temptress. *Well played, Mac. Well played.*

If I took my revenge, I knew both of us would eventually end up covered in paint—which wouldn't be the wisest choice right now, considering we still had a long way to go before the painting project was complete. So I decided not to react. Willfully resisting the urge to press a handprint of paint right in the middle of Mackenzie's pretty face, I stepped back and cleared my throat, choosing to let her think I didn't notice what she'd done. "Thanks," I said, feigning gratitude.

She lifted a brow at me as if she didn't buy my act for one second.

Oh, don't you worry, Mac. This little war of ours isn't over.

5

MACKENZIE

J ess set a plate of food on the picnic table and lowered herself to the bench directly across from Tanner and me. "So . . . how do you two know each other?"

"We're neighbors," I answered quickly, hoping to prevent Tanner from revealing more than I wanted Jess to know about our short history together; specifically, *how* we met.

"That's cool," she said, propping an elbow on the table and grabbing a small stick of celery from her plate. "For how long?" Her hazel eyes lifted to mine expectantly as she began nibbling on the crunchy green stalk.

She just had to ask. Heaven knows what my cousin must be thinking after witnessing us flirt shamelessly all morning. Honestly, I was a little embarrassed by my behavior; not that I regretted being playful with Tanner. I just hadn't ever connected with anyone so quickly before, and I hated that my family had front row seats to the romantic display in all its vulnerable glory. Somehow it felt like we had been friends for years.

I shoved a fork-full of my aunt's homemade coleslaw in my mouth, stalling for time while I tried to think of a good way to change the subject when Tanner came to my rescue.

"Let's see," he said thoughtfully, wiping his mouth with a napkin. "We've been neighbors for . . . one whole day now."

Did I say rescue? Wolves. Tanner was feeding me to the freaking wolves, destroying any shred of pride I had left.

"What?" Jess's lips parted in surprise. "You and Kenzie literally just met . . . yesterday?"

"Yep," Tanner confirmed.

My throat went dry. *Here we go.* Jess had absolutely no filter, and there was no telling what she would say next. *Please don't say anything embarrassing.* Bracing myself for her response, I brought a cup of fresh-squeezed lemonade to my lips, hoping the cool drink would lessen my sense of unease and discomfort.

"I never would have guessed!" she gushed. "So was it love at first sight?"

I sucked in a sudden breath, sending a stream of tart, yellow liquid burning down the back of my throat unnaturally. My body reacted immediately, trying to expel the few drops that trickled into my lungs with a series of violent coughs. Somehow I managed to set my drink down without spilling before Tanner pounded on my back and tugged on my arms, raising them high above my head as if I were nothing more than a toddler, choking on a swig from her sippy-cup. Amazingly, my airway cleared fairly quickly after that. *Wow. That wasn't humiliating at all.*

"You good?" Tanner asked, brows creased in concern as he gently guided my arms back down to my sides.

"Yeah," I rasped, clearing my throat once more. Tanner's piercing blue eyes watched me intently as I picked up my cup and carefully swallowed another sip of lemonade—this time, thankfully, without incident.

"So . . . can I assume that was a 'yes'?" Jess asked, a hopeful smile on her lips.

"To love at first sight?" I retorted in disbelief. Why was she making this even more awkward? As attractive as Tanner was with his short sandy hair, athletic build, and baby blue eyes, love at first sight was not even in the realm of possibilities; for obvious reasons.

Nothing sucks the romance out of life quite like believing you're about to be abducted by a man with a gun. "Oh yes," I said sarcastically, "desperately in love since that very first glance."

"Don't let Mackenzie fool you," Tanner quipped, grinning somewhat mischievously. "I'm not ashamed to admit there were some sparks flying between us."

"I knew it!" Jess clapped her hands together in a girlish show of excitement.

"Ah, ha-ha! Okay," I cut in, chuckling awkwardly as heat rushed to my cheeks. It was obvious he was referring to the sparks from my taser, but I wasn't about to explain as much to Jess, or anyone, for that matter. I'd gone along with his flirting thus far, and may have even enjoyed it, but now I was done playing our little game. I stood, lifting my plate of mostly eaten food. "I'm going to go see if Drew needs help painting the bathroom."

Tanner nodded and moved to follow me back into the house. *For the love, Tanner!* I inwardly groaned. It was bad enough the guy wouldn't leave my thoughts since the moment we met, the least he could do was to let me have a little space while I figured out how to guard my heart against his fine physique . . . er . . . personality. *Get a grip! He's just a man!*

A very attractive man.

Tanner's phone rang. He paused just outside the door to answer the call, while I, regrettably, continued on inside. "Hey, Mom," I heard him say as the door closed between us, shutting out any possibility of eavesdropping.

The resulting disappointment that I felt at that moment of freedom was definitely ironic.

I inhaled deeply, reminding myself to relish the small reprieve from Tanner and all his . . . irresistibleness. The flirting, the laughs, the eye contact, the muscles flexing with every paint stroke—it was too much. For the last three hours, I'd been blushing like a teenager, fighting my growing attraction for the obvious ladies' man. Any man who could charm a woman like that couldn't be trusted.

I was afraid of the sizzling connection that flowed between us like a current of electricity. There was no way I was falling for another guy that couldn't commit to one woman alone.

Players—finding them was my curse in life.

Not that I knew without a shadow of a doubt Tanner was a "player," but all the signs were there: acting the part of the white knight, overly flirtatious and friendly when he should hate my guts—all the things that drew women in when they should be building walls around their heart and hanging up signs that said, "keep out."

It all started in senior year of high school with my jerk-of-a-boyfriend, Clint. I was young and naïve, foolishly trusting that I'd found someone special who'd hold on tight and never let me go. I was wrong. Wrong enough to face the ultimate betrayal—catching Clint making out with my best friend, Thea, on graduation night. Hence the driving force that led me to get up-close-and-personal with "The Valley of the Sun."

All throughout my four years of college, I dated nothing but toads with wandering eyes. That's when I decided that maybe there wasn't such a thing as a fairytale ending; not for me—an average girl with average looks and an average job.

My life was just kind of blah. I hated my job. I rarely dated anymore. Since moving off-campus and into the Freeman house when I graduated last year, I've come to realize the only thing I had going for me that brought any kind of joy to my life, was my relationship with my aunt and cousins, and my friendship with my roommates. I wanted to find a career that gave me a deeper sense of purpose and some kind of fulfillment, but I didn't know exactly what that looked like for me; probably not something I could do with a degree in business management.

I tossed my paper plate into the trashcan in the kitchen, thanked Aunt Crystal and Peg for the delicious food they had prepared, then turned toward the bathroom down the hall, intent on working off some of my inner frustration with a paintbrush.

"Mac!"

Tanner's voice stopped me in my tracks, my stupid heart leaping in my chest at hearing the nickname only Dad used. I inhaled a steadying breath and turned.

"Hey," he said, striding up to meet me. "I have to go. My mom needs help with Hunter."

Hunter? Am I supposed to know who that is? "Okay. No worries," I replied, folding my arms across my chest, trying not to feel too disappointed that he was leaving. *Space. I wanted space*, I reminded myself.

Tanner shoved his hands into his pockets. "I had fun today. You can be my painting partner anytime," he offered with a wink.

"I don't know," I argued, fighting the urge to grin as I gestured to my heavily paint-stained clothes and skin. "It's possible we got more paint on each other than the walls."

"You started the second go around," he accused playfully.

"No, no, no," I shook my head, my paint-streaked braid waving stiffly across my back. "You had it coming when *you* decided to mess with *my* hair."

"I swear I didn't know your hair was going to whip right into my paint roller," he countered, trying and failing to appear contrite.

"Uh-huh," I said, my voice dripping with sarcasm.

He shook his head, his crooked half smile slowly melting my insides, like a crayon on the sidewalk in the middle of July, leaving my heart a soft, gooey puddle of red wax. *Ugh. Get it together!*

Tanner slipped out his cellphone and tapped his thumbs on the screen for a moment. "Can I get your number before I take off?" He extended the phone to me.

"Why? So you can have someone to call when your Chevy breaks down?" I teased, the corners of my lips curving upward as my heart raced with nerves. *Maybe we can make a go as friends.*

"Something like that." He smiled, his silvery blue eyes holding my gaze intently.

Our fingers brushed as I took his phone in hand. A tingling warmth lingered on my skin like a whisper when I drew away. *Friends. I can do this.* Silently, I typed in my phone number and hit save, catching a glimpse of the contact name Tanner had chosen for me before handing it back.

"Mac the thief?" I questioned with a mild scoff.

Tanner pocketed his phone and shrugged nonchalantly. "Yeah, well . . . uh." He awkwardly cleared his throat. "I've got to run."

Is he nervous? It was like he was worried I would tell the whole world he was secretly a jerk.

Tanner threw his arms around me for a quick bear hug, and I greedily inhaled his woodsy masculine scent—which surprisingly seemed familiar, though I couldn't say why. By the time my arms remembered to react, sliding around his waist to return the embrace, Tanner stepped away, breaking contact so suddenly, I ached from the loss of his touch.

"See you around?" he asked, slowly backing further and further away from me, his questioning eyes refusing to leave my face.

I was speechless, lost in the memory of a moment gone too soon. Somehow I managed to lift my shoulders helplessly, hoping it conveyed what little approval I had to offer without giving the guy false hope.

His answering chuckle brought an instant smile to my lips. *Friends. No strings attached. I can do this,* I repeated to myself silently.

All the while, my heart screamed: WARNING. Danger. Proceed with caution.

THE SUN DIPPED low on the horizon, illuminating the sky with brilliant oranges, pinks, and purples when I arrived home from my aunt's house. Tanner's familiar Silverado sat in the exact same spot on the street as if it hadn't moved an inch since I left that morning. I reflected on the extreme embarrassment I'd felt at seeing that truck then and laughed at how very unexpected my day had turned out to be. Now, a small ember of hope glowed in my heart. Who would have thought that Tanner Hansen would want to be on friendly terms with me? *Mac, the thief.*

I hopped out of my truck and fingered my stiff, paint-streaked braid as I crossed the lawn to the front door, grinning the whole way there. I couldn't help it; I liked being noticed by an attractive man. But it wouldn't last; it never did.

"Kenz? Is that you?" Sydney greeted me from the living room as I opened the front door.

"Yeah, Syd. It's me," I answered, locking the deadbolt behind me.

"Do you want to go out for ice cream?" she asked. "I'm craving *Andy's* so bad today."

No plans on a Saturday night and sugar cravings? That was unusual for my serial-dater, health-nut friend.

"Ice cream sounds great," I began, tucking my keys into my purse, and crossing the wood-grained tile to hover at the edge of the living room—Sydney was lounging on the recliner, watching her favorite season of *The Office*—"but I should probably get cleaned up first."

The amused inflection of my voice pulled Sydney's gaze away from the TV. She slowly took in my heavily paint-stained appearance, her jaw practically dropping to the floor. "Kenz! What happened to you?"

I tempered my smile and shrugged nonchalantly, trying to play it cool. "I got into a bit of a paint-fight at my aunt's house today." The last thing I wanted was Sydney thinking I had developed some crush that I wanted her to help me pursue. I was attracted to Tanner, yes, but I wasn't stupid enough to give the guy any real power over my heart. I'd met enough "players" to last me a lifetime, and I wasn't signing up to let anyone break my heart again.

Who needed romance, anyway?

A stubborn grin broke free at the memory of running my roller up one side of Tanner's face after he'd sullied my hair. Sweet satisfaction—not at all romantic. It was . . . fun. Yes. Just two people having a friendly bit of fun.

"I know that look." Sydney flashed a smile, then lowered her gaze to the remote, briefly, as she paused the TV. "Who's the guy?" she asked, tucking her legs under her body and shifting to face me more fully, her perfect, platinum hair softly grazing the tops of her shoulders with the action.

My posture grew rigid and my lips pressed into a thin line. *I'm NOT falling for Tanner!* I couldn't let myself be vulnerable again. "It's nothing," I said, shaking my head and forcing my body to relax enough to offer her a convincing smile. "I just had fun today."

"What? No handsome strangers showed up to help?" She lifted her eyebrows in a dance to match her teasing smile.

The tension in my shoulders eased, and my smile became less strained, knowing that I could answer her truthfully. "Nope. No new faces." Tanner was inarguably handsome, but he luckily didn't quite qualify as a stranger. *Not anymore.*

"That's too bad," she said, twisting her lips to one side in thought.

I needed to change the subject before she started asking questions I didn't want to answer. Sydney's Altima had been missing from the driveway when I left that morning, so I questioned, "What have you been up to today?" I folded my arms across my chest and waited for her reply with interest.

"Oh, nothing too exciting," she began with a small lift of one shoulder. "I filled in for a couple of Jake's classes at the gym. He called in sick."

"Again?" I scoffed in annoyance. "That guy needs to be fired."

"Hey! Cool the jets, miss big-shot-manager," she chuckled. "Jake is the only reason I'm getting any Saturdays off at all. I keep him happy . . . he keeps me happy. It's a win-win situation."

"If you say so." I smiled and shook my head at her effort to smooth my ruffled feathers, when she was the one who should be getting irritated with the flakiest instructor she'd ever had to work with.

"What are Kara and Ashley up to?" I asked. They were our roommates—likely out with their latest love interests, if I had to guess.

"At the movies with Marcus and Landon."

"You didn't feel like joining them?" Maybe I should have bit my tongue, but it was odd that Sydney hadn't gone along with her own "date of the week," like she usually did.

She shrugged. "No. Not really." Her deep, ocean blue eyes lowered and blankly stared at her lap.

Something was definitely off with her. "Okay, who are you and what have you done with Syd Freeman, the queen of fun?" I teased, trying and failing to make her laugh.

Not even a chuckle? My brows lowered as I studied her vacant expression. "Hey, are you okay? Something on your mind?"

She exhaled, her breath heavy and slow. "Do you remember that boy I told you about . . . the one that stood up for me when I was being bullied in third grade?"

"Yeah." He was her perfect guy, the man that nobody could ever measure up to. "The guy that moved away before you were old enough to sneak him off to Vegas and claim him for yourself, right?" I added, grinning at the ridiculousness of the whirlwind idea.

"That's the one," she chuckled, her eyes twinkling as her smile returned. "I found out yesterday that he moved back."

"What? To the neighborhood?" I confirmed, completely surprised at the turn the conversation was taking. "Is he still single?"

She grinned. "Yes!"

Sydney's dream guy. Single. Back in the neighborhood. She finally had her chance! "You know, I don't believe in fate, but this is totally fate!"

"Right?" She chuckled. "This is it. I finally get my shot with Tanner!"

Tanner? Wait, wait, wait. *Oh no.* Sydney's perfect man was—

"This is so unbelievable . . . the chance of a lifetime," she gushed with a giddiness that I had never before seen her possess. "I'm ecstatic one minute and terrified the next."

My heart squeezed with each and every painful declaration flying from her mouth. *This. This was why I needed to swear off men from my life.* I was tired of coming in second best, and with Sydney now in the running . . . I had no chance with Tanner at all. There were no words to describe the disappointment I felt. Why wouldn't my stupid heart stop hoping for the impossible?

Sydney sprung out of her chair and began pacing. "He came over for game night, but only stayed twenty minutes before he left to go help you, and then neither of you came back." She paused to look me directly in the eye. "I thought that the two of you . . ."—she gestured to me as she struggled to find the right words—"maybe hit it off?" She shrugged and shook her head, looking somewhat perplexed. "I don't know."

"Whoa, wait a minute," I interjected, uncrossing my arms and raising my palms between us. Blood pounded fast through my head as I tried to process what she was insinuating. Did she think that we had some impromptu date after he came to help me? The idea was laughable, considering I had assaulted him, but Sydney didn't know that. "I came right home after Tanner fixed my truck. I went in through the back because I was in a bad mood and wanted to go straight to bed."

Her brow creased over rounded eyes. "But then, why didn't Tanner come back?" she asked, her tone a mix of hurt and confusion.

I shrugged, not allowing myself to speak the words that would probably explain everything. *I attacked him and stole his truck.* Who wouldn't want to go home and sleep after an experience like that?

"I barely slept last night, worrying that I'd already messed this up!" Sydney said dejectedly, her anguish written all over her face. "And I'm craving sugar like a mad-woman."

Dang, she's got it bad. I had never known Sydney to break down like this over anything. I felt for her anxiety, because I was often put under a lot of pressure at work and knew exactly what it felt like to drown in stress. Despite how much I hated it, I somehow learned to thrive in all the chaos—except where romantic relationships were concerned. Any hint of drama with multiple women involved and I'm gone. Life's too short to be hung up on a relationship that makes you feel insecure. And right now . . . I was definitely feeling like the girl who does *not* get the guy in the end—which was the story of my life. Totally fine. I was used to it. But still, it was a little depressing.

Sydney, however, could have any man she wanted. Why, out of all the millions of men in the world, did I have to feel a connection to the one guy that was apparently off-limits? How was that even fair? *Maybe the universe does hate me.*

I mean, how was I supposed to react? Pretend I felt nothing for the guy—that I wasn't weak in the knees at the very sight of him? Yeah, that's exactly what I needed to do.

I'd just met the guy, for crying out loud! Syd had been in love with Tanner practically her whole life. If anyone deserved a chance with him, it was her.

I watched Sydney bury her face in her hands, groaning in frustration. She really was a mess over this guy. Was it bad that a part of me was secretly relieved to discover even my perfect roommate could use a self-confidence boost now and again?

Ugh! What am I doing? I shouldn't let Tanner, or *any* guy, for that matter, come between Sydney and me. We were friends first and foremost, and that bond deserved my loyalty and support. Right now, my best friend was struggling, and she desperately needed my help.

If winning Tanner's heart was that important to her, she seriously needed to get her mojo back. Lucky for her, I knew just the thing for her to try.

"Hey, look at me," I commanded, grasping her shoulders and capturing her gaze. "You are strong, you are beautiful, and you are enough. Now, say it to yourself!"

She shook her head and bit her lip, likely feeling awkward about self-affirmations when she obviously had never done them before. Unlike me, who had lots of practice—thanks to my ugly breakups.

"Come on, Syd! You need this," I encouraged, squeezing her shoulders.

"Okay." She nodded and spoke in a soft, unassuming voice. "I am strong, I am beautiful, and I am enough."

"Say it again. Louder."

"I am strong,"—her voice gained in strength—"I am beautiful, and I am enough!"

"Yes, you are," I agreed. "Tanner would be a fool not to fall in love with you."

Staying in love with each other is what I was worried about. "Player" meets "serial-dater." What could possibly go wrong?

Her smile emerged, overshadowing any and all doubt in her expression. "You're right. I can do this."

"That's right," I echoed, dropping my arms to my sides and taking a step back. There. Mission accomplished. Now, on to avoiding the pair of them for the foreseeable future.

"And you're going to help me!" she declared.

"Yes, I will." The reply left my mouth before I had the good sense to stop and think.

Wait. *Crap. What did I just agree to do?*

6

TANNER

"Hang on, buddy. We're going for a ride," I said, sliding one arm under Hunter's neck and shoulders, then securing my other arm under his knees. My muscles strained against seventy-five pounds of dead weight as I lifted him out of bed. Hunter grinned, baring a mouthful of worn, crooked teeth. "Good morning to you too." I smiled back and cradled him close, turning sideways to avoid catching his head and feet on the walls as I carried him through the doorway and down the hall.

Mom waited for us in the living room, sitting cross-legged on the gym mat, a change of clothes, a diaper, and a pack of wipes placed neatly beside her. I knelt down and lowered Hunter to the mat, careful not to pull on his shaggy, golden hair as I extracted my arm from behind his neck.

"Good morning, my smiley boy!" Mom crooned. She caressed his face and leaned in close to kiss his scruffy cheek. "Oh, I love it when you're happy!" She shifted to meet my gaze, her eyes sparkling with joy. "I think he likes having his big brother home."

Hunter moaned in agreement, his low voice bursting out like a tortured sigh.

I chuckled, my chest filling with a special kind of warmth that only Hunter could provide. "Love you too, little buddy."

I lived for these perfect moments. Moments where, no matter what kind of crap I was going through in my life, Hunter could always cheer me up and put things into perspective. Happiness wasn't limited to ideal circumstances or once-in-a-lifetime opportunities. My brother, a twenty-three-year-old man, trapped in a body he would never be able to control, was living proof of that. If he could find a reason to smile each day, then maybe I could, too.

My mind drifted to Mackenzie, the woman that somehow accomplished the impossible. She whittled away all my defenses in a matter of hours and surprisingly passed part one of my test with flying colors. I couldn't remember the last time I'd felt so carefree in a woman's presence. What was it about her that drew me in, making me feel like dating her would be the easiest thing in the world?

I'd wanted to text her so many times over the last couple of days but resisted. Was I ready to take that next step—the step where I start to let my heart lead the tiniest bit? Would she even pass part two of my test? I reached for Hunter's hand and squeezed it gently. Not everyone was comfortable around people with disabilities. If she supported me in my career and loved my brother without reservation, I might just have to get down on one knee.

Mom pulled off Hunter's pajamas, changed his diaper, and dressed him in clean clothes with impressive speed—a testament to her many years of experience.

"Come here," I grunted, lifting Hunter once more, then carried him to his wheelchair near the window. I buckled the safety harness around his chest and secured an adult-sized bib around his neck. It protected Hunter's clothes and chair from drool and vomit for the most part.

"Do you want me to give him his seizure meds?" I called over my shoulder. Mom was in the kitchen preparing Hunter's breakfast—the same unflavored liquid he had to eat for every meal. It smelled almost as bad as rotten milk. *Poor guy.*

"Sure. I have the syringe ready right here."

I walked into the kitchen, grabbed the syringe with pink liquid off the counter, and turned to go.

"Oh, Tanner! Here." Mom handed me the extension that hooked up to Hunter's feeding tube in his stomach. It had a special port designed for administering medications.

"Thanks." I chuckled softly. "I'm kinda going to need that."

Mom smiled, then turned back to the task at hand while I continued on to the next room.

I attached the extension to Hunter's stomach and pushed the medicine down the tube. Mom followed after me, rolling the IV pole into the living room with Hunter's pump and feeding bag all primed and ready to go. As she hooked him up and started his feed, I retreated back into the kitchen to rinse out the syringe and set it aside to dry.

"Do you need help with anything else?" I asked, poking my head back into the living room.

She turned and smiled. "No, I can handle the rest."

"Okay. I'm going to go check on Dad."

I went down the tiled hall and turned toward my parents' bedroom. Dad sat on the edge of the bed, grimacing as he attempted to slide his injured arm into the sleeve of his button-up shirt.

"Hey, let me help you with that," I said, crossing the room to his side.

He waved me away. "No, no. I can do it."

"Just because you can, doesn't mean you should." I folded my arms across my chest and gave him a stern look.

He sat up straighter and lifted his chin, a defiant look in his eyes. "I haven't got a foot in the grave yet."

I fought the urge to smile. "Dad, I never said you were old. Come on, you had surgery less than a week ago. If you're not careful, the healing process will take longer. Let me help you."

"Fine." He slouched, looking defeated. "I just hate feeling so useless!"

Even though I understood his frustrations, it was still hard seeing Dad that way. "Dad, you're not useless," I said calmly, slipping his shirt over his arms before starting on the buttons. My thoughts turned to Hunter. He literally couldn't do one thing for himself, and yet, he was the beating heart of the family. Just because he existed, we got to experience something very few could understand—pure, unconditional love. "Think about Hunter. He's the most dependent human being we know, and even he isn't useless."

Dad's face instantly sobered. "You're right." He shook his head slowly, eyes fixed to the floor as I eased his right arm into his sling. "I just wish I didn't have to be another burden for you and your mother."

"It's okay. It's not going to be like this forever," I said, stepping back to help him rise. "All you have to focus on right now is letting your body heal."

Dad put his left hand on my shoulder and nodded. "Thank you, Tanner." His gray-blue eyes softened. "Everything you're doing for your mother and me . . . I'm proud of you. You're going to be a great husband and father someday."

Would I, though? I looked away, my mind flooding with doubts. My parents were childhood sweethearts that got married right out of high school. My sister had been married for the past eight years and had a couple kids of her own. I was twenty-six years old and pretty comfortable being a bachelor. Not very promising.

Although . . . there was one woman in particular that I couldn't seem to get out of my head. It probably wouldn't lead to anything for one reason or another.

But what if it did?

I stared at my paint-stained high-tops and pictured Mac's face, her mischievous smile taunting me to come closer.

I'd never know if I didn't try.

I grinned and met Dad's gaze. "That's because I learned from the best."

Mom walked in holding a plate of brownies. "Look what just arrived from the neighbors!"

Mac. The little devil brought me brownies, anyway. I smiled, lifting the plastic wrap on one side of the plate. "Mmm, breakfast."

I picked up a brownie and took a bite. *Wow. It should be a sin to eat something this good.* I practically moaned and shoved the rest of the warm, chocolaty goodness into my mouth, somehow unsurprised that Mackenzie could bake so well. *I should thank her.*

I was about to pull out my phone to text Mac when Mom laughed. "It looks like Sydney's baking meets with your approval."

Sydney? My hand dropped to my side. Now that was a surprise. I thought she was one of those health fanatics that didn't eat sugar. I shrugged, too proud to admit they were the best brownies I'd ever tasted.

"She's offered to bring us dinner on Saturday. Isn't that sweet?"

Dinner was a thoughtful gesture. Mom was worn a little thin and could use a break, but I couldn't help feeling like there was some ulterior motive. Sydney's had a crush on me since we were kids, and it didn't help that Mom treated her like a second daughter. When were they going to accept the fact that I wasn't interested in Sydney and never would be? She was too much like my ex—high-maintenance, clingy, overly sensitive—all the things that didn't mix well with a police officer's life.

I needed someone driven and independent. Someone who wouldn't buckle under the stress when things got crazy. *Someone like .. . Mac.* I rubbed a hand down the side of my face, a couple days' worth of stubble scratching my palm. How had I let myself fall so far in such a short amount of time?

I shook my head. "We don't need Sydney's charity, Mom. I can take care of dinner on Saturday if you want." Cooking definitely wasn't my strong suit, but I could manage something palatable.

"Honey, the last time I let you cook, you dirtied just about every dish in the kitchen. I really don't think—"

"I'll get take out," I cut in, willing her to understand the way I felt. "Then you don't have to clean."

She smiled softly and shook her head. "Sydney wants to show us that she cares. I think we should let her."

Did she really though? *Not as far as I could see.* A flash of irritation loosened my tongue. "She's just trying to weasel her way into this family!"

"Tanner Derek Hansen!" Mom chastised, scowling. "Sydney has been nothing but kind to us! It won't kill you to let the girl bring us a meal."

Yeah. I may have overreacted a little, but I didn't regret what I'd said. It was the truth.

"Your mother's right, Son," Dad interjected, with a half-eaten brownie in hand. "If these brownies taste like heaven, just imagine what other delicious things she'll feed us."

I crossed my arms, refusing to acknowledge that Dad had a point. Mom looked slightly offended at Dad's enthusiasm, until he kissed her cheek and said, "Of course, no one cooks as good as you do, Sweetheart."

"Mmm-hmm." She shook her head, smiling, then left the room without another word.

"Nice save," I whispered, my mouth lifting on one side.

Dad finished his last bite of brownie and smiled back. "Your mother's a gem. I hope you find someone as kind and loving as she is." He chuckled and added, "And it wouldn't hurt if the girl can cook too." He bumped my bicep playfully with his fist. "Maybe give Sydney a chance. She's always been a nice girl. You don't want to let a good one get away."

Now Dad was turning against me? I sighed, uncrossing my arms and letting them drop to my sides. "Dad, it's never going to happen," I said, hoping the message would stick. "I'm just not interested." It didn't matter how much Mom or Dad pushed, I wasn't going to change my mind. If only I had some way to get them off my back.

Mac.

The solution was simple. Everyone would quit pressuring me if I started dating someone else. And if that someone else happened to be Sydney's roommate? Couldn't send a message any clearer than that.

It wasn't all about avoiding Sydney, either. Mac was the first woman I'd wanted to get to know better in a long time. There was just something special about her—something different.

Dad may have been wrong about Sydney, but he was right about one thing. *I shouldn't let a good one get away.*

TANNER

Hey, Mac. This is Tanner. How's it going?

MAC THE THIEF

Hey. You aren't broken down somewhere, are you?

TANNER

Haha! No. I'm home.

MAC THE THIEF

Good. Because I can't come rescue you right now. I'm about to leave for work.

TANNER

When do you get off?

MAC THE THIEF

8. Unless I have another customer that makes me stay late like the other night.

TANNER

Do you want to catch a movie after?

MAC THE THIEF

Can't. I'm working the morning shift tomorrow.

TANNER

What time do you get off tomorrow? Maybe we could go then?

MAC THE THIEF

Sorry. I've got plans. Sydney's free though. She gets off at 4.

7

MACKENZIE

That was close. When I didn't hear from Tanner those first few days after I gave him my number, I thought maybe he wouldn't try to ask me out after all. Unfortunately, I was wrong. Those brownies were supposed to inspire him to take Sydney out on a date —not me. Why did my plan backfire?

Because you made the man brownies, you idiot!

I rubbed my forehead and muttered to myself, "I knew I should've gone with chocolate chip cookies instead." *Stupid. Stupid. Stupid.* I mean, yes, I was flattered that he asked me out, but I was supposed to be avoiding the guy like the plague. It would've been a lot easier if I'd never given him my number. I locked the front door and turned toward my truck in the driveway, the late morning sun warming my back.

At least Tanner hadn't texted back after I suggested he ask out Sydney. That was a good sign, right? Now all I had to worry about was coming up with "plans" for tomorrow, so I wasn't a complete liar. Then, I needed to figure out the menu for the dinner Sydney would take to the Hansens' on Saturday. Yeah. I was in charge of making that, too, since Syd couldn't exactly be trusted in the kitchen. She's had more cooking disasters than anyone else I knew.

It was fine. I actually enjoyed cooking, and Sydney would never claim the credit for herself. Nobody had to know who actually prepared the food. It could be something oven-ready from the store, and they'd never know. But I wouldn't do that, not when I had an entire day at my disposal. Since moving to Arizona, experimenting in the kitchen had become a new creative outlet for me. It was therapeutic to simply block out the rest of the world and focus on food. And right now, I desperately needed a distraction.

I smiled to myself, started up my Ranger, and headed off to work, looking forward to the fun the weekend would bring.

I PULLED the lasagna out of the oven and set it on the stove. "Food's ready, Syd!"

Sydney entered the kitchen, looking like perfection with soft wavy hair, designer clothes, and flawless makeup. I, on the other hand, hadn't given any thought to my appearance beyond using a hairbrush.

Sydney rushed to my side and hugged me in gratitude. "Kenz, you are the best! It all looks and smells amazing," she said, eying the breadsticks with particular longing as she pulled away.

Going completely gluten-free and sugar-free took a special kind of self-control. I didn't know how Syd did it day after day. I guess when your body can't tolerate something, you just do what you have to do.

"You're going to help me bring everything over, right?"

I forced a smile and stepped away to untie my apron. "Sure," I replied, wishing she had asked anyone else but me. Ashley or Kara could've helped just as easily; they were in the next room doing nothing more than arguing over who had the hottest date for tonight. "Let me grab my flip-flops." I hung up the apron in the pantry, then disappeared down the hall.

When I returned, Sydney was hovering near the pan of lasagna with oven mitts, an eager smile on her face. "Ready?"

"Yep." I grabbed the bowl of salad and the basket of breadsticks, then followed her out the front door.

The closer we got to the Hansens' house, the more my body tensed with nerves. What would I say if *he* answered the door? I hadn't physically seen Tanner in a week, but I couldn't seem to get the guy off my mind. Was it because his blue Silverado was always there, parked on the street every time I left the house, or was it because he'd wanted to go out with me?

Tanner didn't message me again after I completely blew him off two days ago. And he didn't end up asking Sydney out like I thought he would. What did that mean? Was he disappointed that I'd turned him down?

I knew I shouldn't care, but I did. Ladies' man or not, I genuinely liked Tanner. If things had been different, I would have . . . well . . . it didn't really matter now, anyway.

Sydney rang the doorbell, and Mrs. Hansen soon answered with a beaming smile. Her light brown hair streaked with silver was pulled back into a simple ponytail. "Girls! Oh, thank you so much for doing this. Please, come in!"

"It was no trouble at all, Mrs. Hansen," Sydney assured her.

Mrs. Hansen's eyes landed on the bowl and basket in my arms. "Here, let me take those for you." I smiled and nodded, handing them over to her as she exclaimed, "Oh, everything smells so divine!"

"I hope you like lasagna," Sydney said, following after Mrs. Hansen to the kitchen, while I stayed behind in the living room, feeling out of place. It would've been so easy to slip out the door and return home on my own, but I was determined to wait for Syd.

"We do! It's definitely a favorite in this house," Mrs. Hansen replied, her voice quieting as it drifted off into the next room.

I faintly heard a deep-toned voice greet them. Good. It was better this way. Sydney would get her chance to talk with Tanner like she wanted, and I would avoid the two of them like I wanted.

I folded my arms and turned to take in the room. A young man in a wheelchair sat quietly in the corner, next to a wooden rocking chair. I had no idea who he was or why he was there. I pasted on a friendly smile and crossed the room slowly, unsure if he wanted my company. His eyes roamed back and forth, never stopping, never seeming to focus on anything. Was the boy blind? "Hello," I said softly.

He said nothing; his misshapen hands sat unmoving on his lap. *Maybe he's deaf, too?*

"I'm Mackenzie. I live across the street." I tried again. "Do you mind if I sit with you?" Still no response. I sat down on the rocking chair beside him and looked around the room. Two gray tufted sofas, a white end table, and a navy blue wingback chair made up the elegant living room arrangement. A few family portraits hung on display in a whimsical array of mismatched frames. I loved it. My brows lifted when I discovered the young man in the wheelchair in each and every photo.

I turned to study his profile. His golden hair was lighter than Tanner's, and his eyes a deeper blue, but their noses and lips looked the same. Yes, there was definitely a resemblance. Why didn't Tanner mention he had a brother? *And a sister, too, apparently.* She looked a little older than Tanner—slender and platinum, like Sydney.

I turned away from the portraits with a sigh and spotted an old upright piano through a set of French doors near the entryway. *A music room?* I hadn't noticed it before. My fingers automatically curled and stretched, itching to play. Five years had been much too long. "Do you like music?" I continued my one sided conversation, though I wasn't sure why. "I love music."

My gaze lowered to his hands. His long fingers curved inward slightly, with his thumbs tucked against his palms. *Maybe he responds to touch.* I had the sudden urge to take one of his hands in mine but resisted, clasping my hands tightly in my lap. Mrs. Hansen probably wouldn't appreciate my touching her son without permission. "The piano is my favorite instrument," I said, watching him closely for any sign that he could hear me.

The young man bounced his eyes in my direction an extra beat as if he were trying to focus on me but couldn't. *He's aware of me.* A strange feeling seeped into my soul, warming me to my core. I grinned, not really understanding why I felt so happy. "Do you like the piano too?"

"He does." Tanner interjected from across the room, an easy smile on his face.

My heart rate kicked up a notch—whether it was from being startled or from being on the receiving end of that crooked smile again, I couldn't say. "Tanner—" I stood and folded my arms, self-conscious that he'd been watching me. That masculine voice I'd heard earlier drifted to my ears again from the next room. *Guess that wasn't Tanner, after all.* "Sydney's in the kitchen," I blurted. "She uh . . ." I looked away for a moment, trying to gather my scattered thoughts. "She wants to talk to you."

When he frowned in response, I rambled on like an idiot. "You knew she was bringing dinner, right? It's homemade lasagna with breadsticks and salad. I'm just waiting for her to finish talking with your mom." I gestured to his brother and grimaced. "I hope I didn't overstep. I saw him sitting alone and thought—"

"Mac," Tanner cut in, his smile reappearing as he crossed the room toward me.

I shut my mouth and focused on his eyes as he approached.

"It's okay," he assured me. "Hunter likes the attention."

Hunter. That was who he'd helped on Saturday. *Made sense.*

Tanner stepped beside me and picked up Hunter's left hand.

I'd wanted to ask about his disabilities but was unsure if it would be rude to bring it up.

"He had meningitis when he was a baby." Tanner's voice was soft and soothing, though his words broke my heart. "The doctors treated the infection, but it was too late. A stroke destroyed over ninety percent of his brain." Tanner met my gaze; a hint of sadness clouded his eyes. "Mentally and physically, he's like a newborn baby. It was a miracle he survived."

How devastating. "Tanner, I'm so sorry." I placed a hand on his arm. "How old were you when it happened?"

His face was solemn, like he'd seen and experienced things no one should have to experience. "Three."

My eyes widened. The brothers were closer in age than I realized. "How old is Hunter now?"

"Twenty-three."

My age. I never would have guessed. He looked more like a young teen than a man. I braved a personal question. "Is he blind?" I wanted to make sure that moment where I thought he'd looked at me wasn't just a fluke. The warmth I'd felt—it wasn't nothing. It was something special.

Tanner shook his head. "He has cortical visual impairment, which means he can see; it's just the image processing part with the brain isn't so great."

I nodded, glad to know I hadn't imagined what I saw and felt. "I bet he's a real charmer with the ladies," I offered, attempting to lighten the mood. "I was drawn to his good looks the second I saw him."

"Love at first sight, huh?" Tanner teased, a mischievous glint in his eyes. "Does that happen to you often?"

Ugh, why did Jess have to open her big mouth? I rolled my eyes, knowing he was just trying to get a reaction out of me.

Tanner leaned closer to his brother and whispered loud enough for me to hear, "You'd better watch out. I know she talks pretty, but this lady will steal your wheels if you're not careful."

"Hey!" I poked Tanner's arm. "That's not funny."

Tanner chuckled, turning to face me. "Come on. It's a little funny."

My lips twitched, but I refused to give him the satisfaction of a smile. "You're never going to let me forget, are you?"

Tanner grinned, then turned his focus back to his brother. "What do you think, little buddy? Should we cut Mac some slack?"

Hunter tipped his head toward Tanner and smiled. My heart nearly exploded at the sight of seeing his face light up in a way I hadn't expected. A grin broke free on my own lips.

"Yeah," Tanner said, as if agreeing with his brother. "You're right. I should play nice." Tanner turned his head toward me and asked, "Do you want to go out with me tonight?"

Oh boy. My heart picked up speed. I hadn't realized how close we were standing to one another until that moment. His silvery blue eyes held my gaze, inviting—wanting me to give in. I breathed in his earthy-woodsy scent, remembering how good it felt when he hugged me. It would be so easy to have that again. All I had to do was say, "yes."

I opened my mouth, about to give in, when Sydney's melodic voice suddenly reached my ears, halting the words on the tip of my tongue. *What was I thinking?* I took two steps back, hit the edge of the rocker, and lost my balance, falling back into the chair.

Tanner chuckled and moved to reach for me. "You okay?"

My cheeks were on fire. "Yeah, fine." I took his offered hand, trying not to think about how much I liked the rough, callused feel of his skin as he pulled me to my feet. It was like holding a fistful of warm sand at the beach. "Thanks." I dropped his hand and looked away. "Um, I'm sorry, but I can't go out tonight." When I glanced up to meet Tanner's eyes, his expression was unreadable.

I turned to Hunter and forced a friendly smile. "It was nice meeting you, handsome."

Sydney entered the living room with Tanner's mom at her side. "Really, Mrs. Hansen, if you need anything at all, don't hesitate to give me a call."

That was my cue. "Bye," I mouthed, waving pitifully, then turned to go wait by the door.

Mrs. Hansen replied, "Of course! We really appreciate what you've done for us."

I couldn't stop myself from finding Tanner's gaze once more. A sly half smile appeared on his lips. *Oh no.* A sinking feeling settled in the pit of my stomach. What if he thought I was just playing hard to get?

Sydney looked up, her smile brightening when she turned to find Tanner in the room. "Hey, you!"

"Hey, Sydney," Tanner replied in a polite manner, any trace of his usual playfulness gone.

"Tanner thought your brownies were something special," Mrs. Hansen said, her eyes sparkling with mischief.

Sydney turned to Mrs. Hansen, smiling. "Really?"

Tanner stared at his mother for a beat, looking somewhat like a caged bird. *Odd.* Why was he acting so strange? *Did he not like my brownies?* When his gaze flicked to Sydney, he shrugged nonchalantly. "They were . . . edible."

Sydney lifted a brow as if to say, "that's it?"

I was wondering the same thing. *Must not be a huge fan of chocolate.*

Mrs. Hansen chuckled, breaking the awkward tension. "Oh, he's just pulling your leg. He loved them. Ate nearly the whole plate himself."

Oh, that man. I should have known he would try to play it down. *Always the tease.*

"I'm glad you enjoyed them." Sydney giggled and shyly lowered her gaze to her hands. Her platinum hair fell forward, hiding her face. For a moment, she wasn't the confident person I knew her to be; she was hesitant and vulnerable, wearing her heart on her sleeve for all to see.

Tanner's lips curved slightly at the corners—a feeble smile compared to what he normally gave me.

In one quick motion, she whipped her hair in place and drew her shoulders back, confidence restored. "We're going tire-rolling later with a group of friends. Do you want to come?"

Tanner's eyes flicked to mine before darting back to Sydney. "Maybe. When and where?"

I started to get the sneaking suspicion that maybe Tanner was more interested in seeing me than Sydney, which was absolutely crazy. In what world would a guy prefer a cheeseburger when he could have *filet mignon*?

Sydney's eyes beamed with hope. "Eight o'clock at Holmes Park."

"Sounds good." Tanner nodded, then turned away, his attention fixed on Hunter.

"You girls take care now. Thanks again for dinner!" Mrs. Hansen said, following us to the door.

"You're welcome," Sydney and I answered in tandem as we exited the house.

Before I made it to the other side of the street, my phone buzzed with an incoming text.

TANNY

Tire-rolling is your excuse?

Hmm. Maybe he was more of a cheeseburger man. *Not good.* Not good at all.

8

TANNER

I savored every last bite of Sydney's lasagna, because it was the best I'd ever had. How'd she learn to cook so well? I had to admit it surprised me. I didn't think she even ate food like that, let alone cooked it. *Hidden talent?*

It didn't matter. Sydney Freeman could try to impress me all she wanted. It wouldn't lead to anything. I only hoped she wouldn't keep her sights on me much longer. Mom made the mistake of giving Sydney my phone number. Already, in the space of one hour, she sent me three sugary sweet texts, hinting at wanting to spend more time together. *Ugh. Thanks a lot, Mom.*

Since my broken engagement, I'd managed to avoid breaking any hearts, including my own, but politely discouraging a determined woman like Sydney wouldn't be an easy feat.

That was why I needed Mac. Dating her would be the perfect solution to keep Sydney at bay. Was that my only reason for wanting to date Mac? Not at all. But it was definitely a plus.

What had me puzzled was why Mac pushed me away every time I asked her out. I'd thought our interest in each other was mutual. She'd given me her number, after all. Even her cousins teased us about the obvious chemistry we shared. I never expected it would be so difficult to get her to agree to a date.

She'd wanted to say yes; I saw it in her expressive eyes before something pulled her away. And despite what she claimed in her text, that "something" was definitely more significant than tire-rolling with her friends. Tonight, I planned to discover what exactly was holding her back.

Just after eight o'clock, I turned into the Holmes Park parking lot and pulled into the first empty space I could find down the row of cars. I hopped out of my truck and headed toward the trailer with three large tractor tires loaded in the back. I passed about twenty people standing around, waiting on the grass, while two men lowered the ramp and climbed inside the trailer. By the time I made it over there to help unload, only a couple more volunteers stepped forward to assist them with the heavy lifting. Ridiculous. *Bunch of lazy saps.*

When I tipped the first massive tire up onto its side with the help of one or two more sets of hands, Sydney appeared out of nowhere like a fly to—uh . . . never mind.

"Hey, Tanner! Glad you could make it," she said, sliding a hand over my bulging bicep.

The contact annoyed me, as if I knew she was sizing up my muscles, rather than simply getting my attention.

"Hey," I grunted, lifting the second tire as two strong men rolled the first tire away.

"Wow! I forgot how big those things are."

My muscles? Did she really just—

"Must be really heavy," she added.

Oh, the tires. Duh! Sydney's presence must've been addling my brain —and not in a good way. "Yep," I agreed, trying not to roll my eyes.

She leaned closer, her lavender scent assaulting my nose. My desire to drop everything and run was immediate. "You make it look so easy," she whispered, her breath tickling my ear.

My grip on the tire faltered, tilting the heavy tire toward the poor skinny guy standing just on the other side. I tried and failed to regain control, quite possibly making the situation worse. Slim-Jim's quick reflexes were the only thing that saved him from being flattened like a pancake, though his muscles were shaking from holding up all that weight on his own. *That could've ended badly.*

I quickly shuffled around the tire and helped lighten the guy's load, tipping it back on its side.

"Thanks, man. That was a close one."

I nodded and replied, "No problem," even though it was definitely my fault.

Sydney was smiling when I came back around to wait until the others were ready to roll the tire away.

"Good thing you were here to help," she said, completely oblivious to the dangerous situation she'd just caused.

I didn't know what my parents saw in the woman. When I looked at her, all I could see was a wolf in sheeps' clothing. Yeah, I'd heard about her unseemly habit of exchanging men faster than a bookworm in the library. I needed to get away from her. And more importantly, I needed to find Mac.

After the third tire was on its side, I helped guide it all the way down the ramp, where some random bystanders took over, rolling it to the crest of the retention basin. Sydney annoyingly stayed by my side as we trailed the flow of people gathering around the tires at the starting line. The farther we walked away from the streetlights in the parking lot, the harder it was to see. But that wasn't going to stop me from searching for Mac.

Sydney bumped my arm playfully with her shoulder. "So did you enjoy dinner?"

Fishing for a compliment? She would.

"It was . . ." I paused, searching for the right word, my eyes never leaving the crowd, "tasty."

Sydney's hand brushed mine, her fingers lingering, inviting me to take them. I'd felt nothing from her touch. No heat, no sparks. Nothing. It was like I was immune to her poison. The thought made me smile, knowing I was in complete control. I inched away and cleared my throat, my eyes still scanning faces. "So how did you make your sauce? My mom is dying to know."

"Oh . . . well, actually—"

I didn't hear the rest of what she'd said. My brain had tuned her out the second I spotted Mac. She was climbing into the first tire in the lineup, her devilish smile taunting some guy to join her.

A spark of jealousy rushed through my blood, and my hands tightened into fists. Was *he* the reason she'd turned me down?

Somehow that just didn't feel right. Mac didn't seem the type to string a guy along just for the fun of it. If she was dating someone, she would've told me. There had to be another reason—something that convinced her to keep me at arm's length.

Sydney bumped my hand again, and the answer hit me like a lightning bolt to the brain. The hints through text. The hasty retreat when Sydney entered the room. *You've got to be kidding me.* Mac was bowing out of the ring for Sydney. Not only that, she was trying to set us up! And there I was, at Sydney's side, playing right into their hands.

Mac and Sydney had no idea who they were messing with. Nobody could push me into a relationship I didn't want. One hundred percent guaranteed.

I rubbed my jaw as my mind turned over a dangerous plan budding to life. Did I really want to play their game? *It could work.* "Remind me the name of your roommate—the one that had car trouble." I turned to Sydney and met her low-brow expression.

"You mean, Kenzie, right? The one I was just talking about?"

Now it was my turn to be confused. What had she said about Mac? As much as I wanted to, I wasn't rude enough to make her repeat it. "Oh, that was the same person?" I said, choosing to play ignorant.

Sydney laughed. "Yeah, silly. Who'd you think I was talking about?"

Not wanting to straight up lie to her face, I shrugged.

"Why do you ask, anyway?" Sydney's voice held a hint of suspicion.

I couldn't tell her I was interested if I wanted my plan to play out just right. "Just wondering if she's had any more problems with her old Ford."

Sydney's eyes gleamed. "That's why I like you, Tanner. Always the hero."

Yeah, she was definitely under some disillusion that we would be good for each other. Time to set my plan into motion and prove her wrong. I turned to Sydney, unsmiling. "Being a hero has nothing to do with it. Come on." I grabbed her hand and pulled her down the hill.

"Tanner!" she squealed, nearly tumbling at my fast pace. "Where are we going?"

"To talk to your friend." I slowed down as we reached the tire Mac and what's-his-name were climbing out of on unsteady legs.

The pair of them laughed uncontrollably. "Ryan!" she gasped. "I never knew you could scream like a girl!"

"Neither did I!" he replied, cackling obnoxiously.

Ugh. I hated the guy already.

"Fun ride?" I interrupted, drawing Mac and Ryan's gaze.

"Yeah, man!" Ryan agreed. "Was my first time rolling down. That ride's no joke!"

Mac's eyes flicked to Sydney's hand still in mine, then she quickly looked away. I knew the hand-holding would get her attention. It was just as I'd thought. No matter how much Mac hinted otherwise, she didn't actually want me to date Sydney.

Now, on to phase two—convincing Sydney that she didn't want to date me.

"Do you guys want to get out of here? Maybe get some dessert?" I planned to take them to the fattiest, sugariest place I could think of, hoping it would make Sydney's health nut side come out and squirm a little.

Sydney flashed a beautiful smile, which I'm sure had blinded more than her fair share of men. "You read my mind."

Mac looked about to give some lame excuse of why she couldn't go when Ryan spoke up, "Sure, I'm down for that. Kenzie?" He turned his smiling eyes on her.

"Sure," she replied, tucking a strand of hair behind her ear. "I could go for some dessert."

Perfect. Everything was going according to plan.

I STARED in silence as Sydney scarfed an entire cinnamon roll, followed by a large cookies 'n cream milkshake without one word of complaint. In fact, she looked happier than a kid at Christmas. To say I was shocked would be an understatement.

She eyed my half eaten cinnamon roll with wanting, like the way a drug addict looks at her next hit. "Would you like to finish this for me?" I offered, just to see what she would do.

"Oh, no. I couldn't. You go ahead." She looked so embarrassed, I was sure she was blushing under all that makeup.

"I'll take it—if it's up for grabs," Ryan volunteered.

"Go for it." I pushed the plate his way. "My eyes were bigger than my stomach tonight."

"Sweet! Thanks, man." Ryan grabbed the roll and turned to Mac. "Do you want some?"

She smiled and shook her head, her unfinished ice cream nothing but a cup of soup now. "No, I had a big dinner." Her eyes flicked to Sydney, as if there was some unspoken message she was trying to convey. It was a look of disappointment if I ever saw one.

Mac had been avoiding my gaze all night. Maybe inviting her along to witness "my failure" to impress her roommate hadn't been my best idea.

"Speaking of dinner," Sydney said, turning to Mac. "Tanner's mom was asking about your sauce in the lasagna. Care to share your secrets?"

Mac's sauce?

Mac shrugged and finally made eye contact with me. "I can try to write up a recipe and bring it over. I don't measure my ingredients, so I can't promise it will taste exactly the same."

She was the one behind the amazing food? I smiled and replied, "My mom would really appreciate it." And me. And my dad. Heck, my dad would raise the banner for team Mac forevermore the second he found out she was the cook.

Mac nodded and looked away, back to ignoring my existence again.

"This was fun. We should do it again sometime," Sydney suggested.

And that was my cue to move on to phase three. I pulled out my phone and looked at the screen. "Excuse me, I've got to take this call." I stood and walked towards the exit. "Hey, Mom. Is everything okay?" I said aloud. Nobody was on the other end of the call, but Sydney didn't need to know that.

After about sixty seconds, I returned my phone to my pocket and came back inside. "Hey, sorry to do this, but I need to take off." Without waiting for Sydney to reply, I turned to Ryan. "Can you give Sydney a ride to her car?"

"Yeah, but that's not cool, man. First you forget your wallet, now you're ditching your girl?"

She's not my girl.

Ryan shook his head. "Bad manners. Sydney deserves better than that."

That was exactly the point.

"It's okay, Ry." Sydney soothed. "His mom needs him right now, and I'm sure he'll make it up to me later. Won't you?" She pinned her innocent eyes on me.

Run. Just turn around and run.

It took everything in me to force a smile and nod. How had my plan completely backfired? Any hope I had of a one and done operation was toast. Sydney was in it for the long game, so I had to cut my losses and regroup.

I turned and hurried out to my truck, wasting no time as I started the engine and shifted into drive.

Back to the drawing board. I gathered my thoughts as the street-lights whizzed by. If I was going to push Sydney away for good, I needed to attack where it hurt the most. Play off of her fears maybe? But how could I do that without appearing downright sinister? And did I even know what she was afraid of?

Wait.

An idea started taking shape. *Yes.* It was so awful . . . *it just might work.*

9

MACKENZIE

I peeked out the window and sighed in relief when I saw Tanner's truck missing across the street. *Finally.* It had taken a few days for the timing to work out, but now I had the chance to visit Mrs. Hansen alone. No Sydney, and more importantly, no Tanner.

Any inkling of doubt I had about whether Tanner was a player or not had been smothered the second I saw him holding Sydney's hand. He wasn't interested in me, not really. *And neither was Ryan.* It stung more than I cared to admit. Not the Ryan part—I'd known about his thing for Syd for some time. He just hadn't had the courage to ask her out yet. It was the whole flirting thing with Tanner . . . and the way he looked at me when he'd asked me out—he made me think he actually preferred me! *And I almost believed him.* Why did I always have to fall for the stupid jerks that thought women were nothing more than things to be played with?

I knocked on the door, and Mrs. Hansen soon appeared with a friendly smile. "Well, good morning. It's Mackenzie, right?"

I returned her smile and nervously tucked my hair behind my ear. "Yes. I just came to bring this recipe for you. It's my homemade tomato sauce." I extended the instructions I'd typed up for her.

She took the paper with a measure of excitement. "Oh, thank you!

Tanner mentioned you might be bringing this by, and I'm so glad you did." She stepped back. "Won't you come in and visit for a few minutes?"

My eyebrows lifted. I hadn't planned on staying. What if Tanner came back?

I was about to politely decline when Mrs. Hansen added, "Hunter would love the company—if you have the time."

Visit that sweet and pure soul? My heart took to the idea instantly, urging me to accept. "I'd love to." I remembered the special feeling I couldn't quite explain the last time we'd met. I didn't understand it, but I knew I had to see him again.

Mrs. Hansen's smile brightened. "Wonderful!" She shut the door behind us and crossed the living room to her son's side. "Hunter, look who came to visit!"

"Hello, handsome," I said, standing a couple of feet away.

His eyes darted back and forth like before, forever searching.

"Here, come closer," Mrs. Hansen instructed. "Let him see you better."

I moved forward and stood directly in front of him. "Do you remember me?" I asked. "I'm Mackenzie, your neighbor. We met on Saturday."

"You can take his hand if you want to. It helps."

When I looked up to meet Mrs. Hansen's gaze, she nodded as if to encourage me. I reached out and slid my hand around Hunter's, tucking my fingers against his palm. My thumb stroked the backside of his hand. *His skin's so soft.* I lowered my body nearly into a squat so we were at eye level with each other. "It's good to see you again."

Hunter's fingers tightened around mine gently. *He knows I'm here.* His eyes slowed, bouncing my way an extra couple beats, and his breathing increased. Every time he exhaled, a barely audible moan escaped his mouth. Was he trying to speak to me in his own way? Again, a special warmth enveloped me, filling my soul with something new but familiar—like receiving a much needed hug from a loved one. The type of embrace that makes you feel wanted and whole. "You little charmer." I grinned. "I hope you're staying out of trouble."

Mrs. Hansen chuckled. "Tanner was right. You're a natural with him."

Tanner had been talking about me? *Why?*

"You look confused." Softening her smile, Mrs. Hansen explained, "Not many take to Hunter so easily."

I stood and turned to face her, Hunter's hand still in mine. "What do you mean?"

She sighed, sadness dimming her smile. "Most people feel uncomfortable talking to him, so they usually ignore him. Just because he can't respond doesn't mean he doesn't want or need human interaction. It gives him something to look forward to each day."

Sydney didn't acknowledge or even look at Hunter when we had come by over the weekend. She'd known their family for years. What was there to be uncomfortable about? "I'm sorry people can be so thoughtless. They don't know what they're missing. He's got a smile that could brighten any day."

"He does, doesn't he?" Mrs. Hansen's eyes shined. "Would you like to sit down?" She motioned to the gray sofa behind me.

I nodded and perched myself on the edge of the couch, shifting so I could continue to hold Hunter's hand.

Mrs. Hansen settled into the rocking chair, set my recipe aside on the white end table beside her, and picked up Hunter's other hand. "Tell me a little about yourself. Are you from Mesa?"

I shook my head. "No, I was born and raised in Tulare, California. I moved out here for college and never looked back."

Her brows lifted. "Oh, I'm not familiar with Tulare. Is that in northern California?"

"It's right in the middle, actually," I offered, unsurprised that she'd never heard of it. Not many people knew of the beautiful little farming town where I grew up. "It's about forty-five minutes south of Fresno."

"Oh, I see. And have you ever been to the Sequoia National Park?"

"Yes, many times." I smiled. It was only an hour away from home. Standing next to the massive trees always made me feel as though I'd stepped into a fairytale—one where I was a small woodland creature in a world of giants. It was humbling, to say the least. "Have you?"

"No, but I have always wanted to visit." Her smiling eyes crinkled at the corners. "I hear some of the trails are handicap accessible."

"Yes, there are quite a few. I think Hunter would really enjoy it." I squeezed his hand.

Mrs. Hansen nodded. "I think so too."

I'd never realized how much I took for granted in life until that moment. As a kid, I didn't think our annual family trips to the beach or Disneyland were anything out of the ordinary—as far as family vacations go. Now I wondered if the Hansens had ever been able to do anything like that. Not because they couldn't afford it, but because it wasn't something Hunter could safely participate in.

"Tanner mentioned we have a mutual acquaintance," Mrs. Hansen remarked casually.

We do? My brows lowered in confusion, prompting Mrs. Hansen to confirm. "Crystal is your aunt?"

Oh yeah! "Yes! I forgot that you're her client. How long have you been seeing her?"

"Let's see . . ." Her mouth pulled to one side in thought. "Her twins had just started kindergarten the first time she cut my hair."

"So about twelve years, then." I smiled and added, "You must know her pretty well."

"Oh, yes. I consider her a dear friend. I attended her husband's funeral a few years back," she said, her smile dimming. "Very sad for one so young to lose a spouse."

I nodded, my eyes dropping to my lap. "It's been really hard for her. She's good at putting on a smile, even though it still hurts."

"The hurt never does go away, but as she finds the little things that bring her joy, the pain won't seem as impossible to bear."

When I looked up and met Mrs. Hansen's gaze, I knew she spoke from experience. Who had she lost? A parent? Maybe a sibling? I wondered if she ever mourned for the life Hunter would have lived if he hadn't caught meningitis. My eyes drifted to the IV pole standing next to his wheelchair with bags and tubes hanging from it. How did Mrs. Hansen have the strength to deal with it all—the trauma, the loss, the sacrifices, the physical burden of raising a severely handicapped child? I couldn't even imagine what it must be like.

"Well, isn't that a pretty picture?"

I turned to see Mr. Hansen, right arm in a sling, smiling at us from across the room. He had sandy blond hair the same shade as Tanner's, with the addition of graying sideburns.

"Mackenzie brought by her recipe for us. Isn't that nice?" Mrs. Hansen said to her husband.

"That's wonderful!" Mr. Hansen sat on the sofa near his wife. "We sure appreciate you sharing your talents with us. Your food was absolutely delicious!"

My cheeks warmed, secretly pleased by the praise. "Thank you. I enjoyed preparing the meal—cooking is sort of a hobby of mine."

"Well, feel free to cook for us anytime." His eyes gleamed.

Mrs. Hansen nudged her husband and whispered, "William."

I bit back a grin.

Mr. Hansen hurried to add, "Oh, uh . . . maybe my wife would like to return the favor?"

Mrs. Hansen looked utterly shocked; her eyebrows couldn't lift any higher if she tried. It would've been funny if his words didn't give me cause for concern.

"She makes a mean pot roast," Mr. Hansen continued. "We'd love for you to join us for dinner on the day of your choice."

And there it was—the thing I hoped he wouldn't say. I couldn't have dinner with Tanner and his parents! I had to think of an excuse. The rumbling sound of the garage door opening increased my panic. "Oh . . . that's very kind of you to offer, but you really don't need to do that."

Despite her initial surprise, Mrs. Hansen was quick to echo her husband's invitation. "Really, it would be our pleasure to have—"

"Mom! Dad! I'm home!"

Oh no. My gut twisted, and my palms began to sweat. *I shouldn't be here.*

"We're in here, Tanner!" Mrs. Hansen replied, her face all aglow. "Come and see who came to visit."

I needed to leave. Fast. I squeezed Hunter's hand and stood. "I'm sorry, but I really need to get going."

"Mac?" Tanner entered the room, his genuine smile bringing a blush to my cheeks.

"Hi . . ." *Why does he have to look at me like that?* I turned toward Hunter to avoid Tanner's gaze. I couldn't let him fool me again. "I was just bringing by the recipe for your mom." I dropped Hunter's hand and smiled at Mr. and Mrs. Hansen. "And now I really need to head off to work."

"Of course," Mrs. Hansen said, then stood to follow me to the door. "Thank you for stopping by." She placed a gentle hand on my arm and lowered her voice. "Think about dinner and let me know if you'd like to join us sometime. It won't offend me if you'd rather not." She indicated Tanner with a tilt of her head. "And don't you worry about him. If you decide to come, I'll make sure he behaves."

Did Mrs. Hansen know her son was a ladies' man? I chuckled, almost convinced to agree right then and there. Almost. No matter how delightful Mr. and Mrs. Hansen were, it didn't change the fact that I couldn't stand to be around their oldest son. It wasn't that I didn't want to be near him. The problem was . . . I did. *Way too much.* Sydney would hate me forever if she knew how much I wanted him to be my man.

"If you ever need an extra pair of hands with Hunter, you know where to find me," I said, hoping she knew my offer was sincere. I didn't understand where the desire had come from or if Mrs. Hansen would even welcome my help. All I knew was that being near Hunter filled something inside me, something I'd been missing from my monotonous life.

Mrs. Hansen smiled and replied, "Thank you. I'll keep that in mind."

Tanner walked up behind his mom and spoke over her shoulder. "Enjoy your shift at the studio."

I flashed him a feeble smile. "Thanks. I'll try." *Try* being the key word. To be honest, I wasn't looking forward to it at all. Another day, another dollar, right?

"See you around." His eyes found mine, tempting me to drink in his presence a little while longer.

He's not yours. Blinking away the bitter thought, I waved and turned to go.

"Bye, Mackenzie!" Mrs. Hansen called. "Come visit us anytime."

If only I could, Mrs. Hansen. If only I could.

SYD

Kenz! Tanner's taking me out this weekend!
Just the two of us!! I hope he's a good kisser.
You never can tell with cops.

MACKENZIE

That's great, Syd! I knew he'd come around.
What's he got planned?

SYD

I don't know. All he said was to come hungry
and wear jeans and close-toed shoes.

MACKENZIE

Hate to break it to you, but it sounds outdoorsy.

SYD

Are you sure?

MACKENZIE

Yep! The man's got off-roading tires. Trust
me. It'll be outdoorsy.

SYD

No, no, no! I'm about to freak! What am I going to wear!??

MACKENZIE

No freaking out. Just borrow some of my stuff.

SYD

You're the best!!

MACKENZIE

How's your stomachache?

SYD

Miserable enough to give up cinnamon rolls for the rest of forever.

My body hates me. Why does bread have to taste so good??

MACKENZIE

Sorry you're still suffering. Got to be strong, girl! That stuff's bad for you!

SYD

I know. I just couldn't help it. Tanner makes me nervous. Apparently, I stuff my face with all the things when I'm nervous.

MACKENZIE

Do I need to worry about you?

SYD

No, no. I'll be fine.

10

TANNER

Dad rubbed his chin in confusion. "So . . . tell me again why you're taking Sydney on a date instead of Mackenzie?"

"Because Mackenzie won't agree to go out with me until Sydney sets her sights on someone else," I said, stuffing the sandwiches into a gallon-sized ziploc bag.

"And why would Sydney lose interest when you're finally showing interest?"

I loaded the sandwiches into a small cooler box with a smirk, giving nothing away.

"You're going to sabotage the date."

I shrugged, letting my devious smile speak for itself.

Dad lowered his voice. "Don't tell your mother."

I chuckled. She'd definitely have my hide if she knew what I had planned.

A few minutes later, I was all packed and ready to go, right on time. So I spent the next fifteen minutes hanging out with Hunter, just to be sure I was late.

Instead of crossing the street to knock on the door, I hopped into my Silverado and sent Sydney a text.

TANNER

Ready to go? I'm outside in my truck.

SYD THE MAN-EATER

Almost. I'll be out in a min.

She wasn't ready yet? It's not like it was an early morning date. It was after six p.m. on a Saturday. *Ugh.* Women and their infernal beauty regimens. Looked like the joke was on me.

One minute turned into ten. *Finally.* Sydney exited the house, for once not looking like a runway model. She wore an oversized tee shirt, jeans, and ratty old hiking boots. I actually liked the look. Definitely more practical than her usual expensive tastes. What took the woman so long?

Sydney opened the passenger-side door with a hesitant smile. "Hey, Tanner."

There was a big Chevy symbol across the front of her shirt. "Dressing to impress tonight?" I teased.

Her smile fell. "I knew this outfit was all wrong. I'll be right back." She started to turn.

Oh no. Not again.

"Sydney, wait!" I called before the door closed. "I was joking. Your outfit is perfect. Now, please, get in the truck."

She grinned, obediently climbed up, and buckled her seatbelt. Why did I get the feeling I said the wrong thing?

After a quick stop to top off the gas tank, we were finally on our way. Traffic on the sixty was smooth sailing since rush hour was nearly over. Sydney had chattered happily about a variety of topics— working at the gym, her favorite songs and movies, her life aspirations ...

I was surprised. I never took Sydney as the motivational type, but that was what she wanted to do—to help kids with low self-esteem build confidence in themselves through goal setting and exercise.

"That's a worthy cause, for sure," I said, my eyes never leaving the road.

I didn't have to look at her to know she was smiling. I needed to quit being so nice.

Sydney rested her hand on my arm, and I recoiled away from her touch, quickly placing my right hand higher up on the steering wheel. She cleared her throat. "Tell me what it's like being Officer Hansen."

Perfect. The golden opportunity to tell her what my job was really like had come—and I didn't even have to bring it up. "Well, when I'm working, I actually go by Trooper Hansen, because I work for the state instead of the city."

She giggled and tested out the title. "Trooper Hansen. I like it. Why have I never known this about you? All this time I thought you worked for Mesa or Scottsdale or something."

I shrugged. "You've never seen me in uniform. How could you know any different?"

"I thought maybe your parents would've said—"

"They don't talk about my job much," I cut in, "for their safety and mine."

"What do you mean?" There was obvious confusion in her voice.

I sighed and shook my head. "Not everyone loves the police, Sydney. The world is a lot scarier than you know."

She stayed silent, so I continued. "There are people out there . . . very bad people, who would target me, my parents, my wife and kids. If they knew where I lived, there's no telling what they might do—break in . . . vandalize my property . . . violence . . . kidnapping . . . murder. All because they hate the badge I wear and what it represents. My job isn't all sunshine and rainbows, rescuing people in need. A lot of the time I have to deal with the absolute scum of the earth."

For about thirty seconds, she said nothing. *Good. Maybe my warning had hit the mark.*

"That's awful. Why do you do it?" she finally asked.

Sydney was not the person I wanted to be having this conversation with, so I shrugged and teased, "Maybe I just like drivin' fast, shootin' guns, and kissin' all the pretty ladies."

Sydney laughed and leaned over the center console. "I'm sure you do."

I made the mistake of glancing her way; her focus was razor sharp, pointed directly at my lips, like she was hungry for a taste. *Uh. . .* I'd never been more glad for bucket seats than at that moment. Sydney was much too close for comfort, and it was all because of my stupid mouth. Why couldn't I think of something less flirty to say? *Idiot.*

One step forward, two steps back.

At last, I pulled onto the dirt road turnoff with a measure of relief. Now the real "fun" could begin. *Come on, desert. Work your magic.*

The first leg of the trail was pleasant for an evening ride, fairly bump free. For the first time in my life, I wished I didn't have such good suspension. Sydney seemed to be enjoying herself way too much. She smiled and commented on how beautiful the desert looked bathed in the fading light of sunset. I didn't disagree. If Mac had been the one beside me, I would have pulled off to the side of the road to watch.

I turned off the air conditioning and rolled down the windows to let the desert air rush through the cabin. Instead of some complaint about her hair tangling into a mess like I'd expected, Sydney said, "Mmm, that smells so good."

Yes, it did. So far, the desert was giving me the wrong kind of magic. The next turnoff had better be as rutted out as I remembered.

I reached into the center console and pulled out two ice cold water bottles, extending one to Sydney. "Need a drink?"

"Thank you." She took the bottle and unscrewed the lid, while I put mine in the cup holder for later.

Perfect timing. We'd reached the turnoff, and her wild, wind-blown hair blinded her to the drastic change in terrain. Just as she lifted the bottle to her lips, I gave the engine a little gas and plowed over the rocky path, thrashing us from side to side.

I didn't see the water explode all over her face, but I heard the shuddering gasp that accompanied it.

I glanced her way and busted up laughing. *Yes!* She was completely soaked.

"Um . . . do you have any napkins?" She put her mostly empty water bottle in the cup holder and peeled away the wet hair plastered to her face as best she could. It wasn't easy with the car rocking us from side to side. Her makeup had turned into a smeared mess.

"Nope," I said, chuckling at the fact that I had removed my stash of napkins earlier that day. "It's just water. It'll dry soon enough."

"Great. Could you maybe slow down a little? This road is giving me whiplash," she complained.

Finally, a negative reaction. *Thank you, desert.*

"We're off-roading," I said, grinning. "The whiplash is half the fun."

"If you say so," she replied with a bit of sass.

After a few minutes of silence, Sydney asked, "We are planning to eat at some point, right? You did say to come hungry."

"Yep. Just about ten more minutes, and we'll be at the perfect spot for dinner."

She nodded and kept her eyes ahead, where the headlights sliced through the haze of twilight.

I didn't have any perfect spot in mind. Honestly, I was just driving until it was dark enough out for the next activity on my agenda.

"We're here." I pulled off the road into a small dirt clearing with a fire-pit someone had constructed out of rocks.

"Thank goodness. I'm starving." Sydney hopped out of the cab and looked up at the night sky. "Wow! Now I can see why people would want to come out here. The stars are beautiful!"

"Yep," I agreed. "One of the reasons I love being out in nature." I grabbed my flashlight and gathered up a few dead twigs and brambles for kindling, then placed them in the fire-ring. "Sydney, could you help me find a few dry branches we could use for the fire?"

"Sure," she said, coming to stand next to me.

I shook my head. "No, you go look over there."

"But you have the flashlight!" she protested.

I barely held back a grin. "You have your phone, don't you?"

"Yeah," she said.

"Use the flashlight app."

"Okay." She obediently slipped her phone out of her pocket, tapped on the light, and slowly walked away.

Not one minute later, she screamed and bolted to my side, clinging to my arm for dear life. "Tanner! It almost got me!" She was shaking like a leaf.

"What almost got you?" I asked patiently, secretly pleased that she was still terrified of just about anything with little legs. When we were kids, she'd scream bloody murder every time a cricket or gecko so much as crossed her path.

"I don't know!" Her nails dug into my skin. "Something creepy and crawly! One minute it was there, and the next it was gone!"

"What? You're scared of a little bug?" *I know, I know, I'm a jerk.*

My uncaring response hit a nerve because her voice instantly changed from scared to angry. "This was no little bug, Tanner Hansen! This thing was huge with lots of little legs! Yuck—" She shuddered. "I swear it was the ugliest thing I've ever seen. And! It almost killed me!"

When I started laughing at her, she dropped my arm and shoved me. "Ugh! I'm going to wait in the truck." She stomped away and called over her shoulder, "You can bring me my dinner when it's ready."

Finally, a glimmer of the prissy princess I knew Sydney to be. Getting her to drop the mask of sweetness she was so fond of wearing was turning out to be harder than I expected. The sooner we could level with each other and part ways, the better.

The fact was, no matter how much she hinted otherwise, Sydney couldn't handle being a trooper's wife. The salary alone would never be enough for her name brand clothes and manicured nails, not to mention her outright hatred of guns. Even if my profession weren't an issue, she'd never enjoy roughing it in the woods or hiking the Grand Canyon rim to rim, like I'd always dreamed of doing. Then there was the way she misunderstood my sense of humor, which created extra awkwardness when all I'd wanted was to ease the tension hovering around us for years.

Perhaps the biggest thing against Sydney was the way she avoided Hunter. Which was a shame. He was everything good and pure, a shining light when my world felt dark. Who wouldn't want someone like that in their life?

I set to work on building the fire, my grin long since faded. For all Sydney's wanting, we would never work. And as much as I hated manipulating her, the only way the message would stick was to make her come to the conclusion herself—with the help of a few harmless pranks.

After I'd charred Sydney's sandwich over the open flame, I brought it over to her on a paper plate. She accepted the food with a smile of gratitude. "I'm sorry for how I acted before. I've been an awful date." She looked down, embarrassed. "I guess I can get a little overly emotional when I'm hungry. Do you care if I come sit by you?"

And the man-catching act was back. I was too shocked to say anything at first. How could she go from terrified and snarling to "let's get cozy by the fire?" *Women.* I'd never understand them.

She looked up at me and said, "I promise not to freak if I see any more bugs."

Ha! She'd be seeing more bugs alright, and I was counting on her to freak. "You'll have to sit on the dirt," I warned.

"That's okay," she replied. "I can handle a little dirt."

Doubtful.

I swallowed a sigh and turned away. "Follow me."

Well, the one good thing about Sydney joining me was now I could see her reaction to the peanut butter, sauerkraut, and grape sandwich I'd made for her. Mine was plain old peanut butter and jelly, but she definitely didn't need to know that.

Sydney took a nice big bite and chewed. "Wow! This might be the strangest sandwich I've ever eaten, but it actually tastes pretty good."

Seriously?

I watched her take a second and third bite with a smile. *Didn't see that coming.*

"I actually shouldn't eat this," Sydney admitted between bites. "I'm gluten intolerant."

You've got to be kidding me. "You are?" If she couldn't have wheat, then why was she eating cinnamon rolls and sandwiches?

"Yep. Bread's my weakness." She giggled good-naturedly.

Nothing about this date was turning out the way I'd thought it would. And now I felt like an even bigger jerk than I already did. I knew Sydney had been a health nut for years, just never knew the reason why. A food intolerance made sense. Why hadn't she told me before now? I never would've brought sandwiches had I known it would mess up her insides. Guilt burned through my conscience like a festering splinter, but I couldn't change tactics now; not when my freedom from this woman was on the line. Rather than apologizing or saying something gallant that made her feel better, I opted to say, "That sucks. You should take your health more seriously." To be fair, Sydney needed to learn better self-control for her own well-being. She could end up in the hospital if she wasn't careful.

Sydney nodded, her face instantly sobering. "You're right." She tossed her paper plate and the last few bites of her sandwich into the fire and watched the flames turn them to ash.

An awkward silence fell between us.

Time to move on to dessert and get this date over with. I stood and headed toward my truck.

"Where are you going?" Sydney asked.

"Just need to grab something," I called over my shoulder.

I opened the driver's side door and leaned in to retrieve my other flashlight from the center console.

Gravelly footsteps quickly approached from behind me. "What are you getting?" I should've known Sydney wouldn't just wait by the fire alone. For all her attempts at acting brave, she was still terrified of the desert wildlife—which was great for my plan but bad for my attempts at physical distance. I hadn't considered how clingy she would become.

"This." I turned around and held out the light for her to see.

She lifted a brow. "What do we need another flashlight for?"

"This one's special." I clicked it on to show her the purple glow of the black light.

"Oh." She folded her arms across her chest. "What do we need it for?"

"We're going hunting," I said, closing the truck door behind me.

"For?"

"A healthier option for dessert." In reality, I hadn't brought anything else for dessert; cooking scorpions was my endgame. There wasn't one female I knew who would try it. And I was banking on it being the straw that broke the camel's back. If worst came to worst and I had to eat one, so be it. I couldn't think of a better way to keep her from trying to kiss me.

Sydney's eyes widened, though she said nothing.

"Can you show me where you saw that thing with all the creepy legs?" I smiled encouragingly. "It sounds like a good place to start."

Her jaw fell slack. Instead of protesting like I thought she would, she nodded, grabbed my arm and led the way. "It was over there," she said, pointing to a Manzanita branch near a bunch of rocks the size of bowling balls. "Under that stick."

Perfect. She'd found something creepy and crawly alright. Rocks were prime real estate for scorpions. "Here, I'm going to need you to hold this for me while I flip a few rocks over." I handed Sydney the black light.

"Okay," she said in a wobbly voice.

"Good. Now, when we find the scorpions, I need you to hold the light steady while I catch one. You can't scream and run away. Got it?"

She swallowed and nodded her head.

"Good."

Just as I reached for the first rock, she said, "Wait!"

I turned to look at her, feigning annoyance. "What?"

"Why do you want to catch one?"

I lifted a brow, trying not to enjoy her obvious discomfort. "I told you. It's for dessert."

"You can't be serious!" She was incredulous, looking at me as if I were from another planet.

"Oh, I'm dead serious. Scorpion is very nutritious. Tastes just like chicken. You'll love it."

"But!" she sputtered. "Aren't they poisonous?"

"Sure they're poisonous. That's why we'll cook them before we eat them."

She squeezed her eyes shut and moaned, bouncing up and down on her toes. "Okay, okay, okay. I can do this."

She's toast. "Good." I rolled over the first rock, and a scorpion nearly as big as my hand glowed under the stream of purple light. It scurried and snapped its pincers, trying to escape the sticks I used to pin it down.

Sydney whined and shook her head, backing away. "Mmm nope, never mind. Can't do it! Tanner, this is crazy and disgusting! I don't want to do this! Please, can you just take me home?"

"Are you sure?" I asked, lifting the scorpion in the air with my homemade tongs for good measure.

She jumped back and screamed. "Get that thing away from me!"

"Alright, alright. Calm down. Let me just set this little guy back in his home, then I'll put out the fire and clean up so we can head out."

"Great." She looked relieved. "I'm going to go wait in the car." She turned and headed toward my truck, taking my flashlight with her.

I didn't even care. Nothing could spoil my mood now. I'd won the war! All at once, I felt lighter than air, a rush of euphoria filling my chest. My lips curved up in the darkness. Things could only get better from here.

TANNER

You still awake?

MAC THE THIEF

Yeah. What's up?

TANNER

Um . . . I kinda need a favor.

MAC THE THIEF

What kind of favor?

TANNER

Sydney and I are stranded in the middle of the desert. Can you come rescue us?

MAC THE THIEF

What's the damage?

TANNER

Two flat tires and only one spare.

MAC THE THIEF

Dang! That's unlucky.

TANNER

That's not even the worst part. There's a rattlesnake coiled up right next to my most recent flat. So . . . even if I had another spare, I wouldn't be using it just yet.

MAC THE THIEF

Creepy. What do you want me to bring? Fix-a-flat? Shovel?

TANNER

That would be perfect.

MAC THE THIEF

What's your exact location?

TANNER

Sending you a pin now.

> Oh, one more thing. Do you think you could help my mom get Hunter in bed before you head out? I was supposed to be home to help a few minutes ago.

MAC THE THIEF

Yeah. I'll head over now.

TANNER

Thanks! I owe you one!

11

MACKENZIE

I knocked softly on the Hansens' door. Tanner's mom soon appeared with a warm smile and a hushed voice. "Mackenzie, thank you so much for coming to help."

"No problem at all," I replied, careful to match her quiet tone. I followed her into the living room, which now had a gym mat spread out on the floor.

"Okay, I just need you to help me move him from his chair to the mat. After I change his diaper, we'll put him back in the chair, move the mat out of the way, wheel him to his room, then lay him in bed."

I nodded, hoping Hunter wouldn't be too much weight for us to handle. "Sounds good."

Getting Hunter down on the mat went smoothly enough. I cradled him like a baby and locked my fingers together to lower him as carefully as I could, while Mrs. Hansen supported the weight of his head. Lifting him up off the floor to set him back in the wheelchair was another story. The dead weight combined with the length of his body made it really difficult to stand without losing my balance. I didn't think I'd ever lifted anything so awkwardly heavy before in my life. In the end, it was pure determination that gave us the strength to accomplish our goal safely. There really was no way Mrs. Hansen could've done it on her own.

"Wow, for a minute there I wasn't sure if we were going to get him off the floor," I said, breathing hard from the exertion. "It's a good thing you have Tanner to help out on a daily basis."

"Yes, he's such a blessing to us," she said, folding up the mat and pushing it off to the side. "I couldn't ask for a more caring son."

But Tanner couldn't take off several months of work while his dad healed, could he? I tilted my head and voiced the thoughts in my mind. "So how much time does Tanner have off from work? I assume you'll have to get someone else to help out when he goes back?"

Worry lines creased her brow. "That's true. He's scheduled to go back in a little more than a week." She exhaled, her shoulders drooping from the weight of the burden she carried. "To be honest, I'm not sure what we'll do. We've been searching for a respite nurse for months without any luck. The staffing shortage makes it nearly impossible. The only other option is to get a lift installed in our home, but that takes time and money we don't have." She shook her head and continued. "Tanner says he'll find a way to work around his schedule and drop in when I need him in the morning, but the reality is, he won't be able to. His job is too unpredictable. I need to find another solution."

Mornings? I typically worked the closing shift at the studio Monday through Friday. Occasionally, I worked the morning shift if I felt like it, but I didn't have to. Making my own schedule was a perk of being the manager. *I could be consistent.*

Of course, I might not be her best option, since it took everything in me to lift him. Then again, I could add weight lifting to my workout regimen to help build up my strength a little at a time. *I can do this.*

The more I thought about it, the more I wanted to step in and help. It had been far too long since I'd had any real sense of purpose in my life. I was tired of the daily grind. Helping Mrs. Hansen would break up the monotony and make me feel like I'd done something worthwhile. And the best part? I'd never see Tanner because he'd be at work. Avoiding him at all costs was imperative. Distance was the only way I'd keep my heart in check.

Mrs. Hansen released the brake on Hunter's wheelchair and pushed him toward his bedroom down the hallway. I followed behind, feeling a newness of energy budding to life, willing me to speak. "I know I'm not the strongest candidate, but I would love to come help you in the mornings when Tanner goes back."

She paused and turned to face me, her eyes gleaming with hope. "Are you sure?"

I knew it wouldn't be easy, but I'd never felt more sure of anything in my life. "Absolutely. I'm happy to help."

Mrs. Hansen's eyes filled with tears. Without warning, she wrapped her arms around me. "You dear girl," she sniffled, "you're an answer to my prayers."

All at once, a feeling of peace pricked my heart and warmed my body from the top of my head to the tips of my toes. The moment felt important, as if deep down I somehow knew that because of this decision, the whole course of my life was about to change. *For the better.*

WHEN I FINALLY SPOTTED TANNER'S BLUE Silverado in my headlights, I pulled up beside him and rolled down my window. Tanner followed suit, revealing one very haggard version of Sydney, who was clearly having a miserable time. *Poor Syd.* She'd never been a fan of outdoorsy things.

"Thanks for coming," Tanner said, his voice full of relief.

"You're welcome." I handed over the grocery bag with the fix-a-flat in it. "I had to go to two stores to find this, so don't screw it up."

His half smile appeared, making my stupid heart flutter. "You wanna come show me how it's done?"

I shook my head. "Not a chance. I'm not getting out of this truck with rattlers slithering around."

"Fair enough." He brought his arm up to rest on the door frame. "Speaking of snakes, did you bring that shovel?"

"Yep. It's in the back," I said, hooking my thumb over my shoulder. "You're welcome to go get it."

"If you pull forward a few more feet, I will."

"Kenz?" Sydney poked her head forward before I hit the gas. "Can you take me home?"

She'd rather leave with me than let her dream guy take her home? Must've been some date. "Sure. When I get in position, hop in the back. You can climb through the window."

"Okay."

I pulled forward until Tanner's driver's side door lined up with my truck bed, shifted into park, then twisted around in my seat to slide open the rear window. Tanner climbed over to grab the shovel without setting one foot on the ground; Sydney carefully followed suit. While Tanner hopped back to his own truck and settled into the driver's seat with the shovel in hand, Sydney squeezed through the small window and flopped onto the bench. Her hair was in knots, and her makeup was a smudged mess. Had she been crying?

"Hey," I said gently, after sliding the window shut. "Are you okay?"

"Yeah." She buried her face in her hands. "I don't know." She shook her head and sighed. "The whole night has been one disaster after the next. Worst date ever."

"He's your dream guy," I reminded her, trying to cheer her up. "Was it really that bad?"

"Oh, trust me. It was." She groaned in frustration. "I never want to see this stupid desert again." She clicked on her seatbelt and threw her shoulders back. "Come on, let's go home."

"You got it." I flipped around my truck and paused at Tanner's open window to check on him before we left. "You good?"

"Yeah, don't worry about me," he replied, then winked in our direction. "Drive safe, ladies."

"We will," I called back before slowly rolling away.

"Now he acts charming," Sydney grumbled under her breath.

"What do you mean?" I asked, confused. "Isn't he always?"

"If you count laughing at me when I spilled water all over my face or making fun of me when I saw a creepy crawly and freaked, then yes, he was the perfect gentleman." She scoffed and continued. "Oh! And don't forget the best part—when I told him I was gluten intolerant, he offered to cook me scorpion for dessert. So, so, gallant!"

I couldn't stop myself from laughing. The things she complained about described Tanner to a T. She obviously hadn't experienced his teasing side until now. Did she know the guy at all? Sydney just glared at me. "I'm sorry," I said, finally getting my giggles under control. "You have every right to be mad."

"I've been holding in my pee for the last two hours too!" she whined.

"Let me guess—" I tried to hold back a smile. "He forgot to bring toilet paper?"

"I didn't even ask. You couldn't pay me enough to squat out there with all the cactus and snakes!"

I grinned and teased, "True, I wouldn't recommend mooning a rattlesnake. You'd be in for one nasty surprise!"

She shuddered. "Ugh! I hate the desert! Please, just get us out of here."

I pressed on the gas in response to help hurry us along.

"Ooo!" She cringed, bracing her hand against the door. "Slowly. My bladder can't handle all these bumps."

I knew it was kind of traitorous for me to think, but I felt more sorry for Tanner than I did for Syd. Dealing with that emotional wreck for hours must've been a nightmare. It would be a miracle if either one of them was interested in a third date now.

I smiled to myself in the darkness, thinking that maybe the torture was finally over. No more stupid scheming to throw them together. Sydney wouldn't act like a lovesick puppy all the time and I . . . well, I could be my usual boring self that avoided dating most guys. Yep. Bring it on. I was ready for my life to get back to normal.

12

TANNER

I arrived home well past midnight, completely exhausted. I couldn't believe the date had ended with two flat tires. And a rattlesnake! The desert had worked its magic alright. Even I wasn't very eager to return; at least for a few weeks.

I deserved it after the way I'd treated Sydney. Because of me she'd never set foot in the desert again. But . . . knowing that she'd give me the space I wanted from here on out was worth it. No more texts, no more annoying notes left on the windshield of my truck, no more following me around and hanging on my arm, no more staring at my lips like they were a piece of chocolate cake. Yep. I'd do it all over again in a heartbeat. Except maybe the sandwiches bit; I still felt bad about the physical pain that would cause her.

"Thanks for sending Mackenzie over last night," Mom said as I laid Hunter on the gym mat for his morning ritual. "She was a big help."

I still felt guilty about that, too. I'd tried asking a few of my squad mates for help before reaching out to Mac. Rogers was off the grid, Wilde and Butcher were unavailable, and Martin was wasted. I knew it was a long shot since it was the weekend, but I had to try. Mac and her kind heart and four-by-four truck had been my saving grace. I didn't know what I would've done if she hadn't come to my rescue.

"Sorry I wasn't home on time." The worst part about getting the second flat tire was I couldn't be there for Mom when she needed me.

"It was meant to be." Mom guided Hunter's head through the bottom of his shirt, smiling. "Mackenzie volunteered to help me in the mornings when you go back to work."

The major weight pressing on my mind for weeks suddenly lifted, a sliver of hope settling in its place. "She did?" Carrying Hunter was not easy. Was she really okay with it? If so, I owed Mac big time.

Mom nodded and tugged off Hunter's pajama pants. "I like her. She's sincere—doesn't try to impress anyone with her words or actions. She's kind for the sake of being kind, like her aunt."

It was true. She was probably the most genuine woman I'd ever met. That was a big reason why I liked her as much as I did.

When Mom finished changing Hunter's diaper, she pinned me with her knowing gaze. "Why haven't you asked her out yet?"

I smiled and folded my arms across my chest. "Who says I haven't?"

Her eyes widened in surprise. "Did you?"

"A couple times, actually," I admitted, chuckling. "She seems to think I'd be better off with Sydney."

Mom shook her head and laughed. "Roommate drama. I should've known." She guided Hunter's feet into his pant legs one at a time. "How did the date with Sydney go last night? Besides the flat tires."

I pulled my mouth to one side, choosing my words carefully. "Awful. Guess we aren't as compatible as you thought."

Mom's mischievous eyes bored into mine. "Or maybe you were too preoccupied with someone else to give her any real consideration."

When I only smiled in response, she laughed.

"I know you haven't been keen on dating for the last few years, but I'm glad you're finally getting back out there," she said, rising to her feet. "Having the right woman at your side will make all the difference in your life."

I cradled Hunter in my arms and carried him over to his wheelchair, saying nothing. Mom and Dad's constant love and easy friendship had seen them through all the ups and downs of life. She was right—finding that someone who would love and support me through anything would make my life significantly better. If only finding the *right* woman was as simple as ordering custom parts for my truck.

At least with Mac I had somewhere to start. She wasn't afraid of defending herself in a dangerous situation, she respected my job, she accepted my brother and treated him with kindness, she was an amazing cook, she was selfless, and a loyal friend—not to mention beautiful and fun. She checked all my boxes and then some, turning my "wife material" test on its head. The only thing left to do was build a relationship and see where it led.

But . . . the path forward would be tricky. Just because Sydney and I were toast didn't mean that Mac would jump at the opportunity to date me. I needed to tread carefully—build on our friendship in a non-threatening way, if she'd let me. I could tone down the flirting a notch, too. If I could manage that, I just might stand a chance.

I slipped my phone out of my pocket, intent on sending Mac a message. But what should I say? My thumbs hovered over the keyboard, my mind drawing a blank.

"If you're thinking about texting Mackenzie, don't," Mom said before disappearing into the kitchen.

How did she . . . ? I followed after her into the kitchen, my phone still in hand. "Why not?"

Mom was already in the middle of counting scoops for Hunter's breakfast, so I waited until she finished. "The woman lives right across the street. Go over there and talk to her." She tightened the lid, vigorously shook the bottle in her hand and turned to look at me. "And don't go empty-handed. She just saved your bacon. You should bring her something to show your gratitude, don't you think?"

Yeah. She deserved an extra effort on my part. I would bring back her shovel, at the very least. What else should I bring? A bouquet? I slipped my phone back in my pocket and rubbed my jaw, thinking.

I pulled open the refrigerator and scanned the top shelf. *Perfect.* "Hey, Mom?" I grabbed the pack of bacon, then turned to face her. "Where do you keep your gift wrapping ribbon?"

Mom lowered her brows in confusion. "You aren't planning on giving her raw bacon, are you?"

I chuckled and shook my head. "You'll see."

I KNOCKED on the door with Mac's shovel in one hand, a bar of chocolate and a bouquet of perfectly crisp bacon in the other. Maybe it was a little cheesy, but I had a feeling Mac would appreciate it more than a bouquet of roses.

She cracked the door open with brows lifted high. "Oh, hey."

When she pulled the door open wider, I stood there transfixed. Her hair was down, draped over her shoulders in soft waves nearly to her hips. I hadn't realized how long it was since she usually kept it pulled back.

Just when I thought she couldn't get any more beautiful, she smiled. "Uh . . . Tanner?"

Stop staring like an idiot and say something! I swallowed and returned her smile. "Hi."

"Glad to see you made it home in one piece," she said, her curious eyes lowering to my hands.

"All thanks to you." I set down the shovel, leaning it against the house, then offered her the bacon bouquet and chocolate. "For saving my bacon."

Mac chuckled and took the gifts, her brown eyes twinkling. "I have to say, this is the most unusual bouquet anyone's ever given me. I like the red bow. Gives it a nice touch." She held up the chocolate. "How did you know Symphony bars are my favorite?"

I grinned and shrugged. "I'm a man of mystery." I didn't know; it just happened to be what Mom had on hand in her chocolate stash.

"Well, thank you." Her hair fell forward, covering one side of her face. She tucked it behind her ear and met my gaze. "You really didn't have to do this."

Oh yes, I did. "I wanted to."

Her answering smile warmed my insides.

Remembering the cash I'd meant to give her, I pulled out my wallet. "I almost forgot. This should cover the fix-a-flat and gas." I offered her two twenty-dollar bills.

"I'm not taking your money," she stated. I opened my mouth to protest, but she shook her head and argued, "You rescued me first, remember? Now we're even."

"Are we?" Without warning, my eyes lowered to her mouth, her perfect lips tempting me to find out if they were as soft as they looked.

"Yes."

I inched closer and propped my free hand on the door frame, all coherent thoughts dancing around one thing and one thing only—how badly I wanted to kiss Mac. I lifted my gaze to her amber-colored eyes, searching for any sign of interest on her part.

She stepped back and looked away, her cheeks coloring slightly.

I'm an idiot. I blinked and pushed off the door frame, giving her the space she wanted. The last thing I needed was her thinking I was jumping from one girl to the next. *Slow and steady.*

I cleared my throat and stuffed the twenties back into my wallet. "Well, if you won't take my money, then I'll just have to find some other way to repay you." I folded my arms across my chest. "Can I mow your lawn?"

She lifted a brow. "Sydney's parents pay someone to take care of that for us."

"Then how about I wash your truck and rotate your tires?"

She shook her head and narrowed her eyes. "Why are you doing this? I said we're even. You don't owe me anything."

"Yes, I do," I countered. "If not for the rescue last night, then for you volunteering to help my mom when I go back to work. You don't know how much that means to us."

Her eyes softened. "I didn't volunteer to make you indebted to me, Tanner."

"Then why did you do it?" Normal people didn't give so selflessly of their time.

She shrugged. "Because she needs me. If I were in her situation, I'd hope someone somewhere would be willing to do the same for me."

I was face to face with a living, breathing angel on earth. "Are you always this amazing?"

Her cheeks darkened from pink to red. "Shut up. I'm just doing what any decent human being would do."

If only that were true. I shook my head, my lips curving up on one side. "Will you join us for dinner tonight? My mom's making pot roast. She wants to go over a few things about helping out with Hunter."

"Um . . ." Her wheels were turning, trying to decide if she wanted to take the risk or not. "What time?"

"Does six work?"

Come on. You know you want to.

Finally, she nodded. "Yeah. I'll be there."

Yes! I was so stoked I fought the urge to fist pump the air right in front of her. Time to leave before I did something even more stupid—like lean in to steal a kiss. "Well . . . I should probably get going. See you later, Mac." I stepped back and waved before turning to go.

"Tanner?"

I paused, my heart rate kicking up a notch as I met her gaze one last time. She was chewing on her lower lip. The woman couldn't be more attractive if she tried.

"Did you really try to feed Sydney a scorpion last night?"

I chuckled and admitted, "I may have teased her about it a little. She didn't think it was funny."

"Yeah, she was pretty upset on the ride home." Mac smiled and looked away. "Maybe stick to something simple, like the movies next time."

Next time? She didn't think there would really be a next time, did she? *I should tell her.* "Mac—"

A white Altima pulled into the driveway, setting me instantly on edge. *Sydney.* Time to run. "We should talk about this . . . later," I said, backing away. "I really need to—"

"Go," Mac cut in, waving me away. "It's fine. See you at six."

"See ya." I turned to leave just as Sydney stepped out of her car. "Hey, Sydney," I called out as I passed her by, hoping she wouldn't try to stop me for once.

"Hey," she replied politely, then continued on to the front door in silence.

Victory! My mission to shift Sydney's unwanted attention to anyone but me was a success. I could definitely get used to this.

Now, on to convince Mac that she wanted to date me. I was pretty sure I'd figured out the easiest way to achieve that—to tell her the truth. But it was risky. If Sydney caught wind of how I'd purposefully sabotaged our two dates, it could ruin everything.

On the other hand . . . what was life without a little risk?

13

MACKENZIE

S ydney walked into the kitchen with a huff of annoyance. "What was Tanner doing here?"

"Bringing by a little gift for rescuing you guys last night," I said, holding up the bouquet of bacon briefly before setting it back down on the counter.

"So he takes the time to bring you a gift, but he doesn't even bother apologizing to me?" She shook her head and muttered, "Typical."

I untied the ribbon and began moving the strips of bacon to a ziploc bag as she slunk onto a barstool across from where I stood.

"I don't get it," she complained. "He's such a nice and thoughtful guy. Why does he treat every woman like a freaking queen except me?"

I shrugged, not truly understanding it myself. "Maybe you make him nervous or maybe he feels intimidated by you." Even as I said the words, I knew it wasn't true. That man wasn't afraid of anything.

"No, that's not it," she said, folding her arms on the cool granite countertop. "It's like he's toying with me—like he's trying to make me jealous or something."

"You, jealous?" The thought was laughable, though I didn't dare laugh now. Syd was being completely serious. "What do you have to be jealous of?"

"You," she whined, resting her head on her arms.

Me? I let out a humorless laugh. "Very funny. Are you going to tell me the real reason now?"

"I'm serious!" She lifted her head and looked me square in the eyes. "Tanner's always flirting with you! He never acts like that with me. Maybe . . ." She shook her head hopelessly. "Maybe he likes you more than me."

"Whoa, whoa, wait a minute." I held up my hands in front of me, shocked that we were even having this ridiculous conversation. "The only reason Tanner flirts with me and treats every woman like a queen is because he's a player." He had no real interest in anyone; he was just like every other jerk I'd ever dated, going after the thrill of the catch. *That's it!* The answer zinged into my thoughts as clear as day. "If you want to catch his interest, you have to play hard to get."

She sighed and laid her head back down on her arms. "It's too late. He had his chance. I deserve better than that jerk."

Go Syd! I was proud of her for deciding to give Tanner up like I had. It couldn't have been easy—finding out that her dream guy was not the man she thought he was. There always seemed to be a line of men waiting to take her out, anyway. She'd move on soon enough. Maybe she'd meet someone tonight at the *Dropout*—Ash said she was bringing some "friends."

"You're right," I agreed. "There's a guy out there somewhere that loves exercise, eats healthy, and would never even think about eating a bug. When you two meet, you won't be able to deny the fireworks going off. He'll adore you and shower you with all the love you've been waiting for."

"Sounds amazing." Sydney tilted her head to smile at me. "Bring it on."

Tanner opened the door and smiled. "Mac, come on in." He stepped back and motioned me inside.

"Thanks." I ignored the fluttering in my stomach and entered the house. Just because Sydney didn't want Tanner anymore didn't mean that it was okay for me to give in. Players were strictly off limits; no matter how handsome and charming they were.

I gravitated toward Hunter sitting in his usual corner in the living room. "Hello, handsome," I said, reaching for his hand.

His face lit up with a smile just for me. My heart melted right then and there.

"Hunter remembers you."

I turned to face Tanner, unconvinced. "How do you know?"

"He never smiles for strangers."

He really remembers me? Warmth filled my chest at the thought. "Well, I'm happy to see you too," I said, turning back to Hunter. I noticed the bag of food hanging from the IV pole at his side with a long tube connected to his stomach. "And what are you having for dinner tonight? Something delicious, I hope."

Tanner chuckled and slipped behind Hunter's wheelchair to release the brake. "Let's just say he's lucky he doesn't have to taste it." His brows lowered in thought. "Well . . . not unless he throws it up."

"Poor guy." I let go of Hunter's hand and stepped back so Tanner could push him wherever he was intending to go.

"Could you roll the IV pole along beside us? I'm bringing him to the table so he can at least smell what we're eating."

How sweet. "Sure." I grabbed the pole and followed Tanner into the kitchen.

"Mackenzie!" Mrs. Hansen said. "We're so glad you decided to join us tonight." She set a platter of roast beef on the table next to a bowl of garlic potatoes and buttered carrots.

"The pleasure is mine," I replied, smiling. "The food smells delicious."

"I told you it would be, didn't I?" Mr. Hansen's eyes gleamed from the head of the table.

I held back a chuckle and nodded. "You did."

Mrs. Hansen finished setting the table and sat beside her husband. Tanner wheeled Hunter over to the empty space on her left, set the brake, then moved to sit on his father's other side. After positioning the IV pole beside Hunter, I walked around the table and lowered into the last remaining chair on Tanner's right.

To my surprise, everyone bowed their heads as Mr. Hansen offered a prayer. It reminded me of Sunday dinners back home in Tulare, when life was good. Simpler. Easier. Mom, Dad, Justin, and I would sit around a table much like this one, filled with delicious home cooked food and very little worry in our hearts. In the last few months leading up to high school graduation, Clint would often join us. Everything seemed so straightforward then. I was happy, thinking life would continue on much in the same way for many years with the people I loved at my side.

How wrong I'd been.

I hadn't meant to hurt my parents by staying away for so long. I just couldn't bring myself to go back to the place where my dreams had been snatched away; the place where friendships and trust had been irreparably broken. In five years, I still hadn't figured out how to find my place in the world—to feel like I belonged. How much longer would it take? One year? Two?

I hated feeling so lost.

When everyone murmured "Amen," I looked up at the kind people around me. Mrs. Hansen smiled at her husband lovingly and dished generous portions of food onto his plate. His quiet, "Thank you, my sweet" brought a small smile to my face.

Tanner turned to me with the bowl of garlic potatoes in hand. "How much would you like?"

My lips parted at the gentlemanly gesture. *He never misses an opportunity to woo a girl, does he?* "One scoop is fine, thanks."

Dinner passed by effortlessly. The food was delicious, and the conversation flowed easily. It didn't feel nearly as uncomfortable as I expected. Tanner put forth a gallant effort to be on his best behavior, which I appreciated. I imagined he wouldn't be quite so polite if his parents hadn't been there with us. Thankfully, it didn't feel like a date at all—at least to me it wasn't.

The trouble was . . . it was hard not to like someone when they were so easy to like. Now that Sydney wasn't competing for Tanner's attention anymore, it was going to be even harder to resist him.

After clearing away the dirty dishes, we gathered in the living room and settled onto the gray tufted sofas—apart from Mrs. Hansen who sat in the rocking chair next to Hunter. While Mrs. Hansen and I discussed the particulars of what to expect on the mornings when I would come help her out, Tanner and his dad chatted quietly about trucks and trail riding.

By the time Mrs. Hansen finished the breakdown, Tanner and his dad had gone quiet. I turned to find that Tanner wasn't even in the room. *Where did he go?*

Mr. Hansen smiled at me and tilted his head toward the hallway. "He'll be right back; went to change his shoes."

"He takes Hunter for a walk on Sunday evenings," Mrs. Hansen explained as she stood to disconnect the feeding tube from Hunter's stomach. "Gives them both a change of scenery."

"Would you like to join us?"

I turned and met Tanner's gaze as he crossed the room. My heart fluttered when he smiled that familiar half smile I was coming to love. He really was too handsome for his own good. Should I spend time with him in a more intimate setting? Probably not. Did I want to?

Oh yes.

"The weather is perfect tonight," Mrs. Hansen encouraged.

"It certainly is," Mr. Hansen agreed. "In a couple more weeks, we'll all be hiding in our air-conditioned homes until the summer monsoons hit."

It was true, summer always came early in the Phoenix Valley. Guess I'd better soak up the nice weather while I still had the chance. "You've convinced me," I said to them, smiling. "Are you two coming with us?"

"Oh, no," Mr. Hansen replied. "The back porch is far enough for us."

"William built us a lovely bench swing for our thirtieth anniversary," Mrs. Hansen added, taking her husband by the left hand and gazing into his eyes. "It's perfect for nights like this."

"That's sweet." They were a match made in heaven if I ever saw one. Clearly, they loved and cherished each other the way a husband and wife should. I ached to have that kind of relationship someday, though I wasn't sure I believed I ever would.

Tanner maneuvered Hunter out of the corner and asked, "Ready to go?"

"Yep. I'll get the door." I hurried toward the entryway, feeling somewhat nervous. Was this really a good idea?

A little walk with Tanner and his brother would be harmless. *No reason to panic.*

"Thanks," Tanner replied, carefully wheeling Hunter backwards over the doorstep.

"You kids have fun!" Mrs. Hansen called as I closed the door behind me.

This isn't a date.

I fell in step beside Tanner, walking down the sidewalk towards the green belt at the end of the street. All the streetlights were aglow, dispelling the darkness just enough. Hunter's wheelchair methodically hummed and thumped over the cracks and dips in the cement, almost like a child whizzing by in a pair of roller blades. A slight breeze teased the ends of my hair and tickled my skin. It really was a beautiful night.

"Can I ask you a question?" Tanner glanced my way, eyebrows raised.

As long as it has nothing to do with Sydney. I was over playing matchmaker. "Sure." I prepared myself, folding my arms across my chest like a shield.

"Do you feel—" He struggled to find the right words. "Like certain people are placed in your life for a reason?"

Was he talking about me? My stomach twisted in anticipation. "What do you mean?"

"Like . . . take Sydney, for example."

Sydney. Of course it would be Sydney.

"When we were kids, she got bullied pretty bad on the bus one day. Some jerk from our neighborhood sat behind her, pulling her hair and calling her names the whole ride home. She just quietly endured it in tears. I knew I had to put a stop to it, so when the bus driver drove away, I decked the kid in the nose. He never bothered her again."

Syd had never told me the details before; just that Tanner was there when she needed him. *And she's loved him ever since.* Maybe Tanner really did care about her. Should I help him get back in her good graces?

"It was that experience that led me to become a cop," Tanner continued when I said nothing. "So in a sense, if I hadn't met Sydney, I wouldn't be in a career I love."

He was talking about his job. Not romance.

"I'm not sure if that's happened to me, exactly, but it makes sense. Some things are just meant to be." I wish I'd felt that way about my career choice. Where was my person, inspiring me to take the right path when I needed direction?

Tanner gave Sydney hope in her darkest moment. Did he really not see how he'd affected her life as well? "You know . . . Syd could say the same about you. You changed her life that day too."

"Yeah." He rubbed the back of his neck. "There's something I've been wanting to tell you."

A good something or a bad something? "What is it?" My shoulders tensed as I waited for him to speak.

He sighed and met my gaze. "The only reason I asked Sydney out was to show her how wrong we are for each other; to help her move on to the next guy."

Wait, what?

He was never interested in her? I looked away and chewed on my lower lip, dropping my arms to my sides. It had to be a lie; everyone loved Sydney. Tanner was just telling me what I wanted to hear.

Hold on. Sydney did say he never flirted with her like he flirted with . . . *me.*

Could it be true? Did I completely misread him from the start? Or was I being played?

"The woman I would like to go out with is you."

I glanced his way, and for one blissful moment I let myself believe that he wanted me. Tingling warmth radiated from my chest. My stomach danced with nerves as my gaze darted to his lips. Oh, those tempting, full lips. He'd wanted to kiss me earlier that day. What would happen if I kissed him now? I drew closer and inhaled his spicy cologne, momentarily closing my eyes. I drank him in and then . . . I tripped over my own clumsy feet. Floundering into Tanner's side, I threw my arms around him to steady myself.

He stumbled back, holding firm to Hunter's wheelchair for support and chuckled. "You okay?"

"Yeah, I just . . ." My eyes flicked to his lips again, distracting me from fully forming my thoughts. "Tripped. I tripped on my foot." I pried my gaze away and shook my head.

"So what do you say to going out with me on Saturday?"

All at once, the reality of my situation came crashing in. There I was, about to make the same stupid mistake I always made with men. I couldn't let him manipulate me into another cycle of misery. I needed to be in control of my own future. *I will not be weak!* "I like you Tanner, I really do. But I can't date you."

His brows lowered. "Because of Sydney?"

"No. She told me she's finally over you. It's just—" I pressed my left temple, trying to ease the sudden headache budding there. "I don't trust easily. I've been hurt too many times by guys like you."

"Mac." I tried to walk away, but he placed a gentle hand on my shoulder and turned me toward him. "I'm not those guys. I would never hurt you."

He sounded so sincere. I wanted to believe him—to give him a chance. But the glaring evidence stacked against him convinced me otherwise. Based on his actions in the short time I'd known him, he proved to be a ladies' man through and through. And I swore I would never trust a ladies' man again. I shook my head, smiling sadly. "You have no idea what I've been through. I'm sorry to disappoint you, but I just . . . can't."

"Alright." He nodded and pulled his hand away. "If you don't want to date me, I'll respect that." He turned and started walking again.

That was easier than I expected. Massive relief washed through me, the pain in my head lessening the tiniest bit. "Thank you." I hurried my steps to keep up with his quickened pace. "Still friends?" My voice carried a wave of uncertainty. As sure as I was that I couldn't date him, I didn't want things to become cold and weird between us. We'd become friends over the past few weeks, and I didn't want that relationship to change.

"Friends," he agreed with a nod, a hint of his good humor returning in his expression.

I was proud of myself for proving that I wasn't as weak as I felt. No matter how much I'd wanted to give in, I was determined to have the final say in my future. And that future didn't include any more pain from doomed relationships.

"As my friend," Tanner said, flashing a devilish smile, "why don't we take Hunter to the movies on Saturday? One last hurrah before I go back to work. He'd love it."

Ha! We haven't even had a first hurrah. I grinned, shaking my head. "You don't give up, do you?"

"It's not a date," he argued. "We'll go see whatever kid movie they have playing. Nothing romantic. No expectations. Just three friends hanging out. What do you say, Mac?"

Sounded safe enough. But if he tried to pull anything, my taser would keep him in line. "Okay." I pointed a finger in warning. "But only because Hunter's coming with us."

14

TANNER

I backed the minivan out of the garage, threw it in park, then lowered the motorized ramp on the passenger side entrance. Mom wheeled Hunter up the ramp and into the back, anchoring his chair to the floor.

"Here's his diaper bag," Mom said, handing me the red backpack. "Remember, he needs to be home to eat by five."

"Don't worry." I smiled to reassure her. "I'll bring him home on time."

She nodded and turned to kiss Hunter on the cheek. "Have fun, my sweet boy."

As she exited down the ramp, I heard her call out, "Hello, Mackenzie!"

I glanced over my shoulder and watched Mac cross the street toward Mom, smiling. "Hi, Mrs. Hansen."

"I was just telling Tanner that Hunter needs to be home by five," Mom said when Mac reached her side. "You'll help him remember, won't you?"

I chuckled quietly to myself. Mom never stopped worrying.

"Of course," Mac replied. "I'm sure we'll be back well before then."

Hopefully not too much before. I planned on taking advantage of every minute Mac would give me. Her offer of friendship was my olive branch—the way I could earn her trust. I didn't know the details of how she'd been hurt in the past, but she wasn't the only one with emotional scars. I'd been hurt, too. I was just beginning to believe I didn't have to go through life alone. And if I didn't have to be alone . . . *neither did she.*

Mom waved goodbye, then disappeared into the house, closing the garage door behind her. I folded up the ramp with the remote as Mac climbed into the passenger seat.

"Hi, Tanner." She smiled, looking as beautiful as ever. Her hair was braided today, like the day we covered each other in paint.

I smiled at the memory. "Hey, Mac. How's your day going so far?"

"Good," she said, reaching for her seatbelt. "I hung out at my aunt's for a few hours this morning. Jess has prom tonight, so we had fun playing around with hair and makeup for a while."

"You played dress up?" I grinned, clicking my own seatbelt in place before backing out of the driveway.

"Technically, Jess and my aunt did all the 'playing' while I watched." She shrugged. "Somebody has to be the cheering section."

I chuckled and shifted into drive. "Is Drew going to prom too?"

"No." She shook her head with a sigh. "He thinks school dances are lame. Maybe when he gets a girlfriend he'll think differently."

Not likely. School dances are the worst. "Did you go to prom in high school?" I glanced her way again.

She nodded. "My senior year. How about you?"

"Same." Nearing the stop sign, I slowed down and said, "Your cousin's right, though. Even with a girlfriend, I thought it was pretty lame."

"What? Why?"

I pulled onto Twenty-Fourth Street, explaining, "After spending all that time and money on dressing up, we waited in line the entire night to take pictures. When they called the last dance of the evening, we finally gave up and ditched the line so we could say we danced at least once."

"Wow." She chuckled. "That is pretty lame. We definitely didn't have that problem in my small town."

I smiled. "You're from Tulare, right?"

"Yep."

Mom had told me where Mac was from after her visit the other week. I had to look it up on a map to figure out where it was, since I'd never heard of it—only a couple hours away from a place on my bucket list. "Have you ever been to Yosemite?"

"You know . . . it's sad. I've only been there once, and I guess my parents aren't very adventurous because we didn't even do any amazing hikes. It was so beautiful, though. I'd love to go back."

"Got to take what you can get out of family vacations."

She smiled and agreed, "So true."

"I've always wanted to hike Half Dome," I said, turning onto Baseline Road.

"Me too!" she exclaimed. "Seeing it from afar was breathtaking, but to be up there looking down on the rest of the world would be incredible."

I loved her enthusiasm. The second Mac had recognized my off-roading tires the night we met, I knew she was the outdoorsy type, but learning she also loved hiking was like the stars coming into alignment. Everything I learned about this woman drew me in and always left me wanting more. An idea struck me. "Have you ever hiked Flatiron?"

Her forehead wrinkled. "Never heard of it."

What? Hasn't even heard? I shook my head. "How many years have you lived here?"

"Five."

"And you've never even heard of Flatiron." *Shameful.* "We need to fix that."

She chuckled. "What's so great about it?"

"The view! You're at the top of the Superstitions, looking down at the whole valley!" It was no Half Dome, but it was the best the desert had to offer. "I can't promise you'll see a lot of the color green, but it's a sight you won't want to miss."

"Sounds amazing. We should get a group together and go sometime."

"Deal." I was a little disappointed about the group part, but if it meant spending more time with Mac, I'd take it.

Mac turned to look over her shoulder. "And how's my favorite handsome man doing today?"

I checked the rearview mirror and saw Hunter's face perk up. There really was something special about her, and Hunter wasn't the only one to see it.

"I bet you're excited to get out of the house," she continued. "We'll see the big screen; smell some popcorn. It's going to be great!"

Yes. Even though we were going to see some lame cartoon, I had a feeling it would be.

I PUSHED Hunter out of the theater, laughing loudly. Mac was as red as cinnamon candy—when she'd taken the lid off her cup and tipped it back to get one last sip of her drink, ice cubes came sliding out, spilling all over the floor. The poor teenager waiting to clean the room glared at her as she dropped the cup into the trashcan and bolted for the door in embarrassment.

Mac playfully smacked my arm with the back of her hand. "Okay, you had your laugh. Now cut it out. People are staring."

I didn't care. I was used to people staring when I was out with Hunter. *But Mac wasn't.* A few deep breaths later, I was back in control, cool as a cucumber.

"Do you care if we take a detour to the car?" I asked as we stepped out of the building.

Mac shrugged. "Where to?"

"The pet store. I think Hunter would enjoy seeing the animals." Really, it was an excuse to spend more time with Mac.

"Okay. You sure you don't want to drive? That's kind of a far walk."

"Trying to get rid of us already?" I teased.

"No." She chuckled, shaking her head. "Just want to make sure we get Hunter home when we need to. If we drive, we'll have more time to see the animals."

She did have a point. "Alright. To the Batmobile!"

Mac laughed at my nineteen-sixties Batman impersonation and said, "I knew there was a superhero hiding in there somewhere."

"Shh! Don't tell anyone. You'll blow my cover."

"What cover?" she countered. "Saving lives is your profession."

"True. But not everyone sees it that way." When her brows lowered, I explained, "The people I arrest seem to think I ruin lives, rather than save them."

She scoffed and shook her head in disgust. "That's because they're too childish to take responsibility for their own mistakes."

I grinned. *Couldn't have said it better myself.* "It's true. Even when I'm taking wrecks on the freeway with your average Joe, most people try to shift the blame on anyone and anything but themselves."

"That's sad." She shook her head and folded her arms across her chest. "You never know who to trust these days."

I unlocked the car and lowered Hunter's ramp, hoping that someday, if anything, she'd learn to trust me. Honesty was key in any relationship. Without it, we wouldn't stand a chance. The more I learned about her, the more determined I was to earn that shot out of the friend-zone.

When we walked into the pet store, the combination of hamster pellets, chew toys, and Puppy Chow assaulted my nose. Considering how many animals they housed there, it could've been much worse. I slowed the wheelchair to a stop and turned to Mac. "Where to first?"

Mac looked to her left and pointed. "How about the fish?"

"Sounds good," I said, wheeling Hunter toward the wall lined with glowing tanks.

"My brother and I had a few different kinds of fish over the years," Mac said, eying the little scaly swimmers as we walked. "Sadly, we couldn't keep any of them alive for more than a few months."

One side of my mouth curved up. "I never would've guessed you were the fish killing type."

Her cheeks colored slightly. "It wasn't intentional, but I still feel a little guilty about it."

"You've got nothing on me." I admitted, chuckling. "I think my record was two weeks."

Her eyes widened. "Wow! That's pretty bad."

I shrugged. "I had better luck with my pet tarantula. Had her for four years before I released her back in the desert."

"Good job keeping her alive." Mac teased good-naturedly. "What was her name?"

Points for not freaking out over a spider.

"Harriet."

She smirked. "Very fitting for a hairy spider."

"Thanks. I thought so too," I agreed with a smile, then turned down the aisle of reptiles. "Did you have any pets besides fish?"

She nodded. "We had a golden retriever named Beau."

Dog person. Another point in her favor. It's not that I hated cats as much as I hated sneezing. *Dang allergies.* "Nice."

"And we had a cockatiel named Wally."

Funny name for a bird. "Why Wally?"

She shrugged. "My brother picked the name."

"What? No story about the bird getting his name because he flew into the wall all the time?"

She bumped into my shoulder playfully and chuckled. "No."

Mac seemed more laid back and less on her guard the longer our "not date" went on. I wasn't going to get my hopes up, but it was nice to see that this friendship thing might actually work. "Tell me about your brother," I suggested. "Is he older or younger?"

"Justin is a couple years older," she said, her eyes scanning the reptiles as we walked. "He's in med school. Starts his residency next year."

My brows lifted. "Oh really? What's he specializing in?"

"Orthopedics." She smiled and met my gaze. "You could say he likes putting things back together because he wants to become a surgeon."

Bone surgeon. Hunter had one of those on his team of specialists. "That's cool. Sounds like a smart guy."

"Yeah. I think he'll do well." Her attention shifted to something past my shoulder. "Check out that bearded dragon! I almost didn't see him."

I turned and observed the creature that caught her notice. His dirt-colored scales blended in perfectly with his surrounding habitat. "Wow. If he holds still, he's pretty much invisible."

"Yeah. Sometimes I wish I had that superpower."

"Really?" Why would anyone want to be present but unseen?

Mac nodded and walked on, offering no explanation. "So you and Hunter have an older sister?" she asked casually, changing the subject.

"Yep," I said, pushing Hunter along beside her. "Jennifer's about three years older than me. Lives in Texas with her husband and two kids."

"Awe. Do her kids call you Uncle Tanny?" Mac's teasing eyes sparkled.

I fought a smile and shook my head. "Here, let me show you." I pulled out my phone and opened up a short video I had taken when we were all together last Christmas. Mac stepped closer to see the screen. I inhaled her vanilla scent as I turned up the volume and pressed play.

In the video clip, Lacy ran up to me and jumped up and down. "Uncle Tan-nuh! Uncle Tan-nuh! We see pity whites now?"

"Are you sure you're ready to see all the pretty Christmas lights?" I answered in the background. "I think maybe we need to get you a cup of your very own hot chocolate first!"

"Yay! Choco-rat!" Lacy said, running away. "Mommy! Mommy! Uncle Tan-nuh give me choco-rat!"

The clip blurred to a stop.

Mac met my gaze, smiling. "How old is she?"

"Lacy is four," I replied, easily matching her grin.

"She's so adorable."

"Yeah." I slipped my phone back into my pocket. "I sure miss the little squirt."

"Do you have any nephews?"

"Nope. Just Lacy and her sister, Hannah—who will be seven in a couple months."

She nodded and started walking again.

I followed after her, maneuvering Hunter's wheelchair around the corner and down the bird aisle. "So I was thinking"—Mac turned toward me with eyebrows raised expectantly—"if you're serious about hiking Flatiron, we need to go within the next week or two, before it gets too hot."

She smiled and said, "I was totally serious. Are you available next Saturday? I'm free all day."

Perfect. I liked that she was finally "free" to spend time with me. "Great! Let's plan on that, then. Are you good with an early start?"

She lifted a brow and folded her arms across her chest. "How early?"

"Four."

"Hmm," she said, thoughtfully. "Might be hard finding anyone else willing to get up that early to join us."

Exactly. "There might be one or two. It's a three to four-hour hike if you can keep a decent pace. The bigger the group, the slower it'll be. My mom's going to need help with Hunter when he wakes up, so I was hoping we could be back by eight-thirty."

"Okay." She dropped her arms to her sides and gave a determined nod. "Four o'clock it is."

15

MACKENZIE

M rs. Hansen opened the door, her eyes crinkling into a welcoming smile. "Mackenzie, good morning! Please, come in."

"Good morning, Mrs. Hansen." I smiled and stepped into the house. "How's Hunter today?"

"You're just in time to find out," she said, closing the door behind me. "Come with me!"

I followed her down the hall and into the first bedroom on the right. The walls were painted in a yellow and white striped pattern. It made the room feel cheery and warm. A chocolate brown dresser sat in the corner of the room, next to what looked like a toy chest. The black gym mat was folded and laying on the floor, partially tucked under the twin-sized hospital bed on the other side of the room.

Hunter lay in the bed, blankets pulled up to his chin with his head tilted toward the window illuminated with morning light. His eyes were open, sleepily shifting back and forth; his face pale and expressionless.

Mrs. Hansen motioned me closer and whispered, "Watch his face." She folded back the blankets and leaned over her son so her face was hovering a foot directly above his. "Good morning, Hunter!"

she said, rubbing gentle circles on his chest. "How's my sweet boy doing this morning?"

Hunter turned toward his mother, his blank face transforming into a grin of pure joy. His entire countenance beamed, like the golden glow of sunlight coming in from the window, only stronger. His happiness was contagious. I smiled, feeling so elated I thought I might burst. Hunter suddenly squealed, catching me completely by surprise. A giggle escaped from my lips.

Mrs. Hansen turned to me, radiating with happiness, too. "It really warms your heart, doesn't it?"

I was grinning like a fool. "Yes! It's so incredible to see him light up like that." I shook my head in amazement. "Does he do this for you every morning?"

She nodded. "Just about. He does have his off days, though."

"Well, I'm so glad I was able to see it my first day on the job."

"Me too," she agreed, smiling.

Mrs. Hansen bent over to pull the gym mat out from under the bed, then paused mid-task. "You know what?" She stood upright and tapped her lip with a thoughtful expression. "I think I have a way to make this easier on us." She turned and walked out of the room, calling over her shoulder, "I'll be right back."

I watched her leave, then sat on the bed next to Hunter. His grin had faded, but he still looked generally happy to be awake.

"Hey, handsome," I said, grabbing his soft hand. "I loved getting to see your big smile and hear your voice today. You can cheer anyone out of a bad mood with that smile of yours, can't you?"

Remembering how his mother had leaned over him so he could see her, I positioned my face in his line of sight. "I'm going to carry you today while your brother is at work." Hunter's eyes bounced my way an extra couple of seconds. "Hopefully, it won't be too uncomfortable for you. I know I'm not as strong as your brother, but I'll do my best." The enormity of the task before me weighed on my mind. Was I strong enough to do this? I hoped so.

Mrs. Hansen returned, carrying an armful of towels, clothes, a diaper, and wipes. "Okay," she said, dropping her load onto the end of the bed. "This is what we're going to do." She picked up a towel from her pile, shook it out, then folded it in half. "You're going to lift up his legs so I can stuff this under his bum to protect the sheets. Then I can just change him here instead of us having to lift him up off the mat again."

It was a genius idea. Take away the hurdle of getting him off the floor and our goal would be completely attainable for my weak arms. *This is going to work.* "Sounds good."

Mrs. Hansen worked quickly, getting Hunter changed and dressed with surprising speed. The initial lift to get him out of bed and swivel him to the wheelchair was challenging but not impossible. Overall, the whole process ran a lot smoother than I expected. Was ten measly minutes of my time really all she needed?

"What else can I do to help you?"

Her eyes shined with gratitude. "Would you like to learn how to feed him?"

I smiled, feeling a sense of excitement bubbling up, though I couldn't say why. "Absolutely."

The whole feeding process fascinated me. The fact that a person without the ability to do something as simple as swallow could be nourished through an exterior hole to their stomach was incredible. And the invention of a pump that administered food as slowly or as quickly as you wanted? Ingenious.

Hunter even had a pump implanted into his abdomen that automatically administered medicine directly into his spinal fluid, to keep his muscles from permanently tensing up. *Medical advances never cease to amaze me.*

"Would you mind sitting with Hunter while I go check on my husband?"

"Not at all," I assured her.

"Thank you," she said, then quickly disappeared down the hall.

I settled into the rocking chair and smiled at Hunter. "Your mom sure does a lot to keep everyone healthy and comfortable, doesn't she? You're one lucky guy to have a mom that cares so much."

Unlike mine. My own mother wasn't an awful person. I loved my childhood and wouldn't wish to change it for the world. She just didn't understand why I had to leave. The betrayal I'd experienced didn't matter to her. She refused to see it as a valid excuse to pack my bags.

"*You're being irrational!*" she'd said. "*Throwing away everything you've worked for over some stupid boy is a mistake!*"

"*I'm not throwing it all away!*" I'd shot back. "*I'm still going to college, just not to Fresno State!*"

"*Then where?*"

"*Arizona State.*"

She laughed mirthlessly. "*Go right ahead. You can stay with Crystal. One summer in that furnace and you'll be transferring back before fall classes even begin.*"

That first summer was especially brutal, but I'd stuck it out just to prove to Mom that I could. By the time I finished up my sophomore year of college without coming home once for the holidays, she'd finally accepted that I wasn't transferring back. Her calls became more and more infrequent over junior and senior years. And after graduation, when I decided to stay in Mesa permanently, completely nonexistent.

I knew I'd hurt her, but I was afraid that if I went back, even to visit, all that pain from the past would drown me all over again. Why would I wish that misery on myself when I'd only just begun to feel free of it?

Why couldn't Mom understand?

Enough dwelling in the past. I shook my head, desperately needing a distraction. I let my gaze wander until I spotted the piano in the music room. Playing the piano had always been my escape in my teenage years—when life wasn't nearly as complicated. I ached to play again, wondering if it would still have the same therapeutic effect now as it did then.

Tanner had said Hunter liked music. *Maybe I could play for him...*

"William will be out in a minute," Mrs. Hansen said, hurrying across the room toward me. "Thank you for all your help today. Truly, I couldn't have done it on my own."

I guess that's my cue to leave. I stood and stepped away from the rocker, trying not to feel too disappointed. "You're welcome."

"Now, I know we've never discussed payment, but my husband and I agree that you deserve compensation for your time. So we'd like to offer you fifty—"

I held up my hands in protest before she could finish. "No, no, please. I don't want your money, Mrs. Hansen."

"Well, there must be something we can do in return," she replied with determination in her voice.

My gaze flicked to the music room, an idea forming fast. "Actually"—I grinned, letting the excitement of the chance to finally play again take flight—"I know exactly what you can do."

16

TANNER

After taking almost a month off work, I'd been antsy to get back on the road. I wasn't used to being home twenty-four seven—made a man feel stir crazy after years of consistently pushing four tens a week.

I'd been relieved when I hopped into my patrol car this morning, grateful to get back to my normal routine. But as the morning wore on, going from call to call, the excitement soon faded into exhaustion. By the time eleven o'clock rolled around, I was ready to go home.

Only four more hours. The morning rush had been so hectic I hadn't even had the chance to stop for lunch. Seeing that Butcher and Wilde were finally in the green, I took the next exit off the highway toward home for my break. Rogers messaged, asking if I wanted to catch lunch together since I'd been gone so long, but Mom needed help with Hunter's midday diaper change. I typed up a reply into the chat. *Sorry, brother. Can't. Want to grab dinner later?*

S. Rogers: Yeah. I could really use your advice about something.

T. Hansen: Annie again?

S. Rogers: Yep.

Sounded like Annie was being her difficult, stubborn self. *Redheads.*

T. Hansen: I'll pick you up at six.

When I turned down Javelina Avenue, I noticed Mac's Ranger sitting in her driveway. I hoped things had gone well with her and Mom today; I planned to text her later to find out.

I parked my patrol car behind my truck and radioed dispatch. "Eighteen-fifty-six. I'll be code seven at my forty-two."

"Eighteen-fifty-six. Ten-four," dispatch confirmed through the speaker.

I used my key to unlock the front door and stepped inside. Piano music filled the living room. It wasn't a song I was familiar with. *Did Mom buy some new sheet music?* I closed the front door behind me and headed toward the music room to let her know I was home.

Wait a minute. That's not Mom. I froze in the doorway, my eyes fixed on Mac sitting at the piano. Her fingers flew effortlessly over the keys as her body swayed with the rhythm. She looked completely in her element, like she was born to play. Not one sheet of music sat in front of her; she played completely from memory.

"She's good, isn't she?"

I turned to face Dad, who had walked up beside me. "Yeah. Amazing. I didn't know she played so well."

"Apparently this is the first time she's played in five years. She must be enjoying herself because she's been at it for nearly two hours." Dad's eyes twinkled in amusement.

I looked over my shoulder and noticed the living room was empty. "Where's Mom and Hunter?"

Dad gestured to the music room. "They've been in there, soaking in every minute of it."

I poked my head in the room and saw Mom relaxed on the recliner with her feet up and eyes closed, a pleasant smile on her face. Hunter was fast asleep in his wheelchair beside her.

Their day must be going well, at least. I smiled at the thought.

"Tanner!" Mom lowered the footrest and rocked back to try to stand. "Are you home for lunch?"

"Yeah." I crossed the room to give her a hand up.

She accepted with a grateful smile.

The music stopped. Mackenzie spun around on the bench, her brows lifted in surprise. "Hey, Tanner."

"Hey, Mac."

"I'll go make you something to eat," Mom said, before slipping out of the room.

I turned to face Mac, motioning to the piano. "That sounded amazing."

"Thanks." She tucked a lock of hair behind her ear and gave me the once over. "You certainly clean up nice."

"Oh yeah? You like the uniform?" I grinned, milking the compliment for everything it was worth.

"It has its charm." She smiled in that mischievous way of hers, making me wish I knew what she was really thinking. "So . . . lunchtime already?" Mac watched me expectantly as she rose from the bench.

"Yep. This is actually a late lunch for me. It's been a pretty busy morning."

"Late?" She drew out her phone, her eyes widening at the time. "It's eleven-twenty? Crap!" She shoved her phone back in her pocket and hurried to the front door. "I didn't realize the time!" she called over her shoulder. "Please tell your mom I had to run to work!"

"Okay. Drive safe!"

"I will!" She ran like mad across the street and through her yard.

I chuckled when she dropped her keys as she rushed to unlock the front door. I already couldn't wait to see her again. If I were lucky, maybe I'd catch her at lunch tomorrow—preferably before she had to rush off to work.

I turned back into the house, shutting the door behind me and went to get Hunter out of the music room. His eyes were wide open, looking for a familiar face. He must've woken up when the music stopped. "Hey, buddy. Don't worry, I got you." I patted him on the shoulder and wheeled him toward the kitchen. "Let's go find Mom."

"Hunter! Oh, did you wake up already?" Mom left the counter to stroke Hunter on the cheek. "You had a nice nap, didn't you?" Her eyes flicked to mine. "Thank you for grabbing him."

"Of course. Thank you for the sandwich."

"You're welcome." She turned back to the counter to grab my plate and take it to the table. "Did Mackenzie leave, then?"

"Yeah. She had to rush off to work." I wheeled Hunter over to the table next to Dad—who'd just started eating his own lunch—then I sat down on Hunter's other side.

"She's not trying to avoid you again, is she?" Dad asked, a look of concern furrowing his brow.

"No." My mouth curved up on one side. "We're making progress. She just lost track of time." I picked up my sandwich and took a bite.

"Good." Dad gave me a satisfied nod. "You know"—he paused to take a drink of water—"your mother and I had a bit of dating drama back in the day. Didn't we, Maggie?"

Mom placed her plate on the table and sat beside Dad. "Oh, yes. I was so mad when you broke up with me. One of the worst months of my life."

They broke up for a month? My brows shot to the ceiling. I thought they'd been together from the moment they met. "Okay, why have I never heard this story before?" I set down my sandwich and folded my arms across my chest, waiting for an explanation.

"Because I'm not proud of how I acted," Dad began. "If I had just asked her about what happened and trusted her, everything would've been fine."

"Your father thought I was cheating on him with Nathan Phelps," Mom filled in.

"Dad's lawyer friend?" I guess I could see it. He was one of those Paul Rudd types, good looking—always appeared at least ten years younger than his actual age.

She nodded. "That's the one."

"It was all just a huge misunderstanding," Dad said. "She was having a girls' night out. I happened to go to the same restaurant with the guys. Nathan was running late. I went to the restroom. When I came out, I spotted Nathan and Maggie hugging by the fountain and assumed the worst."

"He broke up with me the next day." Mom picked up the story with a sigh. "Didn't give me a reason why or anything."

"That's brutal, Dad." I shook my head, completely surprised they hadn't mentioned it before. "Now I get why you've always been such a strong advocate for open communication."

Dad chuckled. "What can I say? Most of us poor saps learn wisdom by experience."

True. I wondered what experiences led Mac to mistrust men so much. If I could just understand where she was coming from, maybe I could help her take that little leap of faith and take a chance on me.

If everything worked out the way I hoped, we'd get a few hours alone to talk on our hike. Saturday wouldn't come soon enough. The thought of spending time with her again lifted me so high, it'd take a thirty car pile up to bring me down. My only problem now was patience; which, unfortunately, wasn't my strong suit. I didn't want to settle for hurried lunchtime visits and texting, but what else could I do?

TANNER

Did you make it to work on time?

MAC THE THIEF

Clocked in one minute late.

TANNER

That's not too bad.

MAC THE THIEF

Yeah. I got lucky. Traffic was good.

TANNER

Thanks again for helping my mom with Hunter.

MAC THE THIEF

No problem. She taught me how to feed him.
It was fun.

TANNER

You'd make a good nurse.

MAC THE THIEF

Ha! Maybe if I didn't hate needles.

TANNER

You're afraid of a little needle?

MAC THE THIEF

It freaking hurts!

TANNER

Maybe you just had a bad nurse.

MAC THE THIEF

Every time? Lucky me.

TANNER

Haha! Sorry.

I've got to get back to work. Hope you have a
good day!

MAC THE THIEF

Yeah . . . I should probably do something
productive too. Be safe!

TANNER

Always.

17

MACKENZIE

My first week carrying Hunter had been a success. Each and every day that sweet, young man never failed to lift my spirits; and I needed it more than I realized. What was it about his gentle, quiet way that made me feel so capable and important?

Working as the office manager of Ellwood Photography had a completely different dynamic. I worked hard to keep everything running smoothly, earning praise and appreciation from my boss easily enough. So why did it feel like I was missing out on something even better?

If only someone had inspired me to know what I wanted when I was young, like Tanner experienced, then maybe I wouldn't feel like I was wandering aimlessly through life. He definitely wasn't. The man seemed to have everything—the love of a supportive family and his dream career, looking way too good in his tan uniform than should be allowed. He exuded confidence and purpose. Anything he wanted, I was sure he had all the right tools and determination to get it. That was the way of the player. Always manipulating, only thinking of themselves.

What baffled me, though, was how Tanner had been acting lately.

When I'd told him I couldn't date him, I wasn't expecting him to take it in stride as well as he did. Instead of flirtatious and persistent, he seemed more relaxed and consistent, which I liked. It took all the pressure out of our relationship to become anything more than friends, which was exactly what I needed right now.

My roommates were always busy chasing after guys, as if having a man interested in them was the only way to prove their worth. I guess I used to believe that, too. And even now, I had no place to judge because it was my growing bond with Tanner and his family that lit up my darkened world like a beacon of hope. I needed them as much as they needed me. I couldn't see where my future would lead, but I knew that somehow I'd find my way.

I did worry about Sydney, though. Despite the few dates she'd gone on in the last two weeks since the Tanner fiasco, she didn't seem her normal, cheerful, confident self. *He must have really broken her heart.*

I glanced at Sydney through the bathroom mirror, my hands still searching for the last few bobby pins holding my hair hostage in a bun. She folded her arms and leaned against the door frame, pouting.

"Are you sure you don't want to go running with me in the morning?"

Even if I hadn't made plans to hike Flatiron, I wasn't about to agree to her torture. Syd's idea of "running" was more like long distance sprinting. *No thank you.* At that pace, my stamina was bound to fizzle out before the hundred yard mark, being more of a slow and steady kind of girl. "You know I'd never be able to keep up." I smiled as I finally tugged the last pin free, then turned to face her. "You should come hiking instead."

She cringed. "Nope. No more desert for me, thanks."

"Come on," I encouraged, brushing out my hair with my fingers. "I heard the view is one you won't want to miss. Don't you want to see the valley from the top of the Superstitions?"

She shook her head. "Sorry, Kenz."

I nodded, trying to think of how I could cheer her up. *Ryan.* He loved running; and he had a crush on Sydney. Why he'd never worked up the courage to ask her out was beyond me. He was just the guy to distract her from her heartache. "You should ask Ryan to go running with you."

She wrinkled her nose. "Why him?"

I chuckled. "Because he's the only one I know that can keep up with you."

She sighed and dropped her arms to her sides. "I'll think about it."

Good. Ryan may not be the most handsome guy in her line of suitors, but he was thoughtful and kind—everything she professed to want in a guy but never seemed to find.

If only I could find the perfect guy for me just as easily.

TANNY

Ready when you are.

HE WAS A FEW MINUTES EARLY, but I didn't mind. I finished tying my hiking boots, grabbed my Camelbak, and quietly slipped out the front door, locking up before texting him back.

MACKENZIE

I'm out front.

Thirty seconds later, the Hansen's garage opened and Tanner emerged from within, carrying his own backpack. I tried to will away the instant fluttery feeling in my stomach as I crossed the street and joined him at his truck under the glowing streetlight.

"Morning, Tanny." I was so tired I almost didn't realize I let the nickname slip.

"Good morning, Mac." His mouth curved into a smile. "Did you sleep well?"

"Yeah," I said with a yawn, then chuckled. "Just not enough, apparently. You're used to getting up this early, aren't you?" I kept my gaze firmly on his eyes. His handsome smile was extra distracting today. No need to give any attention to his perfectly shaped lips.

"Yep. Every workday." He pulled open the passenger side door for me.

"Thanks." I climbed in, set my Camelbak on the floor, and clicked my seatbelt in place.

Tanner hopped into the driver's seat and twisted around to set his backpack on the floor behind him. "Here." He held out his hand. "Let's get your Camelbak out of your foot space."

The small backpack wasn't bothering me, since I didn't have long enough legs to feel crowded in the space, but his thoughtfulness was appreciated, nonetheless.

"Thank you." I lifted it off the floor and handed it to him; his warm fingers brushed mine in the exchange, making me crave a connection I shouldn't want. *No hands. No lips. I can do this.*

"So none of your friends could make it, either?" he asked as he started the engine and buckled his seatbelt.

"Nope." I shook my head, wondering how many people he'd invited to come along. I didn't know why I even bothered asking my roommates. Not one of them wanted to come. *No big surprise there.*

He shifted into drive and nodded, his eyes never leaving the road. "Their loss."

"Yeah," I agreed, yawning again. To be honest, I wasn't disappointed we were hiking alone. *As long as Tanner knows this isn't a date.* Hunter needed us to be fast. The smaller the group, the quicker the pace could be. That was the only reason I was okay with it being just the two of us.

Well . . . that was the lie I told myself to believe, anyway.

When we arrived at the trailhead, it was still dark out—and would be for another hour or more. "Are you ready?" Tanner turned to face me, his headlamp shining right in my eyes.

I squinted and reached for his light, tilting it down toward the ground. "Yes, but you really need to stop blinding me with that thing."

"Sorry." He chuckled, turning away to adjust his light back to the way he liked it before starting down the path. "I just won't look at you anymore."

I bumped into his arm, smiling. "That's fine as long as you and your long legs don't leave me in the dust."

"There's a rope in my pack somewhere. Want me to make you a leash so you don't wander off?" he teased.

I chuckled and picked up my pace to walk a couple of steps ahead of him. "Nope. I don't plan on getting left behind."

He easily lengthened his stride to walk beside me once again. "Neither do I."

As the sun slowly lit the sky, I basked in the quiet stillness of the morning and marveled at the beauty that surrounded me. The jagged cliffs, the Saguaro Cactus, the Teddy Bear Cholla, the orange and yellow desert wildflowers, the Creosote bushes that smelled so divine when it rained; I loved it all.

"Enjoying the scenery?" Tanner smiled in my direction, his forehead finally free of that ridiculous headlamp.

"Yes." I shook my head in amazement. "It's crazy how different this place looks up close. There's a lot more green than I expected."

"That's what I love about the desert; even though it's rough and prickly on the outside, there's always beauty hiding just beneath the surface." He picked up something off the ground and held it out for me to see.

It was a dull gray rock shaped like a heart. I chuckled. "Nice."

"People can be like that too," he continued, tossing the little rock aside.

My brows lifted. *Not all people.* "Or they can be the complete opposite—charming and perfect on the outside, ugly and heartless on the inside."

"True." He nodded and focused on the steep, rugged incline ahead of us. "I take it you've met one or two?"

"Four actually." I didn't know why I told him that. The last thing I wanted to do was talk about my exes.

"I'm sorry." He climbed up the eight-foot rock face in our path and turned to point out the hand and footholds to help me do the same. "I was engaged once," he admitted as I pulled myself to the top.

"You were?" That didn't sound like a player. I stood, brushed off the dirt on my pants, then looked into his eyes. "What happened?"

"Her name was Emily." He looked away and trudged up the path. "She was beautiful and confident, a little too obsessed with fashion, but I was crazy about her."

A spark of jealousy twisted in my gut. *Do I really want to hear this story?*

"When I'd asked her to marry me, she didn't hesitate," Tanner continued. "She'd said she loved me more than anything. Life was great up until a week before the wedding, when all of a sudden, she refused to marry me unless I quit law enforcement."

That's why he was so defensive about his job when we first met. And to have it all end like that right before the wedding? *Awful.* "Tanner, I'm so sorry." I put my hand on his arm.

He slowed his steps, met my gaze, and shrugged. "I fell for the wrong woman." His eyes held a secret, something he wasn't telling me. If I looked long enough into his mesmerizing crystal blues, maybe I could figure out what it was. "It was a hard lesson to learn." He blinked and turned away, unsmiling. "But it's in the past. I'm over it now."

Yeah, because you decided that being a player was easier than facing the pain of loving again. I couldn't blame him, though. I was scared to take that risk, too. "Eh, love's overrated anyway," I joked halfheartedly.

He smiled and shook his head. "I've been telling myself that for the past three years. Now, I'm not so sure."

Did that mean he was ready to try again? With who? *Me?*

"He must've been a real piece of work." Tanner's comment sliced through my racing thoughts.

I looked up, meeting his gaze. "Who?"

"The guy that broke your heart."

Dare I open up about my past? It couldn't have been easy for him to talk about his ex. *Trust goes both ways.* "Clint Masterson," I said, my voice dripping with derision. "Cheated on me with my best friend the day we graduated high school."

Tanner winced. "What a dirtbag."

I nodded, completely agreeing with his assessment. "I never saw it coming from either of them. The three of us had plans to go to college together."

He shook his head. "That must've been hard."

I shrugged and surprised myself by continuing, "It gets even worse than that." I focused on the path ahead. "After I moved here, there was Nick, who wanted an open-ended relationship." I held up a finger as I listed each name. "Xavier, who wanted to get married after only a few weeks of dating, when he was secretly already married. And then there was John, who moved on to the next girl the week after I told him I loved him."

"Wow, Mac." He stopped to look me in the eyes. "I can see why you don't date. I'm sorry you had to go through that."

Warmth and peace enveloped me. It felt so good to open up with Tanner and feel validated for once. He seemed to understand my pain and didn't try to brush it off like it never happened. Like it didn't matter.

"I hope you tased the crap out of all those losers."

An unexpected chuckle escaped my lips. "I should have."

When we reached the top of the mountain, the sun's golden rays shone bright all around us, nearly blinding us with its brilliance. Tanner took my hand and led me to the lookout point to the west with the sun at our backs. He didn't let go as we stood side by side on the precipice overlooking the entire Phoenix Metropolitan Valley. I didn't complain—we were standing on the edge of a cliff after all, and having someone strong and steady to hold on to was comforting. Civilization stretched out before us in every direction as dots of white and gray, like the bird's-eye view you see from an airplane. And in the distance, blue mountains covered the horizon as if they were majestic gates guarding the vast cities within. It was breathtaking.

"Beautiful view," I said, turning to smile at Tanner.

His gaze was fixed on me. "It sure is."

I squeezed his hand and looked away, feeling completely safe at his side; safe in knowing I had a friend that understood my pain, a friend I was beginning to *trust*. And maybe, just maybe, someday we could be something more.

18

TANNER

What I wouldn't give for an excuse to see Mac. It was Wednesday—my one day off in the middle of the work week, so, naturally, Mom didn't need her to help out. Work had been so busy the past couple days, I couldn't stop at home for lunch and chat with Mac like I usually did. In fact, I hadn't seen her since Saturday.

The hike had been everything I'd hoped it would be. We'd talked easily, creating a bond that ran deeper than casual friendship; more than flirting and attraction; more than mutual interests. I finally understood where she was coming from and why she was afraid to put her faith in me. I had to prove to her I wasn't like those other guys. No secrets. No deception. Honest and open communication—everything I wanted in a relationship, too.

I felt like we had a chance to make things work between us . . . if we ever got to actually spend some time together.

I grabbed my guitar out of the music room and settled onto the couch near Hunter, tuning each string one by one. I strummed a few random chords until I found a progression I liked, then got lost in the music for a while. Lyrics came to mind as I pictured Mac staring out at the valley on the top of Flatiron; her brown eyes filled with wonder.

She'd glowed like some ethereal being with the golden sunrise on her back. I'd wanted nothing more than to pull her close and show her how much I cared for her, to give her a piece of my heart. But I couldn't chance ruining the trust we'd built. The ball was in her court. If she wanted something more than friendship, the first kiss was up to her. But that didn't mean I couldn't help move things along.

I saw movement in front of the Freeman house through the open blinds. I stood, propping the guitar against the couch, and stepped closer to the window to investigate. Mac was the only one home at this time of the morning. She was rolling a floor jack over to her Ranger, which she'd parked on the street instead of the driveway. Was she having car trouble?

Perfect.

I watched her jack up the front end of the truck and crawl underneath. "Mom?" I called over my shoulder.

"Yes, Tanner?" she answered from the kitchen.

"I'm going across the street to help Mackenzie with her truck. Call if you need me."

"Alright! Take your time."

I smiled to myself. *I plan to.*

I crossed the street and silently crouched down to get a look under the Ranger. Mac laid on her back beside a collection pan with her arms suspended above her, working a wrench. *She's changing the oil.* Another reason I liked this woman. She was resourceful, and she wasn't afraid to get her hands dirty.

When she finished loosening the drain plug, the oil came out too fast, splattering off the collection pan. "Crap!" She dropped her wrench and reached for the blue paper towels she'd placed nearby. Instead of grabbing them, she'd clumsily rolled them further away. "No, no, no!"

"Need some help?"

She jerked up, bumping her head on the oil pan underneath the truck. "Ouch!"

Oh, that's got to hurt. I should've known better than to sneak up on her. "You okay?"

Mac chuckled and covered her face as she lay back down. "I think so. More embarrassed than anything."

"Hang on. I'm coming around." I hopped up and jogged to the other side of the truck to grab the paper towels, then crawled under to join her.

I leaned in beside her and slowly pulled her hands away from her face. Several black smudgy streaks ran down from her forehead to her jawline like war paint. I grinned, trying to hold in a laugh.

She kept her eyes closed, probably because of the oil on her eyelids. "Go ahead. Say it. I look like a chimney sweep, don't I?"

"Yeah." I chuckled, ripped off a paper towel, and gently wiped the oil from her eyes. "The cutest chimney sweep I've ever seen."

She smiled and her eyes fluttered open, focusing on my lips. My heart rate increased. She reached up and put a hand over mine, stopping me from wiping her cheek.

This is it. She's going to kiss me.

I leaned in part of the way and froze; the smell of grease mingled with her vanilla scent intoxicated me. *Mmm.* All she had to do was tilt her head to make our lips meet. My eyes shifted between her eyes and her mouth, waiting. Wanting.

Her hand moved to rest on my cheek. "Tanner," she said softly. "Thanks for coming to help me"—her gaze lifted to my eyes—"but if you sneak up on me again, I'm whipping out my taser with no mercy."

I grinned, wanting to kiss the woman even more. "Fair enough."

Her gaze shifted to my cheek. She dropped her hand and chuckled. "I'm sorry. I just got oil on your face."

I didn't care. I'd wipe our faces off with my favorite shirt if she'd just let me kiss her. "That's alright. It'll wash off."

She turned away, reaching for the new oil filter sitting beside the collection pan. "Care to do the honors?"

Dang. Mac was torturing me. One minute we were prepared for liftoff, the next, I was left behind as she bailed out the window. *So close.* "Sure." I took the filter and asked, "Got a wrench?"

She leaned over and picked up some channel lock pliers off the ground. "I use these."

"Sounds good." I set down the filter at my side, took the pliers, and began loosening the old filter above. "You know . . . you can change the oil without jacking up the front end."

"I know," she said, watching me work. "I'm just not a big fan of cramped spaces."

"Are you claustrophobic?" I set the pliers down and glanced her way as I finished loosening the filter by hand.

She shook her head. "I wouldn't say I'm afraid of tight spaces— they're just not my favorite."

"I feel like there's a story there."

"Well, you can't become the queen of hide and seek without getting a little uncomfortable," she teased, nudging me in the ribs.

I smiled and flinched away from her pointy elbow just as the old filter came free. A tidal wave of dark brown oil splashed over the side, running down my arm and dripping off my elbow right onto Mac's shirt. *Crap.* "Uh . . . sorry." I quickly dumped the rest of the contents of the old filter into the collection pan and reached for the paper towels.

She chuckled, taking a section off the roll and dabbing up the mess. "It's fine. I've had worse mishaps." She moved to wipe off my forearm next.

I tried to ignore the fiery tingles spreading up my arm at her gentle touch. *Keep it together.* "Thanks."

When she finished, I picked up the new filter, applied a ring of fresh oil on the gasket with my finger, and began twisting it into place by hand. "So who taught you how to work on cars?"

"My dad and my brother. Every summer growing up, I'd follow them around the garage since I had no sisters to play with." Her wistful smile was telling, like she wouldn't have had it any other way.

She traded her dolls in for tools—didn't surprise me one bit. How had her mom felt about that, though? "Where was your mom when you were off getting covered in grease?"

"Working." Mac sighed in a way that made me think her relationship with her mom wasn't what she wanted it to be. "Her dream was to climb the corporate ladder until she made it to the top, which I'm incredibly proud of her because she did exactly what she set out to do. I just—"

"Didn't get to see her a lot?"

"Yeah. My dad was the one who cooked dinner every night and told us bedtime stories."

I grabbed the pliers and finished securing the new filter on there nice and tight. "Does he work?"

She nodded. "He's a history professor at Fresno State."

"Nice." I set the pliers down and turned to face her. "Is that where you were planning to go . . . before . . . ?" I let my unfinished question hang in the air, trying to decide if I should bring the loser up or not.

"Before my ex cheated on me?" she provided, speaking the words I was hesitant to say.

"Yeah."

"Yep. That was the original plan." She shimmied out from under the truck. "But I think things turned out for the best. Being anywhere near Clint and Thea would've been a huge mistake."

Agreed. I was glad she got away from the jerks that betrayed her. Coming to Arizona was the right choice, even with all her failed relationships since. I felt like she really believed that, too. But did she want to stay indefinitely?

I crawled out from under the truck, pulling the oil collection pan along with me. "Do you miss your family?"

"Yeah." Mac started gathering up her tools. "Having my aunt just a few miles away helps, though."

"I'm sure it does." I folded my arms across my chest and leaned against the truck bed. "Do you think you'll ever move back?"

She shook her head, pressing her lips into a thin line. "Nope."

Just what I wanted to hear. I wondered why she was so adamantly against it, but I wasn't about to complain. "So you've become an Arizona girl at heart?" I winked, trying not to grin too widely.

She chuckled, slinging her tool bag over her shoulder. "I guess you could say that."

"I'm glad," I said, dropping my arms and pushing away from the truck. "I don't want you to leave."

"Because your mom needs me?" Her teasing expression couldn't hide the serious undertone of her voice.

Because I need you. As much as I believed it, I couldn't say the words aloud. It was too much, too soon. "I'm not arguing with the fact that she needs you, but it's more than that. I'd miss our friendship most of all."

She smiled warmly, her eyes practically sparkling. "Me too."

I sank to my haunches and lifted the oil collection pan off the ground, wondering how the heck I was going to claw my way out of the friend zone, because in my mind I was already there, willing and ready to give her the world. "Where do you want it?"

"Follow me." She turned and walked up the driveway towards the carport, her grease monkey look drawing a grin from my face.

Anywhere.

19

MACKENZIE

The customer studied the first enlarged proof with a critical eye for the hundredth time. "Hmm . . . You're right. His smile is more natural in this one, but I don't like the way he's slouching." Her gaze shifted to the second photo. "His posture is better here, and the smile doesn't feel forced, but he's not showing his teeth." She gestured to the last proof. "And this one, I'm just not convinced he looks happy to be graduating."

An hour past closing time and my patience was running thin. Not only did my head throb with stress, my left eye started twitching, making it even more difficult to keep a neutral expression. *Remain calm. It will all be over soon.* "If you'd like, I can schedule him for a few retakes free of charge."

"Oh no, these are fine," she assured me. "I just need to figure out which one I want to stare at on my wall for the rest of my life."

"Take your time," I said calmly, though internally my brain was screaming, *"Get on with it!"* This was the part of the job I really hated —bending over backwards to please each and every indecisive customer. I'd already sent the rest of the staff home. No need for everyone to stay late for one measly order of cap and gown pictures.

It was maddening how long someone could stare at three nearly identical poses and search for each and every flaw. Humans aren't perfect, so why should we expect them to look perfect? It was those flaws that made a person unique, gave them character, life—beauty. People shouldn't be expected to strive for celebrity standards. Just because some appear more physically blessed than others doesn't mean they're magically happy with their circumstances.

Take Sydney, for example. On the outside, she appeared flawless —perfect hair, perfect body, perfect makeup, her every action exuding confidence and grace. But I've come to realize that underneath it all, she was every bit as scared of failure as I was—not to mention the health struggles she'd dealt with her whole life. Being different weighed on her more than she cared to admit.

Then there was Hunter. By the world's standards, he was deeply flawed in appearance—crooked teeth, disproportionate, crippled. And yet, when he smiled, he was the most beautiful person I'd ever met. I guess true beauty wasn't about looks; it was about who you were on the inside; how you made others feel.

Tanner had a knack for making me feel beautiful, but it was rarely with the words he'd say. It was in the way he'd look at me, like I was the most important person in his world. The more we were together, the more I believed it. Little by little, I was coming to realize he was different from the other guys I'd dated. He respected me and the boundaries I'd set. Underneath all the flirting and good looks, he was more kind and selfless than I'd given him credit for. I was almost ready to admit I'd misjudged him, but I couldn't understand one thing. After all that we'd been through, why did he want to be with me?

My phone vibrated. I subtly slipped it out of my pocket behind the counter and read the message while the customer continued to stare at her son's proofs.

TANNY

How was work?

My lips curved up at the corners. Ever since Tanner helped me change the oil in my Ranger last week, he'd started texting me every day after I got home from work. We'd chat about random things for an hour before he'd go to sleep. Honestly, it was the best part of my day—besides our short visits when he'd come home for lunch—which he didn't get to do today. It was irritating that this customer not only made me work late, but she made me sacrifice my limited time with Tanner as well. *Come on, lady! Just choose!*

"Okay . . . I'll take the first pose."

Hallelujah! And just like that, the dark clouds parted and the angels started singing. *I'm going home!* What was especially annoying was the fact that she'd chosen the pose I told her I liked the best. I could've had this order done in five minutes if she'd only trusted my professional opinion from the start. *Oh well.*

Fifteen minutes later, I rushed out of the building toward my truck and pulled my phone out of my pocket, opening up the messaging app to send Tanner a reply. My thumbs hovered over the keyboard for a moment before I decided to hit call instead. I didn't want to wait until the next stoplight to read his reply. I held my breath, my stomach fluttering with butterflies as I waited for him to answer.

"Hey, Mac."

The sound of his voice instantly relaxed me, melting away any lingering frustrations from my long day at work and soothing my conflicted soul. "Hey, Tanny." I unlocked the door of my truck and climbed in, closing it behind me.

"Don't tell me you just got off work."

"Yeah." I put Tanner on speaker-phone, set my cell in the cup holder, and buckled my seatbelt. "Another indecisive mother came in to order right before closing time."

"I'm sorry," he said, his tone far from teasing. "That's a test of patience, for sure."

"Yeah. It was pretty brutal." I started up the engine and shifted into drive, grateful to have a listening ear to talk to after a long day. Not that Sydney wouldn't listen when I needed to vent, she just never seemed to understand, trying to tell me how to work through my problems when all I needed was to let off some steam and feel seen.

"Should we make an ice cream run?" Tanner suggested, catching me completely by surprise.

Yes. Ice cream with Tanner was exactly what I needed. Did he have time, though? "But tomorrow's Friday. Don't you have work in the morning?"

"Yeah, but some things are more important than sleep."

"Like eating ice cream?" I teased.

"With you? Definitely."

I grinned like a lovesick fool, grateful he couldn't see my face at that moment of pure girlish weakness. "Can you meet me at *Andy's* in five?"

I heard a car door open and shut in the background, followed by an engine roaring to life. "I'm on my way."

Someone couldn't wait to get out of the house. I grinned even wider. Yeah. The walls around my heart were definitely cracking fast, like shattered glass. If he kept up this "friendship" thing much longer, my heart was toast.

Crunchy. Burnt. Toast.

WE SAT side by side at the outdoor picnic table, our cups of silky smooth chocolate, caramel, marshmallow cream, and brownie deliciousness in hand. "Mmm . . . I'm in heaven. This was a good idea," I said, then helped myself to another bite—any thoughts of how much I hated my job completely wiped from the forefront of my mind.

Tanner chuckled softly as he dipped his spoon back into his cup of frozen custard. "Happy to help."

My lips curved into a smile. The ice cream wasn't the only thing improving my current mood; the company was even better medicine. Tanner had dropped everything, sacrificing sleep to come cheer me up. Nobody had ever made me feel more wanted—like I was enough. *Just the way I am.*

Tanner wasn't a ladies' man in the way I'd first assumed. He was kind, always quick to offer a helping hand to not only me but to anyone in need. I'd been too blind to see beyond the flirting—to see that he wasn't the manipulator I thought him to be. Beneath it all, he genuinely liked me. Me! The girl who never put on much makeup, never wore designer clothes, and rarely fussed with her hair. I didn't get it. Why did he choose me?

"I pulled over Emily's little brother today."

His ex. That's it! I was the exact opposite of her—at least by the way he briefly described her; it felt like we were. *That's why he chose me.* I filed away the revelation for later, unsure of what to think at the moment, and quickly redirected my thoughts to the conversation at hand. "You did?"

"Yep." He sighed, shaking his head in disappointment. "Just barely sixteen and weaving through traffic at ninety like he owned the road."

"Ninety?" I scooped up another bite of ice cream. "Isn't that criminal speed?"

He nodded and scraped the bottom of his nearly empty cup. "I could've arrested him, but"—he shrugged—"I tried to talk some sense into him instead—to help him understand that some mistakes have dire consequences that can't be undone."

"Like getting a criminal record?" I questioned, meeting his gaze, wanting to understand what he was trying to convey.

Tanner set his empty cup on the table and folded his arms across his chest. "More like if he lost control or blew a tire. When you're going that fast on the freeway, surrounded by cars, there's no safe way to stop. Whether it's you or the people you're driving next to, somebody's guaranteed to get seriously hurt, if not killed."

I nodded, thinking about how hard it must be to lose a loved one in that way, and how the teen would carry the guilt with him for the rest of his life if he survived. *An awful burden to have to live with.* I hoped Emily's brother swallowed his teenage pride and took the message to heart. "How did he take it?"

"The kid still thinks he's invincible, but I got him thinking, at least."

"Good." I smiled softly. "You know . . . I think you were meant to be a cop. Even if you never had that experience with Sydney when you were kids, I think you would've found your way eventually."

One side of his mouth curved up in that crooked smile I loved. "You think so?"

"Yeah. I really do." I bit my lip, trying to stem the desire to lean in and press my lips against his. My pulse picked up speed as my eyes lingered on his mouth for a beat. The mouth of a man who'd caught my notice from the very beginning. I wanted him to be mine, but couldn't trust myself to see things clearly. The fear of heartlessly being tossed aside again haunted me and blinded me to how good things could be.

If only I were brave enough to try.

I turned away, lifting the last bite of ice cream to my lips, officially branding myself a coward. I was standing in the way of my own happiness—I knew I was. Tanner had shown me what he was really made of time and again. Why was I still fighting so hard to keep him at arm's length?

"What about you? Have you always wanted to be an office manager?"

I shrugged, then set my empty cup down on the table and stared at my lap, still not knowing what I really wanted. In some ways, I felt more hopeful than I had in a long time. Like, whenever I was around Tanner and his family, life didn't seem so bleak. They uplifted me in ways I didn't even know I needed. But in other ways, I was still standing in front of a ten-foot block wall with no way to go.

"I don't know." I sighed and reached across my chest to pull down on my left shoulder tight with tension, turning my neck from side to side to get a deeper stretch.

"Here, let me help with that." Tanner stood and stepped behind me, placed his sturdy hands on my shoulders and began massaging out the pesky knots.

Shivering warmth instantly spread down to the tips of my toes before I zeroed in on the release of tension in my neck. *Mmm. Sweet relief.* A day's worth of stress slowly melted away, making me feel happier inside; more willing to open up and share my woes. "I hate my job."

"I suspected as much." His voice was soothing, lulling me into a state of peace as his hands continued to work their magic. "What about it don't you like?"

"The monotony of the daily grind, bending over backwards for people that are impossible to please, feeling like I'm swindling the customers when my boss wants me to pretend like a fancy piece of paper is worth the arm and leg we sell it for." It felt good to vent and let my frustrations fly free. "I'm just tired of it all. I want to do something more meaningful with my life. You know?"

"Yeah. I can see how that could weigh on a person day after day," he said thoughtfully, lowering his thumbs to reach the space between my shoulder blades and spine. "So . . . what are you going to do about it?"

That was the million dollar question. What to *do*. "I don't know. I just feel so lost." I wrapped my arms around myself and sighed.

Tanner pulled his hands away from my shoulders and sat down, straddling the bench to face me. His eyes searched mine while he lifted his hand and gently stroked my cheek with the back of his fingers. "You're one incredibly smart and talented woman, Mac."

I closed my eyes at his soft touch and reassuring words, my skin tingling still when he pulled his hand away to tuck a loose strand of hair behind my ear.

"You'll figure out what to do when the timing is right."

My eyes fluttered open as he leaned in and briefly pressed his lips to my forehead, his familiar woodsy scent almost stealing the very breath from my lungs. *He kissed me.* My heart danced in my chest as I repeated what he'd said in my mind. *"When the timing is right."* His words and his nearness were a boon to my soul. I wrapped my arms around his neck, lightly kissed his cheek, then laid my head on his shoulder, feeling more content with my life than I had in a long time. "Thank you, Tanny."

"You're welcome," he replied, his strong arms encased around me like a blanket. He kissed the top of my head before resting his cheek there, proving again that his feelings for me had remained constant these past few weeks.

Tanner had the patience of a saint. He was waiting for me, waiting for the timing to be just right before we progressed in our relationship from friends to something more. He understood my reservations and knew I needed to take things slow. Honestly, I was surprised he'd stood by me this long, because I definitely hadn't made things easy.

Maybe it was time I put in a little effort and show him how much his steady friendship meant to me. "Do you have any plans for the weekend?"

He loosened his hold around me to capture my gaze with his penetrating blue eyes. "Not a thing."

I smiled and stood, taking his hand in mine as he rose to his feet beside me. My heart pounded nervously in my chest. *No turning back.* "Let's change that."

20

TANNER

I yawned as I filled up the gas tank in my patrol car, not at all regretting how tired I felt. Because of that missed hour of sleep, I'd made some real progress with Mac. Something changed between us last night. The barriers she'd kept around her heart were finally breaking. She'd let me pull us into a place just beyond friendship, where deeper feelings could safely grow.

It had taken every ounce of self-control to keep my mouth away from her soft lips, especially when she'd kissed my cheek, but I promised myself I'd wait until she was good and ready, so I settled for a quick kiss to her head with my arms wrapped around her—not a bad alternative. In fact, I needed to do that more often.

For weeks we'd been hovering in the space between friendship and dating. The place where anything was possible. The place where a man decides whether or not he wants something more. I hadn't needed long to realize Mac was someone special, and I wanted more of her in my life. Much more.

I imagined what our life together could be like and smiled. Paint fights, flirting, laughter, four wheeling, music, sizzling chemistry, communication, trust. *Love.* Yeah. I'd be an idiot if I didn't admit that

I'd fallen hard and fast, like a drunk tripping on a crack in the pavement.

Mac was the one I'd been holding out for. I only hoped she needed me just as much as I needed her. *Don't screw this up.*

A call came out for a collision with unknown injuries only a few miles away from where I was at. "Eighteen-fifty-six. I can take that," I answered into my radio. "I'll be ten-nineteen from mile post one-eighty-six."

"Ten-four. Eighteen-fifty-six . . . ten-nineteen from mile post one-eighty-six," dispatch confirmed.

Within a few minutes, I pulled up on scene. Broken glass and debris spread across lanes five and six. A white Nissan Altima lay on its side, driver's side up, in the middle of the mess, with every window busted out except the front windshield. *Rollover.* A utility truck sat off to the side with the smallest dent in the front bumper on the driver's side—the only evidence it had been involved at all.

I parked my patrol car behind the Altima, leaving my red and blue lights on, and watched traffic bottleneck behind me in the mirror, silently praying nobody would crash into me as I radioed dispatch.

"Eighteen-fifty-six. I'm ten-ninety-seven. We are blocking the number six lane. Vehicle on its side. Other vehicle is off right. Start me a nine-two-six and fire, please. And have the next unit come to the front to help move the vehicle off right."

After dispatch confirmed the message, I stepped out of my Tahoe and approached the Altima to locate the driver and assess for injuries. I looked down into the car where the driver's side window should've been and found a woman with blond hair still strapped in her seat, hanging tightly onto the steering wheel like her life depended on it. Her knuckles were scratched and bleeding, which was common when dealing with flying shards of glass.

"Ma'am, are you hurt?"

"I'm stuck!" she said frantically, still clinging to the wheel. "My seatbelt won't unbuckle!"

"Okay, don't worry. I'll get you out real soon, but first I need to know if you have any injuries that might prevent you from safely climbing out of this window."

"Tanner?" Her voice wavered with emotion. "Is that you?" She turned to face me, and her blond hair fell away, revealing a familiar face.

My eyes widened in recognition. "Sydney?"

She nodded and looked away as tears rolled down her cheeks. "Tanner, I'm scared."

"Hey. Look at me."

She turned and met my gaze. A small amount of blood trickled from a few cuts on her cheeks.

Cuts not too deep.

"I'm going to get you out," I promised. "Everything's going to be alright."

She inhaled a shuddering breath and nodded. "Okay."

"Now I need you to tell me if you're feeling any pain."

She shook her head and sniffed. "I don't think so."

"Can you move your legs?"

She extended her legs one at a time, her facial expression remaining unchanged. "Yes."

"That's good." Besides her initial panic and anxiety over the situation and a few cuts here and there, she seemed to be okay. A miracle, considering what she'd just experienced.

I pulled out my knife and mentally formed a plan. "Alright. This is what we're going to do. You're going to hold on to the steering wheel to keep yourself upright while I cut through the seatbelt, then you're going to climb out this window. Okay?"

"Okay," she answered hesitantly, squeezing the steering wheel so tightly the cuts on her knuckles trickled with fresh blood.

"You can do this." I placed a reassuring hand on her arm. "I'll be with you every step of the way."

When she nodded, I moved my knife into position. "On the count of three. One . . . two . . . three!" I sliced through the seatbelt, and Sydney held fast to the steering wheel as her feet scrambled for footing. "Put your feet on the armrest," I instructed calmly.

The panic left her eyes as her feet found what she was searching for.

"Good. Now step up onto the center console and take my hand. You're going to use the steering wheel and headrest as footholds to push yourself up as I pull you through the window. Got it?"

"Yeah."

"Okay. Here we go. One . . . two . . . three!" I pulled with all my strength, guiding her through the final climb without a hitch.

The second her feet hit the ground, she threw her arms around me and buried her face in my shirt. "You saved me!" she sobbed, tears starting to flow freely. "I was so terrified! Thank you for getting me out of there!"

"You're welcome." I awkwardly patted her back, waiting for her to let go. She didn't seem keen on loosening her hold any time soon. "Sydney, we need to get you off the road. It will be a lot safer for you to wait on the embankment until the fire department comes to check you out."

"Okay." She sniffled, got her tears under control, then stepped back, clinging to my arm instead as I walked her over to where I wanted her to wait.

"Now sit tight for a minute. I'll be back after I go check on the other driver."

She nodded and finally released her death grip on my arm, lowering herself onto the gravel embankment without another word.

I walked up to the utility truck, grateful that Sydney had let me leave her side without a fuss, and motioned for the driver to step out of the vehicle. He did so without difficulty and immediately admitted fault before I said a word—which made my investigation significantly easier. I thanked him for his honesty, then began my assessment for injuries. It wasn't surprising to learn he was completely fine. Based on the amount of damage to his truck, or lack thereof, I figured that would be the case. I collected his license and instructed, "Just sit tight for now. I'll be back in a few minutes."

I headed back toward Sydney and updated dispatch through my

radio. "Eighteen-fifty-six. One driver has minor cuts and scratches on her knuckles and face. Other driver has no visible injuries."

Sydney had pulled up her knees and wrapped her arms around them, staring blankly at her car.

"You doing okay?" I asked, moving to stand beside her.

She blinked and met my gaze. "I feel like this is all just a bad dream."

I nodded, looking out at her beat up Altima and rested a hand on my duty belt. "I'm sorry you had to go through that."

Rogers arrived on scene and positioned his Tahoe in front of the Altima; the plan was to push the car back on its wheels and get it into the right shoulder as soon as possible. I turned to Sydney. "I need to go clear the lane for traffic, but I'll be back to ask you some questions for my report in just a few minutes."

I started to walk away, then paused. "Is there anything you'd like me to retrieve from your car before it gets towed away?"

"My purse, please."

"You got it." I turned and headed towards Rogers.

"Tanner?"

I stopped and looked over my shoulder, meeting Sydney's gaze with brows raised.

"Thanks for always being my hero." She formed a heart shape with her hands and tapped it to her chest with a watery smile.

I nodded politely and walked away with a strange sense of foreboding. What did she mean by that heart tap thing? I snuck another glance over my shoulder just long enough to see her grinning oddly at me.

Oh no.

I'd seen that look enough times to know it could only mean one thing.

Trouble.

21

MACKENZIE

I picked up my cell phone off the desk and scrolled through the rapid texts coming in from Sydney.

SYD

> I almost just died!

> Some jerk rolled my car on the freeway!!!

> I was trapped, and you'll never guess who showed up to rescue me! Tanner! Wearing his sexy cop uniform and everything.

> Kenz . . . I think it's a sign. I shouldn't give up on him yet.

> He was so kind and caring too!

> Yep! I'm definitely still in love with him.

> Tell me what to do!!

My heart sank a little more with each and every text. Just as I was ready to take a leap into the uncharted waters of dating Tanner, Sydney decided she was interested again. What was I supposed to do? Support my friend outwardly while I wished her doom in silence or somehow convince her to change her mind?

MACKENZIE

A rollover? That's crazy! You okay?

SYD

Yeah. My car is completely totaled though.

What do you think about Tanner?

Sydney had just been through a traumatic experience and she wanted to talk about what I thought about her being in love with Tanner? *Ugh.*

MACKENZIE

I thought you said he was a jerk to you. Are you sure you want to do this all over again?

SYD

He was so different today though. Thoughtful and kind. Maybe acting disinterested worked like you said it would.

Great. Now I was to blame for her sudden mood swing in men. I racked my brain, trying to come up with any excuse to dissuade her.

MACKENZIE

I don't know, Syd. Maybe he was just doing his job.

SYD

Ash and Kara agree that it's totally fate!!

Fate. *Ha!* I hated the word. But Syd was intent on believing in it. And there was nothing I could do but wish Tanner had some way to cure her of her lifelong fantasy. If he didn't, then our relationship was as good as dead.

I couldn't betray Syd like Thea betrayed me. I refused to go there. What I had with Tanner was incredible and amazing, but it was still so new. Syd and I had been close friends for the past few years. I couldn't ignore that. If our friendship was going to be on the line, then maybe it was best that I gave Tanner up altogether.

I set my phone down and lay my head on the desk in defeat.

It would crush him.

Heck, I would be crushed.

Tanner had really been there for me in a way that Sydney couldn't. He understood my internal struggles and gave me hope for my future. He made me feel happy. Safe. Dare I say, *loved*?

I shook away the stupid thought. *You don't know that. Stop torturing yourself!*

If I were to cut him out of my life now, it would be . . .

A huge mistake.

I squeezed my eyes shut and groaned. I didn't want to let him go. Why did *I* have to be the one to give up my happiness, anyway? Sydney had her chance with Tanner, and it didn't work out. Tanner had told me he didn't like her like that. He wanted a relationship with *me*—and he'd proven it by his unwavering friendship when I'd pushed him away again and again.

"You okay, Kenzie?"

I glanced up to see Addison hovering near my desk with a look of concern. The last thing I needed was to spill my guts to the office gossip, so I sat up and pasted on a false smile. "Yep. Just a little headache." *And a dash of endless roommate drama.*

"That's not fun." She flipped her black hair over her shoulder and smiled. "Hope you feel better."

I wondered if her voice could sound any more insincere. "Thanks."

After she walked away, I turned toward my computer and scowled. *I hate fake people.*

Wait. Was I being fake with Sydney?

If I told her how I truly felt, then maybe *she* could be the one to let Tanner go. The question was, would our friendship survive if she didn't?

I didn't know, but I had to try. I picked up my phone and started typing.

MACKENZIE

> I really don't want to see you get hurt again. Let's talk about this when I get off.

SYD

Okay. I'll be home.

Hopefully, I would know what to say by then.

I DROPPED my keys into my purse and shut the front door behind me, locking the deadbolt, still dreading the conversation I needed to have with Sydney. The background chatter of the TV sounding through the house suddenly halted.

"Is that you, Kenz?" Sydney's voice floated from the living room.

"Yeah, Syd! I'm home." I walked down the short hallway and stepped into the living room.

"Good! I've been waiting for you." Sydney smiled, the cuts and scratches on her face immediately catching my attention.

"Whoa," I said, lowering myself beside her on the couch and setting my purse on the floor. *I thought she said she was okay.* I guess it hadn't truly hit me that my best friend had been in a serious accident until that moment. I mean, yes, she told me, but somehow seeing her now with angry scratches on her cheeks made it all the more real. "Your face . . ."

"I know. It looks awful, doesn't it?" She gazed down at her knuckles—which were in even worse condition than her face. "The firemen told me they were surprised I was able to walk away from the rollover without any serious injuries. So I guess I'm lucky." She looked up at me and shrugged. "I just hope it doesn't scar."

Leave it to Syd to worry about scarring when her life might have been altered significantly in an instant. "It's not that bad. I'm sure it'll heal up fine." I placed a reassuring hand on her arm, causing her to wince and pull away. "Oh, I'm sorry! Are you okay?"

She nodded, then seemed to change her mind, shaking her head as her eyes filled with tears. "It's just a bruise."

She wasn't acting like it was just a simple bruise. "Are you sure? I can take you to urgent care right now if you want to get it looked at."

She released a strangled laugh and shook her head, wiping at her tears. "No, I'm fine. I promise. Just feeling a little emotional about everything."

It would seem the fact that she almost died today did have an effect on her after all. "Come here." I lifted my arms and let her sink into my embrace. "You've been through a lot today. It's okay to cry."

She nodded into my shoulder and began sobbing—the ugly kind of cry.

As I sat there comforting Syd through her release of pent up emotion, I realized our little heart to heart about Tanner wasn't quite so urgent as it had seemed before. It could wait for another day, when the trauma of the rollover wasn't so fresh on her mind. Who knows? Maybe in time, she would change her mind about wanting Tanner on her own.

22

TANNER

Mac's aunt read the next question aloud. "What's something you should never do on a first date?"

I grinned as the perfect answer came to mind, writing it down and folding up my little slip of paper before I lost my nerve. Mac wouldn't be happy, but it would be worth her silent wrath just to see the look on her face. She'd been a little distant tonight, and this was a sure way to get her undivided attention.

Crystal brought the bowl around the room and collected each slip of paper from all of the players—there weren't many of us—me, Mac, Drew, his friend, Trellany, Jess, and her boyfriend, Ben.

Hanging out with Mac's high school-aged cousins wasn't exactly what I'd had in mind when Mac suggested we spend some time together, but I had to admit, it was more fun than I expected. And I figured if Mac was bringing me around her family, she was finally comfortable enough to admit we had the potential for something good. Something lasting.

Crystal stood at the head of the circle and read aloud the answers at random. "Forget your wallet, go to the movies, shave your legs—"

Shave your legs? Ha! Who would write that?

"—act like a jerk, forget to wear deodorant, and steal your date's car."

There it is. I turned to Mac, failing to hold back a smile when she glared at me.

"Hmm . . . I wonder who wrote that one," she whispered, shaking her head.

"I don't know what you're talking about," I deflected with feigned innocence.

The mischievous side of her made an appearance at last. "You're so going down."

One side of my mouth curved up in response. "Nobody knows about that night but you and me." I discreetly threaded my fingers around her own and squeezed three times.

She looked at me with surprise in her eyes, her lips parted slightly. I didn't know if it was my comment or the hand holding that threw her off kilter, but all eyes were suddenly on us and she made no move to take her turn.

"Kenzie?" Crystal said. "What's your guess?"

Mac blinked and looked away, clearing her throat before guessing I was the one that wrote down "shave your legs," which got a few giggles from the room. Why didn't she rat me out? After all that talk of bringing me down, I was sure I was toast. What made her change her mind?

Whatever the reason, I was just glad she was still holding my hand.

When we left Crystal's house an hour later, I pulled out of the neighborhood and glanced Mac's way. "You could've fed me to the sharks back there. Why didn't you?"

She shrugged and rested her arm on the center console in my truck. "I might have decided to show you a little mercy since you were losing every game we played."

I chuckled, reached over and took her hand in mine, sure there was more to it than that. "Nah, I don't think that's it." I squeezed her hand and brought it to my lips, placing a kiss on her knuckles as I kept my eyes firmly on the road. This new closeness with Mac felt good. Like she was always meant to be at my side with her hand in mine. Was she starting to feel that way, too?

After a few seconds, she pulled her hand away and crossed her arms, putting more than a little space between us.

Had I pushed her too far? I'd never know if we weren't open and honest with each other. "Did I cross a line?"

"No. It's just . . ." She shook her head and sighed. "Never mind. It's stupid."

"You can tell me." *Please.*

"Really, it's fine." She forced a smile and changed the subject. "Sydney said you rescued her yesterday."

Rather than take the opportunity to open up about what she was feeling, she'd brought up the one thing that always seemed to be in our way—Sydney Freeman. *Ugh.* I wish I'd never answered up for that call yesterday. The second I saw the hero worship in Sydney's eyes, I knew she'd flipped a switch inside. Plus, she'd sent me a few texts today out of the blue, asking if I had plans this weekend—further evidence that I was in the danger zone with her again. I was just childishly hoping if I ignored the problem, it would go away.

Nope. I wasn't that lucky.

"Yeah." I sighed, feeling like I was forever going in circles around this issue. "She seemed pretty shook up by the experience. Is she doing better today?" I pried my eyes away from the road to get a glimpse of Mac's expression.

Worry lines creased her forehead. "I think so. But it's hard to tell. She's been acting . . . strange lately."

More so than usual? Maybe she'd had a head injury I'd missed. "Strange how?"

"You want the truth?"

"Always," I responded without hesitation.

Mac winced as if it was painful to say the words. "She's in love with you again."

Well, that confirms it. My grip tightened on the steering wheel until my fingers ached. I was hoping I'd been wrong—that she wouldn't be naïve enough to think I cared for her in that way. Especially after all those tricks I'd played on her in the desert. Why couldn't Sydney take the hint and leave me be?

All I wanted was to be free to pursue the woman I loved without all this unnecessary dramatic garbage. Was that too much to ask?

Mac reached out and put a hand on my arm, breaking me from my internal rampage. "Are you okay?"

After all the progress we'd made, Mac was feeling conflicted again. How was I supposed to be okay? Her fingers slid down my arm and grabbed my hand, gently coaxing it away from the steering wheel to rest on the console.

Or was she?

I glanced at our entwined hands and took a deep, calming breath. *Mac wants us to work out.*

That was all the encouragement I needed. "Yeah." I stroked my thumb over the back of Mac's soft hand, feeling my irritation start to fade away. "Don't worry about Syd. I'll take care of it." As much as I hated being the bad guy, Sydney and I would have some words.

Tonight.

I LEANED over the center console and pulled Mac close. "I'll call you tomorrow," I said, wishing I could've held her in my arms a little longer.

Her lips curved up slightly as she pulled away and pushed open the door. "Good luck."

I chuckled and shook my head. "Thanks."

Mac was relieved when I'd said I would handle Sydney. As much as I hated doing what I was about to do, it was necessary for not only my own sanity, but Mac's as well. She didn't want to betray her friendship with Sydney, and I respected that. Admired it, even. But Sydney potentially being upset over Mac and I dating was kind of ridiculous when Syd and I were never a couple. This obsession or fantasy or whatever you want to call it had to stop.

After waiting the ten minutes Mac and I agreed on, I drove around the corner and parked in front of my parents' house. I picked up my phone and sent the dreaded text from the cab of my truck.

TANNER

Are you home?

SYD THE MAN-EATER

Yes! Did you want to come over?

TANNER

I was hoping you had a minute to talk.
Outside.

SYD THE MAN-EATER

Sure! I'll be right out.

Good. I would say what needed to be said and be done with the drama once and for all. Speaking with Sydney face to face was the last thing I wanted to do, but she was just too dang determined to take the hint and give up. I wasn't about to leave things to chance by having her misinterpret a simple text. Blunt honesty was the only thing I could truly count on to get the job done.

Fifteen minutes went by, and Sydney finally emerged from the house. I should've known her version of "I'll be right out" would be another test of patience. Hopefully, that would be the last time I'd ever have to wait on that particular woman.

I stepped out of my truck and crossed the street. Sydney watched from the sidewalk, smiling brightly, a plate of something in her hands.

"Hey, Tanner! I'm glad you texted. I wanted to thank you again for rescuing me yesterday." She pushed a plate of chocolate chip cookies into my hand. They were still warm.

That's why she took so long. "You didn't have to do that."

"Kenzie made a big batch last night, so we're more than happy to share." She grinned and put a hand on my arm, her blue eyes glimmering up at me under the streetlight. "You're actually doing me a favor by taking them off my hands. I don't need the gluten or the sugar."

Feeling uncomfortable with the contact, I shifted out of her reach to scratch the back of my head. "Thanks. I'll just set these on my truck while we talk." She stuck right by my side as I turned and crossed the street.

"What did you want to talk about?"

I put the plate of cookies in the truck bed and turned to face her, trying to decide how to put my thoughts into words in the kindest way possible. "Well, first of all . . . how are you doing? Any new aches or pains from the collision . . . or bumps on the head we missed?"

She smiled and shook her head. "Nope! I'm feeling great today. Super amazing, right?"

"Yeah. Good to hear." I folded my arms across my chest and leaned against my truck, my stomach churning uncomfortably. "So about the other thing I wanted to discuss. We've known each other a long time. We're friends, right?"

"Of course!"

"Good. You've always been something like a little sister to me over the years, and that's been great. But . . . lately I feel like you're expecting something more from me—something I can't give you."

Her smile fell away. "What are you talking about?"

Here we go. "You're an amazing woman, Sydney. Beautiful. Confident. Kind. I just need you to understand that we can't be anything more than friends."

She stared at me in shock for a moment before she parted her lips to speak. "But I *don't* understand. How do you know we can't have something great together if we don't even try?"

"We have tried."

"What, that date in the desert?" She scoffed and shook her head adamantly. "That so doesn't count! You weren't giving us a real chance and you know it."

"We have no chemistry, Syd. It's never going to work out."

"No chemistry?" She closed the distance between us and threw her arms around my neck, trying to coax my head down to her level seductively. "Why don't we put that theory to the test?"

The situation had just taken a nosedive into uncomfortable waters. I quickly uncrossed my arms, placed my hands on her shoulders and inched her away, making my intentions plenty clear. "I'm not the kind of guy who kisses people for the heck of it. I don't play those games."

"Oh, come on. One little kiss won't hurt anyone." She tugged on my shirt and focused on my lips. "If we don't feel sparks flying, then we'll know for sure it wasn't meant to be."

Enough already, woman! "I'm not interested, okay? Just let it go!"

Her arms fell down to her sides, then her face scrunched into a nasty glare. "Fine! Next time you feel like stopping by, DON'T! I don't need your stupid, arrogant ego in my life, anyway." With that final outburst, she turned and stomped across the street.

I watched her disappear into the house and sighed in relief. *It's finally over.* I hated that I had to be so blunt to her face, but her trying to convince me to kiss her was the last straw. I'd had enough of her manipulative games.

And now Mac and I had a real shot at love—the kind worth waiting for.

23

MACKENZIE

Guilt pricked my conscience the moment the front door slammed shut. I knew Tanner was going to break Syd's heart tonight, and not only did I allow it to happen, I wanted it to happen. *I'm a terrible friend.*

Sydney stormed into the kitchen and made a beeline for the refrigerator. "I can't believe I ever fell for such a pigheaded jerk!" she said, pulling the door open with such force, the glass bottles within rattled. She plunked down onto the barstool next to mine, hugging the mixing bowl of cookie dough to her chest.

"I take it things didn't go the way you planned."

"He freaking friend-zoned me! I don't get it, Kenz. Why won't he give me a chance?" She shoved a heaping spoonful of cookie dough into her mouth and chewed.

I should tell her everything. I inhaled slowly and put a hand on her arm. "I . . ." I couldn't put my confession into words when I saw the fresh tears streaming down her face. "I'm . . . uh . . . sorry he broke your heart." *She's going to freak if I just spring it on her. Baby steps.* I pulled my hand away and rested my arms on the island, watching her dig her spoon back into the cookie dough.

"Do you think he might be interested in someone else?" I asked, trying to ease her into the idea that he was never hers to take.

"Ha! I'd doubt it." Syd wiped her eyes with the back of her hand and made another spoonful of chocolate chip cookie dough disappear. "The guy's too in love with himself to care about anyone."

My hands tightened into fists. I should have left it at that and let her believe what she wanted about him, but I couldn't sit there and listen to her say he didn't care when almost everything he did proved the opposite. His job; his family life; how he helped my aunt; how he helped me. He was the most selfless man I had ever met—though I didn't think she'd appreciate hearing that right now. *Better stick to the idea that he's already taken.*

"I'm not so sure about that," I said, trying to keep my voice even and unaffected. "I saw him at *Andy's* the other day. He was . . . with someone." I didn't have the heart to admit that *someone* was me.

The crushing look of hurt on Syd's face made me instantly regret that I'd mentioned it at all. I knew more than anyone that coming in second best in love was like pouring lemon juice on a paper cut— only that cut wasn't just skin deep—the pain seared down to the sinews of the soul. *I'm the worst.*

"Who was she?" Fresh tears glistened down her cheeks.

My stomach twisted uncomfortably at the thought of lying to my best friend, but telling her the truth wasn't going to make things better for either of us. Not now. Not when she was in such a vulnerable state. "Some brunette . . . I couldn't see her face." It wasn't a complete lie—if you ignore the part where I made her believe I didn't know who *she* was.

She nodded and pushed the bowl of cookie dough away. "I shouldn't have eaten that much."

Yeah. She was going to be feeling more pain than heartbreak in the next couple of days. *Poor Syd.*

"Maybe mystery girl snores like a cat with a head cold," I said, trying to lighten the mood.

Sydney sniffed and covered her face.

"Oh—" I lifted a hand excitedly as another ridiculous insult brewed in my mind. "She keeps a secret stash of Tabasco in her purse because she's obsessed and thinks it makes everything taste better. Even ice cream."

Sydney shook her head, still hiding her face.

"I bet she dances like a crow during mating season too."

Sydney snorted, her shoulders finally shaking with suppressed laughter.

There it is! I grinned and bumped her shoulder. "Come on, Syd. Give it a shot. You know you want to."

She uncovered her face and wiped her tears away. "She's got a sugar daddy and six kids."

"Yes!" I laughed and added, "And they're all spoiled brats with names that are hard to pronounce."

Once Sydney got her burst of laughter under control, she lay her head on my shoulder and sighed. "Thanks, Kenz. I needed that. You're the best."

Again, a pang of guilt churned in my gut. I wasn't the best. I was trying to convince her it was okay that Tanner wasn't falling for her—because he'd somehow fallen for me first. But I couldn't just up and admit that. I didn't want to cause my friend anymore pain.

I hooked my arm over Sydney's back and rested my hand on her shoulder in a side hug, feeling like a deceitful snake. I couldn't stand it; I had to make things right.

All I had to do was sort of . . . ease Sydney into the truth.

Just maybe not today.

TANNER'S NAME flashed on my phone, and my heart skipped a beat. I scrambled off my bed to shut the door before accepting the video chat. "Hey. How's it going?" I tried to keep my voice soft enough so my roommates down the hall couldn't eavesdrop.

"Hey, Mac."

Tanner's silvery blue eyes and warm smile filled up my screen, turning my insides to mush. *Mmm.* A girl could get used to seeing that handsome face every morning.

"Things are good," he said, keeping his eyes fixed on me. "How about you?"

"Yeah. Things are good here too." I plunked onto my bed, leaned against the headboard, and stretched out my legs, crossing one ankle over the other. "I actually had Sydney laughing before she went to sleep last night."

"Really?" He raised his brows, clearly impressed. "You're amazing. You know that, right?"

I smiled, feeling warm tingles spread from my chest to my head. "Yep. I'm pretty much the best."

Tanner chuckled, making his eyes crinkle at the corners. "You are —which is why I can't stop thinking about you—about us."

My pulse picked up speed, and my palms started to sweat. This was it. He wanted to have the *"define the relationship"* talk. I nervously tucked my hair behind my ear, then rubbed my left hand up and down my thigh.

"Do you want to come over?"

His voice filled me with hope, like a ray of sunshine on a gray wintry day. Good things were headed my way. I could feel it. But Syd was home. I couldn't exactly cross the street unnoticed. "Well, I'd like to but . . . my roommates are here. Someone's bound to see me."

"Tell them my mom asked you to help out with Hunter for a couple hours. They'd buy that, right?"

I bit my lip and shook my head. "Actually, they have no idea I've been doing that. They're always at work when I'm over there, so I never saw a reason to mention it."

"Okay . . ." Tanner furrowed his brow in thought. "How about we go for a walk?"

I winced, thinking how disastrous it would be if Syd decided to go for a run and saw us together. "I don't think that's a good idea."

"Why do I get the feeling you're still trying to avoid me?"

"I promise I'm not. You and me just need to be a secret right now. If Syd found out, she'd—"

"You and me, huh? I like the sound of that."

I tried not to grin like a fool as heat rushed to my cheeks. "Me too."

"Are you sure you can't come over?" The soft pleading in his voice was adorable.

He had no idea how much I wanted to give in. "I'm about ninety-nine percent positive."

He lifted a brow, his eyes lit with hope. "So there's still a one percent chance?"

I chuckled and shook my head. "I really can't come over. But . . . if you find a way to sneak into my truck bed in the next few minutes"—I lifted a shoulder innocently—"we can go for a drive."

Tanner grinned. "I'm on it."

24

TANNER

After about a mile or so, Mac pulled over her Ranger and slid open the back window. "Coast is clear, Tanny."

"Oh good." I sat up and met her gaze with a teasing smile. "I thought the beating would never stop. How fast were you driving?"

Mac rolled her eyes. "Very funny. You know I drive like a grandpa."

"Except for when you're stealing cars," I pointed out, grinning.

She shook her head, holding back a smile. "You just *had* to bring that up."

"What can I say?" I tipped my head partially through the rear window and shifted my attention from her alluring brown eyes to her tantalizing lips. "It was a memorable night."

"Yeah," she agreed, her gaze drifting to my mouth. "I'll never forget those sparks flying when we first touched."

Ha! "Oh, you think you're being funny, do you?" I lifted my eyebrows, chuckling.

She laughed and covered her face. "I'm sorry. I couldn't resist."

Mac could make fun of our little taser incident anytime she wanted. It didn't bother me one bit. I was just glad she was finally comfortable enough to flirt with me again. Having the freedom to say whatever I wanted to this woman without the fear of it pushing us apart felt so good.

"Mackenzie Parker . . . you are my favorite."

She uncovered her smiling face and bit her lip, staring at me with her sparkling eyes. Mac couldn't be more attractive if she tried.

"I think you're pretty great too," she admitted.

Her eyes flicked to my mouth again, and my heart started racing. If it weren't for the small window preventing a normal-sized guy like me from climbing in there, I would have gone the distance in a heartbeat, no questions asked. I was torn. Should I risk ruining the moment by hopping out of the truck to climb in the cab or I should I sta—

My current train of thought screeched to a blessed halt when Mac closed the distance, caressing my lips with her own. *Yes!* A rush of adrenaline released like wildfire through my veins, consuming every thought, every breath. Everything I wanted. Everything I *needed*. I had it right here. I tilted my head to the side and followed her lead, gently exploring her unbelievably soft lips and loving every second. Her vanilla scent intoxicated me, tethering me to her as everything else around us faded away. The taste of her kiss . . . the feel of her breath on my cheek . . . this moment was everything.

Mac inched away, breaking the kiss and bringing us back from our dance in the clouds. "We should probably go for that drive now," she said breathlessly.

"Yeah, probably." I agreed, now aware of the aching in my knees from kneeling on the hard metal surface. A dog barked nearby, causing me to turn and survey my surroundings for the first time since Mac pulled over—which was a little unsettling for someone trained to always be ready for anything. *Baseball fields . . . volleyball nets . . . dog park. Oh, Countryside.* We were a few minutes away from home. A woman walking her dog passed by, deliberately frowning at us. Did she see us making out? *Awkward.*

"You coming, Grandpa?"

My eyebrows lowered involuntarily. "Grandpa?" I turned to see Mac's face.

She gestured to the empty passenger seat with a tip of her head, her lips twitching into a smirk. "You're taking forever. Get in here already!"

"What?" I teased her, chuckling. "You mean you want me to sit next to you?" I hopped out of the truck bed as she closed the rear window, then I opened the door with an easy smile and slid into the passenger seat. "Admit it, you just want me close by so you can kiss me anytime you want."

She let out that adorable laugh I'd loved from the start. "Dang, Tanny." She tucked her hair behind her ear and shifted into drive. "You figured me out."

Was that my cheeks getting warm? "I knew it!"

She smiled and grabbed my hand, threading our fingers together like she'd done it a thousand times.

This right here was happiness. It didn't matter that I'd been hurt in the past. It didn't matter that I'd nearly given up on love. Right here. Right now. I had something that filled all the cracks in my heart and made me feel whole again.

"Where to?" Mac squeezed my hand. "Canyon or Saguaro Lake?"

"Canyon." I squeezed back. "Let's see how you do on all those blind mountain curves."

Her eyes flashed with challenge. "Piece of cake."

It was lunchtime when Mac turned into our neighborhood and pulled over around the corner from where we lived. She turned off the ignition and faced me. "I'd invite you over to eat if it weren't for Syd—"

"Sydney," I echoed with a nod of disappointment. How long would that woman keep interfering with my life?

Mac bit her lip and looked at her lap. "She's going to need some time before I can break the news to her."

"Yeah." I rubbed the back of my neck and exhaled slowly. "I'm sorry about that. I wish there was something else I could do to help."

"You've done so much already." She looked up, her brown eyes holding a warmth just for me. "I'm just sorry I ever encouraged her to go after you."

"Yeah. What was that all about?" I chuckled, opened my door and stepped out of the Ranger. "It would've been so much easier if you'd just gone out with me the first time I asked."

"I didn't know you then!" She shut her door and circled around the front of her truck to join me. "I thought you were trying to put another notch on your belt or something."

I held back a laugh and tugged on her wrist. "Come here."

She leaned in and brushed her mouth over mine, once . . . twice, teasing me with her perfect lips. *Mmm.* I lifted my hand and cupped her cheek, willing her to come back for more. And she did.

25

MACKENZIE

K issing Tanner was a big step for me—one that I'd been hesitant to take for weeks. But now that I was here, wrapped in his strong arms, receiving the best kiss of my life, I had absolutely no regrets. His racing heart, his gentle touch, and his giddy grin all spoke volumes. It was beyond feeling wanted and safe for the moment. Tanner was in this relationship for the long game; he was a man I could rely on; a man who would stay by my side when life threw its unavoidable curve balls.

Tanner slowly pulled away from my lips to whisper into my ear. "Do you know how long I've wanted to kiss you?"

A shiver of pleasure rushed down my spine. Never had I felt so desired than I did at that moment. I shook my head, practically bursting with happiness. "No."

"The day after we met, at your aunt's . . . you pretended to wipe paint off my cheek, and I pretended to buy your act."

I giggled and nuzzled into his chest, remembering that day well. We had flirted shamelessly for hours—which wasn't something I'd ever really done with anyone before. I guess even then we had an *undeniable* spark, though I never would've believed it on his part. "You really wanted to kiss me that day?"

"I thought about it. We had a connection, didn't we?"

I smiled and tilted my head back to meet his gaze, pleased that he'd felt that way, too. "Yeah, we did. It terrified me, though."

"Why?" He tipped his head and softly kissed the spot on my cheek right next to my nose.

How could a simple kiss on the cheek make me feel so weak in the knees? "Um . . . because you're so attractive?"

"You think so?" He grinned, like he didn't know he was a freaking gift to any woman with eyes.

Duh! I was sure my expression said it all. "I assume you've looked in the mirror before."

He chuckled. "Yeah. I'm no God of Thunder, though."

"A man doesn't need bulging biceps to be attractive." I lifted to the tips of my toes and wrapped my arms tighter around his neck, loving the way it felt to be held by him. "Not to me, anyway."

He brought his smiling lips to mine, stealing more than the breath in my lungs. More than a blissful shudder. *Mmm.* I drank in his woodsy mountain scent, loving this little space between worlds we created together, where only the two of us existed.

Suddenly, all those broken pieces of my heart lying in a junkyard heap somewhere in no-man's-land were gone. Poof. Completely out of reach. Tanner had taken them, picking them up from the crumbly pile, piece by piece, when I wasn't looking. Did he know he was a sneaky little thief?

Maybe one day I'd thank him for it. Because of him, I had more joy and hope in life than I'd had in a long time. For once, I wasn't worried about the future. Somehow, I knew it was all going to be okay.

Until it wasn't.

"Kenz?"

Sydney's voice burned through me like a shock of electricity, hot enough to barbecue my brains. *Not now. Not like this.* I jumped out of Tanner's arms and spun around to face the nightmare unfolding right before my eyes. Sydney was across the street, dressed in running shorts and a tank top, frozen in disbelief like a deer in the headlights. The moment we locked eyes, her face hardened into an icy glare, no longer giving me the benefit of the doubt. I was guilty; caught in the act of betraying our friendship. She tightened her fists and turned, running away towards home.

"Syd! Wait!" I called after her, but it was no use. She wouldn't stop to hear me out. Not in front of Tanner. Not when she was about to fall to pieces.

My chest tightened, and my eyes stung with tears. I was back in high school all over again, watching my dreams turn to ash in an instant over a stupid kiss. Only this time it wasn't my dream being ripped away; it was Sydney's. I had taken that from her. How had I become the very thing I despised? *I'm sorry, Syd.*

Tanner placed a steady hand on my shoulder, offering me comfort I wasn't sure I deserved. "What can I do to help?"

If only he could. I shook my head and sniffed, watching Sydney disappear around the corner. There was nothing he could do now. This was all my fault, and only I could fix it. I stepped away from him and wiped the moisture from my eyes. "I'm sorry. I need to go."

He nodded, his eyes full of understanding. "Call me later?"

"Yeah," I replied absently as I walked to the driver's side of my truck, wondering if Sydney and I would still be friends when this was all over. Worry twisted my stomach in knots. *Please, Syd. Forgive me.* I climbed inside, started the engine and drove away without a word of goodbye or a backward glance, praying I had the words to make this right.

Sydney had just run inside the house when I pulled up onto the driveway. I switched off the ignition and hopped out of the car, racing to catch up to her before she retreated to her room. I burst through the front door and pushed it shut behind me as I hurried down the hall, my heart beating fast.

"What's going on?" Ashley called from the living room couch just as a door slammed further down the hall.

I didn't stop to answer her; I needed to get to Syd.

"Sydney?" I knocked on her locked door, hoping by some miracle she'd let me in. "Please. Let me explain."

Chilling silence filled the air between us, which condemned me far worse than angry words ever could. *Talk to me. Please.* Guilt wracked my conscience like a millstone around my neck. "I never meant to hurt you," I said, sinking to the floor, leaning my back against the door. I wrapped my arms around my knees and squeezed my keys tightly in frustration, blinking rapidly, trying to stem the threatening tears. "I tried not to fall in love with him. I swear I did."

Silence.

Nothing I said was going to get through to her, because I had betrayed her trust. I should have told her about that night Tanner came to fix my truck. I should have told her about painting with him at my aunt's. I should have told her about the hours I spent each week helping his mom with Hunter. I should have told her about Tanner's stubborn persistence. Why didn't I? If I had been open and honest with her from the start, then maybe this wouldn't have felt like an atomic bomb dropping from the sky without warning. And now it was too late. *I'm so stupid!*

Suddenly, the door unlocked and cracked open a few inches as I scrambled to my feet. It was Kara's green eyes glaring at me through the doorway.

"Sydney never wants to see you or talk to you again. You need to pack up your stuff and leave. Tonight. We're posting an ad for a room to rent in the morning." She slammed the door in my face, dismissing me before I even had the chance to say a word.

It didn't matter, anyway. Her mind was made up to never forgive me. Nothing I said now would change that. I *knew* because I'd been there before, five years ago, with Thea—whom I still hadn't forgiven. So why would Syd treat me differently?

An ugly ache settled in my heart as I trudged across the hall to my bedroom. *Another friendship in ruins.* How had I allowed this to happen?

I shut my door and let the tears I'd been holding back fall free, but only for a minute or two. I didn't have time to be emotional because I had a room to pack and sleeping arrangements to make.

The one good thing about hitting rock bottom? Things couldn't get any worse than this.

26

TANNER

I wasn't surprised when Mac didn't call or text last night. She had a lot on her plate, trying to patch things up with Sydney. What did surprise me was finding Mac's truck missing from the driveway when I left for work; it wasn't like her to be up before the sun. I pulled out my phone and unlocked the screen, my thumb hovering over the call button. What if she wasn't awake? For all I knew, she could've spent the night at her aunt's house and wouldn't be up for a couple more hours. I opted to send a text instead.

TANNER

Everything okay?

Throughout the morning, I checked my phone at every opportunity, waiting for a response that never came. I tried not to think too much about it though, expecting I'd see Mac at home on my lunch break—if I could make it there on time.

At eight-fifteen, Mom called. "Tanner, have you heard from Mackenzie today? She hasn't come by yet, and she's not answering her phone."

She's never late. "Did you try knocking on her door?"

"No, but I don't think anyone's home. There aren't any cars in the driveway."

Worry lines creased my forehead. *Where could she be?* "Okay. I'll be there in about ten minutes."

"Oh good. I'm so relieved you can come. Your father was set on lifting Hunter himself if I couldn't get you home soon."

"What?" *He better not!* More recovery time is the last thing my parents needed right now. "You lock him out of Hunter's room if you have to! Promise me, Mom. You can't let him do that."

She paused, making my anxiety increase every second she didn't answer. "I promise."

I exhaled in relief. "Good." Mom never broke her promises, which meant Dad would be safe. "I will be there as soon as I can."

"Thank you! See you soon."

When I pulled up in front of my parent's house, I parked behind my Silverado and messaged dispatch with my laptop, letting them know I was at my forty-two for a quick break before I stepped out of the car. I crossed the lawn and let myself in, heading straight to Hunter's room. Mom was sitting on the edge of the bed, rubbing Hunter's chest with one hand, and holding her phone to her ear with the other.

"Oh no. Don't you worry," she said, watching me enter the room. "Tanner's here now. He'll take care of it." She stood and made room for me to get to Hunter.

I unclipped my duty belt and set it on the bed, still listening to Mom's side of the conversation, wondering who she was talking to. Could it be Mac?

"Really, no need to apologize. I understand completely. I can't even believe how forgetful I've become in the last ten years." She chuckled.

It had to be Mac. Tension I didn't even realize I'd been carrying slowly released from my shoulders. It's not that I'd thought anything terrible had happened to her—it's just, when you truly care about someone, you have this *need* to know they're alright. Mac had a rough day yesterday. Well . . . the second part of the day, anyway. The first few hours of the day were incredible; she was incredible. I was still reeling from how amazing it felt to be wrapped up in her kiss.

"Thank you, Mackenzie. I'll see you tomorrow," Mom said, before slipping her phone into her pocket. She turned back to me and smiled softly. "Mackenzie spent the night at Crystal's. She forgot to charge her phone and woke up late."

That explained why I hadn't heard back from her yet. "Glad she's okay." I bent over and curled my arms under Hunter to lift him out of bed. "Hey there, little buddy. Bet you didn't think you'd be seeing me this early today."

Hunter groaned in response as I cuddled him close and carefully moved him to his wheelchair. Did he sound a little grumpier than usual?

"What? You wish Mac were here instead of me?" I chuckled when he groaned again. "Yeah, buddy. I miss her too."

"Those two have a special bond, don't they?" Mom said, leaning forward to buckle Hunter's harness.

"Yeah. One of the reasons why I love her." I clamped my mouth shut. *Did I really just let that slip?*

Mom straightened, her eyes beaming with excitement. "Have you told her yet?"

I avoided her gaze and cleared my throat, picking up my duty belt off the bed and hooking it back around my waist to busy my hands. "Uh . . . no. Not yet."

"Why not?"

I rubbed the back of my neck and shrugged. "We just started dating, officially. I don't want to scare her away, you know?"

She shook her head and placed a hand on my arm, a gentle smile on her lips. "When I see the two of you together, you know what I see?"

"What do you see?" I tried not to shift uncomfortably under her knowing stare.

"Two people that couldn't be more right for each other," she said, squeezing my arm for emphasis. "Happiness looks good on you. Take that leap and have a little faith that things will work out."

Mom was right. I shouldn't leave any room for doubt when being with Mac was the best thing I had going in my life. I needed to tell her how I felt. *Soon.*

As I walked back to my patrol car, my phone dinged in my pocket. Was it Mac? I picked up the pace and settled into the driver's seat, then slipped out my phone to read the text.

> MAC THE THIEF
>
> Sorry you had to cover for me today. Sydney kicked me out. I'm at my aunt's until I find a new place.

Kicked out? I growled and slammed my palm onto the steering wheel. *What a manipulative little . . . ugh!* Once again, Sydney had found a way to negatively impact not only my life, but Mac's as well. The jealous snake couldn't step back and be happy for her friend. No. She had to go and cut Mac from her life because she couldn't get the man she wanted. *Spoiled brat.*

> TANNER
>
> Dang. I'm sorry she's being a jerk friend right now. I'm going to see if I can convince her to let you stay.

> MAC THE THIEF
>
> No. Please don't. She needs space right now.

> TANNER
>
> Are you sure?

> MAC THE THIEF
>
> Yeah. Trust me. I remember how that feels. She doesn't want to see or talk to either of us. It would only make things worse.

I could see why she felt that way, but this wasn't the same as her high school breakup. Sydney and I never dated. Not seriously. We were barely even friends. The fact that she was acting the part of the betrayed little innocent was ridiculous. It was her own dang fault for believing she could call dibs on a guy in the first place.

It was childish!

I didn't want to stand by and let Mac and Sydney's friendship end like this—not when I knew how much it meant to Mac. But . . . maybe getting involved *would* make things worse. A little voice inside me said I should give the girls a chance to work this one out on their own.

In the meantime, I needed to figure out the perfect way to say those three little words that could make or break my relationship with the woman of my dreams.

No pressure.

27

MACKENZIE

I hugged a throw pillow and leaned into Aunt Crystal's side, grateful her afternoon appointment had canceled. It allowed her to come home early and spend some time with me before Jess and Drew got home from school. "Was falling for Tanner a mistake?"

"No, honey." She wrapped her arms around me and rubbed gentle circles on my back. "You didn't do anything wrong."

Ha! That's debatable. But I wasn't about to go through all the dirty details with her a second time to better explain my tortured thoughts. "Then why is my life such a mess?" I sniffled and wiped at the annoying tears rolling down my cheeks. I hated crying. It made me feel so weak and pathetic when I needed to be strong and figure out how to move forward with my life.

"Your life's not a mess." Her voice held nothing but kind, motherly assurance. "You have a bachelor's degree, a job that provides, and a family that loves you. Not to mention, a handsome guy that's crazy about you," she said, continuing her calming strokes on my back. "Just because you're trudging through a little downpour without a raincoat right now doesn't mean the sun won't come out again."

I nodded, letting her words lift my heavy heart and stem my stupid tears. Everything was going to be okay.

My phone chimed in my pocket. I slipped it out and pulled away from Aunt Crystal's embrace as I glanced at the screen. "It's a text from Sydney."

I'd thought she never wanted to speak to me again. Did she have a change of heart?

"What's it say?"

I held my breath and opened the message.

SYD

He's lying to you.

The meager flame of hope that Sydney wanted to repair our broken friendship extinguished in an instant, leaving behind a gray wisp of dread, slowly poisoning my lungs like toxic smoke.

Deep breaths.

In and out.

Why would she send this? Obviously, there was only one "he" she could be referring to, but I still didn't understand completely what it meant.

MACKENZIE

What do you mean?

SYD

Tanner's playing you.

No! Even as my gut wrenched in fear, I didn't know if I could trust her. Sydney knew how those words would haunt me to my core. But what could she possibly have to gain by deceiving me? *Other than revenge.* My eyes narrowed at the screen clutched tightly in my hand. Either Sydney was lying or Tanner was. I hated that I didn't know what to believe.

Another text came in. This time it was a video. *She had proof.* Tanner wrapped a redheaded woman in his arms and swung her around off the ground; then their heads came together for a kiss before the video cut to an end. I instantly felt sick. *No.* I shook my head. Tanner wouldn't do this to me.

I watched the video again, expecting I'd magically see someone else in the redheaded woman's arms. My eyes hadn't deceived me. They were standing right in front of his parents house. *Syd was right.* My heart shriveled and sank to my feet like a stone to the bottom of a pond.

I stood abruptly, letting the throw pillow fall off my lap and drop to the floor, my throat going dry. "Tanner lied to me," I whispered, stunned that I had been blindsided by a man again.

The lengths he went to get me to trust him were beyond disgusting—it was calculating and manipulative. Why? Why did I allow myself to be deceived again?

Angry hot tears streamed down my cheeks, and I didn't wipe them away. I was too mad to care. I clenched my teeth and squeezed my phone even tighter. If I ever saw Tanner again, I was going to tase his sorry—

"Are you sure?" Aunt Crystal's voice interrupted my rampant thoughts, grounding me, coaxing my emotions back to a more rational level.

"Here," I said, then handed her my phone. "See for yourself." I stepped away from the couch, closed my eyes, and rubbed my throbbing temples with the heel of my hands, my mind running a million miles per hour.

We had plans to go out tomorrow night. *Not anymore.*

"I know it looks bad, but maybe there's an explanation?" Even though her voice was hopeful, her expression held nothing but pity.

I dropped my hands to my sides and shook my head, feeling hollow inside. "No. I don't want to talk to him." Nothing he could say would change the fact that he was a lying cheat.

Aunt Crystal nodded and handed me my phone. "I'm sorry, honey. You didn't deserve this."

"Story of my life," I grumbled.

She stood and wrapped me in a hug. "Things will get better. I promise. Sometimes it takes a little time to find your patch of sunshine."

I nodded and pulled away from her warmth and her optimism, wanting to be alone for a while.

When I entered the guest room—which was where I was staying for the time being—I shut the door and leaned against it. I lifted my phone, intending to text Tanner that we were through, but fresh tears blurred my vision before I could type a single word.

Why? Why does this keep happening to me?

I was going to have to cut all ties just to survive. Which meant I couldn't help with Hunter anymore. I knew he and his parents were innocent of Tanner's wrongdoing, but I didn't think I could face them.

Thick black clouds rolled in, suffocating my pitiful world even further. I wasn't just without a raincoat in a downpour—I was scrambling over sharp rocks and broken glass, barefoot, in the dark. Lost and alone, without even a hope for the sun to shine on me again, I crumpled to the floor, finally hitting my breaking point. *I can't take this anymore.*

I sobbed and cried until my throat ached and my headache flared into a full on migraine. *Ugh.* I laid on the floor and squeezed my eyes shut for what seemed like hours. I prayed the misery would end, that I'd somehow have the strength to carry on with my broken life. When the pain finally subsided and my mind slowly lifted out of the foggy depths of despair, an idea emerged and took shape. The more I thought about it, the more resolved I was to do it, no matter the cost.

I dialed a number I knew by heart, waiting, praying he would answer.

"Mac?"

I started crying again when I heard him speak. "Daddy?"

"What's wrong, baby girl?"

His familiar caring voice warmed my soul like a crackling fire in the middle of December. In that moment, a small piece of my heart, lost and nearly forgotten, found its way home, safe and sound. Why did I stay away so long? "I want to come home."

28

TANNER

I parked my patrol car in the garage, grabbed my rifle and laptop, then walked into the house through the kitchen, heading towards my room to change out of my uniform. All in the house seemed quiet and still. Unusually so. There was no "how was your day" floating down the hall from Mom. I put my laptop on the desk and my rifle in the safe while listening for signs of movement.

Not a sound.

I poked my head into the hallway. "Mom? Dad?"

No answer.

They couldn't have gone anywhere. The van was still parked in the garage.

Unless they traveled by . . . *ambulance.* My heart started racing when I couldn't find my phone. Was Hunter okay? Was it Dad? I had to have missed an important call from Mom. All my pockets were empty. *Where is the dang phone?*

I rushed back to the garage to check my Tahoe, yanking the door open fast, then exhaled in relief when I saw my phone in the cup holder. I picked it up and checked for notifications. No missed calls. No texts.

What? It didn't make any sense. I went back inside, rubbing the back of my head in confusion, when I spotted movement outside the kitchen window.

Mom and Dad were on the bench swing out back; Hunter sat beside them in his wheelchair.

Sheesh. I took a deep breath and shook my head. All that adrenaline pumping for no reason. This was the one thing I didn't like about being a cop—always on high alert with no way to turn it off.

Unless I was with Mac.

I went back to my room, unbuttoned my shirt, and pried open the Velcro of my vest with a smile, thinking about the date I had planned for tomorrow. I was going to take Mac out to the wash for a ride on the ATC under the stars. There was a special place I wanted to show her before I took that leap and laid my feelings bare. I hoped more than anything she felt the same way about me.

When I finished dressing, I headed outside to join Dad, Mom, and Hunter. "You guys almost gave me a heart attack!" I teased, closing the door behind me. "Why are you all out here in this heat?" It was only ninety, but they typically didn't venture outside at this time of year unless they were doing yard work.

"We've received some difficult news," Dad said, gently rubbing Mom's back with his good arm as she stared at her lap.

My smile fell away, and my brows lowered in concern. I crossed the porch and grabbed Hunter's hand, giving it a little squeeze before asking, "What's wrong?"

Mom looked up, dabbed a tissue over her puffy, red-rimmed eyes and sniffed. "We need to find someone else to help us with Hunter," she explained in a wobbly voice.

What?

"Why?" I didn't understand. I thought Mac liked helping out. What would cause her to stop all of a sudden? This wasn't about Sydney, was it?

"Mackenzie's gone."

Gone? Although I knew the meaning of the word, I stared at Mom as if she had spoken in some foreign language.

"Back to California," Dad added, making me feel as though a heavy weight suddenly pressed on my chest.

She'd said she was here to stay. I dropped Hunter's hand and turned away, staring blankly at the block wall several yards away, then swallowed back an unwelcome swell of emotion. Sadness, frustration, hurt—I was feeling it all. My jaw tightened. "She didn't tell me she was leaving."

"Tanner, I'm sorry." Mom stood to give me a hug that brought little comfort.

I sighed and curled my hands into fists at my sides. "Me too."

"Crystal's the one that told us," Mom explained. "She's not sure when or if Mackenzie will be coming back."

I couldn't believe Mac hadn't said a word to me. It didn't make sense. Why would she leave without telling me?

I gently pulled out of Mom's arms, intending to go back inside. "I'll be in my room if you need me." I needed to talk to Mac; to hear her voice; to understand why and if she planned to come back.

"Wait," Mom pleaded.

I turned and met her worried gaze.

"I know this is hard for you right now, but are you going to be able to help out in the morning until we can make other arrangements?"

I nodded and squeezed her shoulder. "Don't worry, Mom. We'll make it work." It might involve getting Mom and Hunter up a few hours earlier than they were used to every morning, but we'd get by.

Something terrible must've happened to convince Mac to leave. *I hope she's okay.*

29

MACKENZIE

After five long years, I was finally home again, lying in the same bed I'd slept in as a child. Gone were the posters of my favorite bands on the wall. Gone were the pictures of my friends and little knickknacks on the dresser and shelves that had once filled this room with memories. I was a stranger in my own home, feeling as empty inside as the whitewashed walls and barren shelves.

The funny thing was, Mom had cleared it all out to make me feel more comfortable. She was worried that reminders of the past would be too painful for me; which, in a way, she was right. But at the same time . . . maybe facing the past was the key to fixing my messed up life. *Worth a try, anyway.*

I turned my head and stared at the beam of light that streamed through the bougainvillea in front of my bedroom window and shined onto the wall in golden patches. At least, that was familiar.

It was humbling to see my parents so changed—grayer, wrinklier, quieter. I guess I had no one to blame but myself. I had kept them at a distance when I should've made an effort to be a part of their life, and in turn, let them be a part of mine.

When Mom had stopped calling, it was easy to assume she was just too busy for me, like it'd been growing up. But the reality was, she sensed I wanted space and decided to give it to me. Before I left, Aunt Crystal confessed that Mom had been calling her to check up on me every week. The thought comforted me more than I expected, giving me courage to confide in both my parents last night about what I was dealing with. They hadn't rubbed my failure in my face or told me to suck it up and get over it; they listened and offered the emotional support I needed.

If only Mom had been as understanding and supportive *before* I left, then maybe our relationship wouldn't have been so strained these last few years. *Oh well.* We all have to live and learn.

I shivered and pulled the comforter up to my chin, hoping to ward off the chill in the air. Who knew I would miss the Arizona heat? Tragically, that wasn't the only thing I missed.

Stupid Tanner.

I hated that I'd cried over him most of the night. I missed him. It wasn't just his crooked smile or his strong arms wrapped around me that I missed. It wasn't just his laugh or his silvery blue eyes gazing into mine like I was the only woman in his world. It wasn't just his achingly tender kisses. It was his friendship and selfless service. His encouragement. I couldn't have dreamed up a more perfect guy. Why did he have to turn out to be a freaking fake?

Tears pricked the back of my eyes. He wasn't my perfect guy anymore than I was his perfect girl. I squeezed my eyes shut and shook away the images, replacing them with thoughts of Mom.

There was something different about her demeanor last night. It was like she was less uptight and not as stressed about things. Easy-going. Happier.

I didn't know what had caused the change in her, but I liked it. I was looking forward to spending more time with her when she got home from work.

The smell of freshly baked bread seeped into my room, causing my lips to curve into a smile. Dad was the same as ever, getting up before the sun to bake before heading off to work. My stomach growled loudly, finally convincing me to throw off the covers and brave the cold house.

"Good morning," Dad greeted as I walked into the kitchen, yawning. "How did you sleep last night?"

I sank into the chair across from him at the table and removed my glasses to rub my eyes. With all the crying lately, I wasn't even going to bother with contacts. "Not great." There had been a lot of tossing and turning in between my bouts of tears during the night.

"Sounds like you could use some cheering up." He smiled, pushing a plate with a giant cinnamon roll, fresh from the oven, toward me.

I put my glasses back on and leaned over the sugary deliciousness, inhaling the heavenly aroma of cinnamon and bread, and sighed. "Dad, you're the best."

His eyes twinkled as he poured me a cup of milk and set it beside my plate, knowing his offering of food would bring a smile to my face on the grayest of days. "What are you going to do while your mom and I are at work?"

"Thought I'd play the piano for a bit," I said with a shrug. "Maybe go to the library."

"Sounds like a good way to take your mind off things."

That was the plan. I nodded and picked up my fork. "When do you have to leave for work?" I took a bite of the cinnamon roll and watched his eyes lower to his wristwatch.

"In a couple of minutes," he said, wiping his mouth with a napkin.

I swallowed my food and took a sip of milk, disappointed I didn't have more time with him. At least he'd finished his breakfast. "I'm sorry I didn't get up sooner. It was hard to leave my warm blankets."

He chuckled, bringing his cup to his lips. "Don't worry about it." He drained the rest of his milk and stood, gathering up his sticky plate and fork. "You up for working on Old Rusty with me when I get home?" His brows danced up and down playfully.

I smiled. Dad had been restoring that old Corvette for years. "Sure."

"Great!" He took his dishes to the sink and rinsed them, then picked up his keys off the counter and said over his shoulder, "See you in a few hours, Mac. Glad you're home!"

Me too. "Bye, Daddy. Drive safe!"

I hadn't felt as empty inside talking with Dad. But now that he'd gone, the deafening silence quickly settled in, bringing my mood back down to the dumps. I propped my palm under my chin, rested my elbow on the table, and sighed. Since Mom had left for work way before I got out of bed, I was alone with me, myself, and I for the next several hours. *Oh joy.*

I thought about calling Aunt Crystal to let her know I'd made it home safely, but ultimately decided against it. I had no intention of powering up my phone for at least a week. It was easier that way—to just cut Tanner out cold turkey. I wasn't interested in seeing whatever lame excuse he had to explain himself. Let him wonder how he'd been found out. He deserved much worse than the silent treatment, but it was the only way I could retaliate; unless I wanted to risk arrest for assaulting an officer.

Well . . . I guess I could ask the man upstairs to send down a lightning bolt or two, to scare the lying cheat right out of him, but that was a special kind of messed up. I pictured Tanner being zapped by nature's taser and cackled like an evil witch to the empty house, quite possibly going unhinged for a minute. Didn't matter. No one was watching. *Wow. I really need to get some sleep.*

After I finished my breakfast and loaded the dirty dishes into the dishwasher, I glanced at the time on the microwave. *Eight o'clock.* A pang of guilt twisted in my stomach. That's when I'd normally go help Hunter get out of bed. It hadn't felt right leaving Mrs. Hansen without saying goodbye or giving her notice to find a replacement, but what else could I do? I had to get away.

I hadn't even told my boss I was leaving the state, just that I needed a couple weeks off for a personal emergency. Mr. Ellwood was very understanding about it, allowing me to use the vacation days I'd saved up to cover the time I would be away.

The thing was . . . I didn't know if I'd be coming back.

I was standing at a crossroads, torn between two imperfect paths.

Should I go back to Mesa and live the monotonous life I'd built for myself, knowing Tanner would be close by but forever out of reach? Maybe there was a slim chance I could fix things with Sydney—she did warn me about Tanner after all. The other option would be to start over in Tulare and figure out what next step to take in life. Whether it be going back to school or . . . what? Some undiscovered professional leap that would bring me the satisfaction I craved? *Ugh.* Sometimes being an adult really sucked.

Either way I would be trying to drown out the painful memories. Old memories. New memories. And all the rotten sludge in between. Yeah. Totally winning at life.

I sat down on the piano bench and started playing a song I'd written back in high school, when all had felt right with the world. My fingers only needed a minute of fumbling around the notes before muscle memory kicked in, taking over the fast moving melody that never failed to lift my spirits.

I could go back to school and get a degree in music. Playing the piano always made me feel better. I could perform professionally . . . or teach? *Nope.* I shook my head, and pushed the thought away as quickly as it had come, knowing I'd never have the patience for it. There had to be something else I could do. But what?

After a while I switched gears and played a few classical favorites I'd memorized as a teenager: *Clair De Lune, Fur Elise,* and *The Turkish March.* My mind drifted to the clouds and cleared out all the stress and turmoil as I got lost in the music. My face and shoulders relaxed. My body swayed with the movements of my hands. This was my safe space. My happy place. A place where no one could bruise or break me.

It didn't really matter what I did for a living or where I lived; as long as I could take my piano with me, I could survive anything.

"I THOUGHT I'd find you two in here."

I paused my wrenching and looked up. "Hey, Mom."

She smiled and crossed the floor, hovering a foot away from the grease zone.

"Hi, honey," Dad greeted, taking one step toward her to lean in for a hands-free kiss.

That was new. I hadn't seen much affection between my parents over the years. I knew they respected each other and got along well enough, but love? I guess I'd never seen much evidence of it in our day to day growing up. Maybe having an empty nest the last few years strengthened their relationship. Was that why Mom seemed happier? *Probably.*

Love always made everything better. Until it didn't.

Ugh. I needed to think about something else.

Dad had resumed working on the intake bolts, so I followed suit.

"I'll have dinner ready in about an hour," Mom said, before disappearing into the house.

Dinner? Mom never used to be home for dinner, let alone make it.

I glanced at the clock hanging on the wall. We'd only been working on Old Rusty for an hour. "Can Mom be trusted in the kitchen?" I asked, completely serious. She hadn't made many of our meals growing up.

Dad chuckled and suggested, "Why don't you go and find out?"

"You sure?" I knew Dad was enjoying my help, even if I didn't exactly love getting grease under my fingernails.

"Yeah, go ahead." He tipped his head toward the door, sending me away with a smile.

After cleaning myself up, I joined Mom in the kitchen, offering to cook the chicken and rice while she chopped vegetables for the stir fry.

"Thank you for the help," she said, blinking her eyes rapidly as she sliced into an onion. "Here I am, fifty-five years old and still not quite comfortable in the kitchen."

I bit back a smile and measured a cup of water to pour into the rice cooker. Made sense when she hadn't had much practice. "I'm surprised you're home from work so early," I said.

"Oh, I've been cutting back on my hours lately."

"Really?" How was that possible? I didn't think she could do that as the VP of the company. I programmed the rice cooker and turned to face her, my brows lifting expectantly.

"I gave up my promotion," Mom said, shrugging nonchalantly, like it was no big deal to step down from her dream position.

What? My jaw dropped to the floor. "You did?"

When had that happened? And why? I couldn't believe it.

"Yes." Mom smiled, her eyes glimmering with a secret. "Being the VP wasn't all it's cracked up to be. I was so stressed all the time. Barely ever home." She scraped the onions into a bowl and moved on to the bell peppers. "About six months ago, a friend of mine invited me to volunteer at the children's hospital with her, cuddling newborns. I never knew you could even do something like that! Anyway, I signed up, took a cut in pay and hours, and never looked back. All my stress practically disappeared overnight."

"Wow, Mom."

Who was this woman? She was smiling and happy—cooking dinner! I'd never seen her like this before. It was different. But definitely a good different.

And not because she'd landed her dream job. It was because she'd given it up. So . . . did that mean I should give up on finding the perfect career if I wanted to be happy? It didn't make any sense.

I turned on the burner and threw a couple tablespoons of butter into the frying pan, not knowing what else to say.

"You know what?" Mom said between slices. "I actually learned about a profession that might interest you."

"Really? What is it?" I asked, while dumping the chopped onion into the melting butter.

"Music therapy."

Music therapy? I turned to face her, my interest more than piqued. I didn't even know that was a thing.

"You get to visit the patients and play and sing their favorite songs. You could work with kids or adults, terminally ill, elderly, special needs—"

People like Hunter? Mom could be on to something. Every moment I'd spent with Hunter, I had this undeniable feeling of peace, as if he were trying to tell me that everything was going to be okay. Maybe Hunter was *my* person, leading me to a path in life I might not have taken otherwise.

A buzz of excitement coursed through me like a dying ember bursting into flames, and I knew in my heart it was right. "How do I sign up?"

30

TANNER

Straight to voicemail again. I'd lost count of how many calls I'd made and texts I'd sent over the last week. But that didn't stop me from trying to get through. Tulare, California. Only a nine-hour drive away, but it might as well have been another continent for how disconnected I felt. Mac was out of reach. And now all I had were memories of her. Was she ever going to come back?

Not knowing was killing me. I thought she would've at least called to explain things by now. I didn't understand what would drive her to run away like that—to run from *me.* Maybe I'd fooled myself into thinking she could love me as much as I loved her. I groaned and buried my face in my hands, trying to ignore the crippling ache in my heart. This was way worse than when Emily had ended things, because Mac was the woman I believed I'd never find—the one woman I could see myself growing old with. How was I supposed to make peace with this and move on?

The truth was, I couldn't. *I need answers.*

I hopped off my bed and walked down the hall with determined strides. "Mom?"

"Yes, Tanner?" she replied from the rocking chair in the living room.

I paused on the way to the garage and met her gaze. "I'm going out. Call if you need me."

"Okay." She turned and smiled at Hunter, squeezing his hand. "We should be okay for a while."

I nodded and continued out to the truck, hoping and praying Mac's aunt would be home.

When I knocked on her door ten minutes later, it wasn't Crystal, but Jess, who answered.

"What are you doing here?" she asked, glaring daggers into my eye sockets.

Someone woke up on the wrong side of the bed this morning. Maybe it was her time of the month? I chose to ignore the unusual hostility and casually folded my arms across my chest. "Is your mom home? I was hoping I could talk with her." I even managed to conjure up a smile to ensure her I hadn't been offended by her misplaced venom.

Her eyes narrowed into slits. "No. And even if she were, you're the last person she'd want to see!" she exclaimed, then slammed the door in my face.

Okay . . . I guess it wasn't her time of the month. She was legitimately mad at me. And Crystal, too, apparently.

"Why?" I called out and knocked on the door again, determined not to leave until I had answers.

"Because you broke my cousin's heart, you lying scumbag!"

What?

Even though her retort was muffled through the door, the message had been clear. Mac left because of me. *Why?* I hadn't done anything wrong. Just as I was about to knock on the door again, it swung open. Mac's aunt was standing in the doorway, telling Jess to go man the stove.

So Jess had lied; her mom *was* home. I dropped my fist to my side and waited, relieved that I would get a chance to speak with Crystal after all.

She turned to face me with an apologetic smile. "Hello, Tanner. Sorry about my daughter. How can I help you?"

Hope flared through me; answers were within my reach. "Jess said

I broke Mackenzie's heart." I shifted my stance and rubbed the back of my neck. "Do you know what she meant by that?"

Crystal studied me in silence for a moment, then nodded. "Sydney sent her a video."

SYDNEY FREEMAN. The bane of my existence. I should've known she'd find a way to make things worse. I was done trying to be nice to the meddling devil woman. As much as I didn't want her involved in my business, she'd made herself a part of it, so now we were going to have a little chat.

I walked up to the front door, scowling as I rang the doorbell. One of her roommates answered. *Ashley, was it?*

"Hey, Tanner." Her dark eyes roamed me over from head to toe, like a feline stalking her next prey. "Mmm. You're looking very fine today. What can I do for you?"

My frown deepened. I folded my arms across my chest and shifted my stance, trying to hold back my irritation. It would do me no good if she slammed the door in my face. "I need to speak with Sydney."

Her catlike smile dimmed. "I'll go get her." She threw her brown hair over her shoulder and turned, hollering through the house, "Syd! Door's for you!"

So much for *going* to get her.

An answering voice drifted down the hall. "Be there in a sec!"

Ashley turned back to me and said, "She'll be out in a second."

Yeah, I heard. "Thanks."

Her cunning smile returned. "So . . . the Diamondbacks are playing tomorrow. I happen to have an extra ticket. You interested?"

My brow lifted, but not in interest. These girls never missed an opportunity, did they? Even if my heart wasn't already taken, it would be a *hard pass*. But . . . I couldn't just say that to the woman's face.

A simple "no thanks" was on the tip of my tongue when Sydney suddenly appeared, saving me from having to reply.

"Oh, it's you. What do you want, Tanner?"

Ashley backed away, making room for the queen bee of the house.

"Did you know Mackenzie went back to California?"

She smiled smugly and leaned against the doorjamb. "Good for her."

"No. It's not good." My arms dropped to my sides in frustration. "That woman you saw me with the other day was my cousin Annie. Ask my mom if you don't believe me. And no, we're not kissing cousins. She came by to tell us she's engaged—which is none of your business, by the way. I'm only filling you in so you understand me when I tell you just how badly you've screwed things up for an incredible woman who has been nothing but a loyal friend to you."

"Loyal?" She scoffed with an ugly glare. "Oh, no! She—"

"I'm not finished," I said over her, trying not to completely lose it to her face. "I realize you think she betrayed you. But you know what? She refused to go out with me for your sake, pushing me your way every chance she got. It wasn't her fault that I fell in love with her anyway. I chased her. Me! Not the other way around. You want someone to blame for your miserable, loveless life? Blame me! You shouldn't hate Mackenzie for wanting to have a little happiness after all she's been through."

Her eyes flashed with hurt, then hardened to stone. "We're done, here." She stepped back and slammed the door without another word.

I headed back across the street and sighed, mentally exhausted. Maybe I'd gone too far with the loveless bit. I was just . . . so angry with her for hurting Mac—for driving her away from me.

All that was left to do now was bring her home.

I STARED at the satellite view of Mac's parents' house on Google maps for the third time today, wishing more than anything I could finally program a route into my GPS and be on my way. I couldn't thank Crystal enough for entrusting me with the address after I explained things a couple days ago, but so far, it looked like I wasn't going to get to use it. Not yet, anyway.

Not until I found someone willing to lift Hunter for Mom around the clock while I was gone. Dad was on track to start physical therapy in a few weeks, but by the time he'd be strong enough to take over, it would be too late. Every passing day was another day Mac spent believing I'd lied to her—that I didn't care about her. If only she'd turn on her dang phone and read the messages I'd sent, then she'd know differently.

I sighed and set my phone in the cup holder of my patrol car, shifting into drive to merge back onto the freeway with a heavy heart.

"Code thirty-four," dispatch radioed. "Black SUV off right at westbound sixty to northbound 101."

Great. Stranded on a blind curve—the worst possible place for a vehicle to break down. Since I was in the green and only a few miles away, I answered the call. "Eighteen-fifty-six. I'll be ten-nineteen from mile post one-eighty-one."

"Ten-four. Eighteen-fifty-six . . . ten-nineteen from mile post one-eighty-one," dispatch confirmed.

My phone rang. I glanced down to see Mom's name pop up on my screen. I was still about three miles out, so I decided to answer. "Hey, Mom. What's up?"

"I have the most wonderful news! MGA just called. They have a nurse for Hunter!" The happiness in her voice was unmistakable. It had been years since Mom and Dad had had a break from Hunters's routine of around the clock care—let alone the stress of wondering if they'd even be able to continue when Dad broke his collarbone. Now, they had a ray of hope to keep going, despite their aging bodies.

"What? That's amazing! When can they start?" I braced myself for disappointment, just in case it would be another month or something ridiculous like that.

"Friday!"

"Really?" I grinned, the weight of responsibility that once felt as endless as time itself slowly lifted from my shoulders. There was finally a light at the end of the tunnel. In just three more days, I would be in California with Mac.

"Yes! It feels like a miracle, doesn't it?"

"Definitely an answer to our prayers," I agreed. The black SUV was just ahead. I switched on my lights and pulled over into the right shoulder, slowing to a stop behind the broken down vehicle. "Listen, Mom. I just got to a call. I'll see you in a couple hours, okay?"

"Okay, bye!"

I got out of my patrol car with a smile, feeling like I was on top of the world. Everything was falling into place. Soon Mac would be in my arms, and before I knew it, I'd be back in my own home again, living my best life with my favorite person at my side—that is, *if* she'd have me.

Cars whizzed past as I walked toward the middle-aged woman standing beside her Escalade. She moved to meet me. I quickly threw up my hands, signaling her to stay where she was. "It's not safe here. Let me come to you!" I yelled over the hum of the freeway.

The screech of skidding tires suddenly pierced the air behind me, and the woman's eyes widened in alarm, my fate inexplicably tied to the warning that I'd given. Fear gripped my chest as my feet lifted from the ground against my will; my lungs gasped for breath. Within the blink of an eye, my helpless body connected with the asphalt, rolling and scraping to a bruising stop. Pain seared through my whole body, my vision growing hazier by the second. I reached for the talk button on my radio, knowing I needed immediate help, but as I fought to form the words, darkness took over, plunging my mind into oblivion.

31

MACKENZIE

I grabbed a shopping cart and pushed it through the grocery store entrance, a peaceful sort of smile resting on my face. It felt good to finally have a plan for my future—to feel like I finally had a purpose for living—using music to heal and comfort those that were suffering.

The debate of "should I stay or should I go" had been resolved as soon as I discovered ASU had a music therapy program. Going back to Mesa made more sense than starting over somewhere new. I had a decent paying job to support me and family just minutes away. Why wouldn't I go back?

Yes, Tanner was there, but as long as I found a place to live far enough away from my old neighborhood, I'd be just fine. Tanner was one of four million people living in the Phoenix Valley. The chance that I'd actually run into the guy was slim to none. I could live with those odds. It's not like I'd had any awkward encounters with any of my other ex-boyfriends.

I pushed my cart to the back of the store, then weaved through the aisles, grabbing the ingredients I needed to make Dad's favorite food for dinner. When I turned down the baking aisle, I noticed a pregnant woman bending down to grab a box of cake mix off one of the lower shelves. There was an adorable little boy sitting in the cart beside her, trying to finagle his way out of the lap belt to get to the cup of frosting in the bottom of the basket, just out of his reach. The woman stood, turned to her son, and chuckled, shaking her head. "No, no, Declan. The frosting is for daddy's birthday cake, remember?"

Why did her voice seem so familiar? *Strawberry blond hair.* Nervous energy pulsed through my body. *No, no, no. Please. Don't be her.*

My hands started shaking. I gripped the handle of the cart tighter and tried to act natural, sneaking a quick glance at her face as I passed by on the left.

Heart-shaped face, upturned nose, freckled cheeks. My worst fear had been confirmed.

The happy and radiant pregnant woman was *Thea.*

After years of carefully avoiding it, fate had given me the chance to confront my ugly past. But at that moment, all I could think to do was escape. I averted my gaze and kept walking—past the spices, past the powdered sugar, and right past the flour I needed for dinner. Nothing was going to stop me from getting aw—

"Kenzie?"

Crap. I froze, my feet refusing to obey my childish impulse to pretend I didn't hear and flee.

And I was having such a good day . . . well, an optimistic one, at least. *Not anymore.*

I took a deep breath and turned, unsure what to say or even how to feel, hesitantly meeting her gaze. My lips parted to speak, but the words wouldn't come. I'd never prepared myself for this moment because I never thought it would happen. What do you say to the childhood friend that stabbed you in the back and ruined your life?

Her eyes brightened in recognition, her lips curving into a smile far friendlier than I felt comfortable with. "It is you!" She pushed her cart forward a few feet to join me at the end of the aisle.

You need to let it go, a voice inside me instructed. I forced myself to speak, though I couldn't manage a smile as she had. "Hi, Thea."

There. I did it. And I did it without snarling in anger. Or breaking down in tears.

"It's so good to see you! What's it been? Five years?"

She seemed genuinely happy to see me, like the reason for our abrupt parting of ways was non-existent. *Unbelievable.* "Yep. It's been a while." My eyes flicked to the boy in the cart, searching for something else to say to get this awkward conversation over with. "You have a son. That's crazy." I wondered who his dad was, though I'd never ask.

"Yeah, this is Declan." She mussed his dark hair lovingly. "He's two. A handsome little handful, but we love him anyway." She furrowed her brow and asked, "Do you remember Jack Brady?"

Jack Brady . . . Jack Brady. I rested my forearms on the handle of my cart and searched my memory until the name clicked in place. "The super shy guy that got valedictorian?"

Thea nodded, her eyes sparkling. "Yeah. Apparently, he'd had a major crush on me since junior high. Finally got the courage to ask me out when we bumped into each other at Fresno State orientation. We've been married four years now."

Four years?

"Oh. Congratulations." If Thea started dating Jack at orientation, then she must not have dated Clint very long. Was my life drastically altered over a summer fling? *Whatever.* I was better off without the jerk, anyway. "So did you and Clint . . . ?" I let the sentence hang in the air, leaving it open for her own interpretation.

"No." She shook her head, her smile turning sad. "When I realized he lied about you two being broken up, I dumped him. I still feel so awful about that, Kenzie. I never should've let that kiss happen. Losing your friendship over a stupid crush has been my biggest regret. I'm so sorry I hurt you."

So she hadn't forgotten. She carried her guilt just as long as I'd carried my resentment. And what was this about Clint telling her we had broken up? Was it possible she hadn't completely betrayed me like I thought? Yes, dating someone she believed to be my *ex* was breaking the number one rule of friendship, but she hadn't meant to steal him from me. Freaking Clint had lied to us both.

I wish I'd known sooner, but back then I wasn't willing to listen. I'd cut them out of my life, just as I'd cut out Tanner now. Maybe I wasn't in a good place to give love—to truly trust. Not until I learned how to forgive.

Quit running from the pain. Face it and let it go.

"Thank you." I swallowed, tears pricking the back of my eyes without my consent. "I didn't know he lied to you too." I sniffed and wiped the gathering moisture from my eyes with my hands.

Thea dug into a side pocket of her diaper bag and pulled out a tissue, offering it to me, her own eyes glistening with unshed tears.

I accepted it, a smile pulling at the corners of my mouth as she grabbed another tissue and began dabbing her own eyes. Here we were, two sides of the same coin, making the same mistakes with men; ruining friendships. But our lives had turned out so differently. She'd found her knight in shining armor.

So where was mine?

Tanner came to mind before I shook the terrifying thought away. I wouldn't allow myself to be in love with a liar—even if he'd treated me better than any other guy I'd ever dated. Maybe that's why losing him hurt so much worse than my other breakups—because I was so sure he was different from the rest.

Some small part of me had this nagging fear that Aunt Crystal was right—that Tanner had an explanation for what I saw in the video—that I'd thrown away the best relationship I'd ever had for nothing. The footage was taken at a distance. What if I didn't actually see what I thought I saw?

Time to turn my phone back on and face the truth; no matter how painful it is.

"Mama sad?" I looked up. Declan put a hand on his mother's arm, watching her with concern.

Thea sniffled and chuckled, wrapping her arms around her son. "No, sweetie. Mama is very happy."

"No cry." He pulled out of her arms and kissed her rounded belly.

She laughed and leaned down to kiss his cheek. "I love you, Declan."

My heart ached with longing. Oh, how I wanted what Thea had, more than anything. But I was tired of being hurt, pretending not to care when things didn't work out. Maybe Thea could give me some advice about how to snatch up a good man...

When I was ready.

"Do you want to meet for lunch?" I asked suddenly, cringing at the desperation in my voice. Even though I wasn't staying in Tulare much longer, having someone to talk to other than my parents would be nice. "It would be fun to catch up."

Her eyes lit with interest. "I would love that so much."

I smiled, a strange warmth enveloping my chest. It slowly seeped through my oldest and deepest scars, softening a hurt I hadn't believed would ever truly fade. Yet, there I was, feeling happier inside, free from the bitterness that had overshadowed my life for so many years.

Hope sprouted like a seedling, finally getting that patch of sunlight it needed to grow. In that moment, I discovered a secret strength I never knew I had. Strength to face my pain. Strength to let go of the past. Strength to make room for a brighter future.

I WALKED in through the front door and dropped my keys into my purse, heading toward my bedroom.

"Mac? Is that you?" Dad called from the office.

"Yeah, Daddy," I answered, poking my head through the doorway. "How was work?"

He swiveled around in his desk chair to face me, his smile warm and welcoming. "Same old, same old. Where've you been?"

"I had lunch with Thea."

"Really?" His brows nearly lifted to his hairline. He knew how big this was for me. "How'd it go?"

I straightened my purse strap over my shoulder and folded my arms across my chest, my face betraying nothing. Then my lips slowly stretched into a smile. "It was fun," I admitted. After lunch, we had talked for hours about anything and everything, just like old times. Amazing what a little forgiveness can do for a broken relationship.

He pointed in my direction, his expression triumphant. "I knew you two would work things out eventually."

I furrowed my brow and waved his comment away. "You did not."

"Okay, okay. I didn't *know,*" he amended, pushing on his armrests to stand. "But I hoped you would." He crossed the room to stand in front of me, a teasing light in his eye. "Now, on to more important things. I noticed you went shopping. What are we having for dinner tonight?"

I laughed. He would joke about food being more important than friends. I'd been cooking dinner for my parents nearly every day over the last week—my version of saying "thank you" for letting me come home while I sorted things out. It was good to know my efforts were appreciated. "Chicken Alfredo."

He lifted a brow. "So you've stooped to bribery now, have you?"

I bit my lip to stem a smile and shrugged innocently, playing along. "Maybe."

He chuckled, placed a hand on my shoulder, and squeezed. "I'm sure going to miss having you around, Mac."

"I'm not leaving for a few more days," I said, fully aware I'd miss him and Mom every bit as much. "And Arizona's just one state away. It's not like I'm going to live on the moon." Things would be different this time. No more pushing Mom and Dad away.

"Worse than the moon," Dad quipped. "You're going to live on the sun."

"Ha. Very funny." I shook my head and continued down the hall towards my room.

"Oh, Mac?" Dad called after me.

I turned, brows raised. "Yeah?"

"Give Crystal a call. Your mother said she's been trying to get a hold of you all day."

"Okay." Aunt Crystal knew I was going unplugged for a while. If she was calling Mom to try to reach me, it must be important.

I hurried to my room and shut the door, setting my purse on the dresser before digging my phone out of the bottom of my suitcase. Time to rejoin the digital land of the living and face the consequences of my negligence. Within seconds of powering it on, alert after alert chimed and flashed across the screen. Nine voice mails and thirty-seven texts. Almost all of them from Tanner. The man didn't give up easily.

As if on autopilot, I opened up Tanner's text chat and began reading, the call to Aunt Crystal no longer at the forefront of my mind.

TANNY

Are you okay?

What happened?

Are you coming back?

Please, Mac. Call me.

Seriously, Mac. You're scaring me. Are you okay? Please answer.

If he didn't actually care about me, why was he so intent on keeping up the act? There were several more similar messages of concern rolling by as I scrolled down the chat. Near the end of the string of texts, something changed.

TANNY

Your aunt told me why you left. I swear to you I didn't kiss Annie. She's my cousin. I would never cheat on you.

His cousin? The smallest glimmer of happiness sparked within me, fighting to overthrow the ugly doubts competing for dominance in my mind. Could it really be just a huge misunderstanding?

If it is, then I'm the biggest idiot who ever lived.

I groaned and flopped face down into my pillow, trying to stifle the fiery rush of shame that seemed to singe through my soul without mercy. Was it true? You'd think everything I had come to know and love about Tanner would be all the proof I needed. But it wasn't easy to ignore what my eyes had seen.

If the redheaded woman was Tanner's cousin, then why did they look so . . . friendly? None of my cousins ever hugged me like that. Then again, I didn't know my extended family well—besides the twins. I guess I could imagine Justin hugging me that way. *Maybe.*

I wanted to trust him—to believe him innocent. I just didn't know if I could.

I rolled over onto my back, picked up my phone, and read through the last remaining texts, the sweetness of Tanner's words steadying my troubled thoughts.

> TANNY
>
> Please, come back.
>
> I miss you.
>
> You're the best thing that's ever happened to me. I don't want to lose you.
>
> I'm not giving up.

Fuzzy warmth spread through my chest, thawing the ice walls I had allowed to encase what was left of my wounded heart. I think I believed him. I needed to hear the sound of his voice, to hear the truth in his words. My thumb hovered over the first voice mail.

Wait.

Aunt Crystal wanted to speak to me about something important.

I quickly pulled up her name in my contacts list and hit call, knowing Tanner's voice messages would still be there when I was done.

Aunt Crystal answered on the fourth ring. "Kenzie?"

"Hey—"

"Oh, thank goodness you called!" she said, an unnerving urgency in her voice. "Tanner's in the hospital!"

I sat up, the shock of her words crashing over me like an angry wave on the sand.

"Tanner? Is he alright? What happened?" My words tumbled out in a strangled heap, my voice almost unrecognizable.

She paused.

Three seconds. Four seconds. Five . . . I held my breath. Waiting. Willing Aunt Crystal to tell me he was okay.

"He was hit by a car on the freeway."

No, no, no. My throat went dry. This couldn't be happening. It had to be a nightmare. *Wake up!* I squeezed my eyes shut and shook my head, as if it would somehow transport me to an alternate reality, though in my heart I knew it wouldn't. "Please, tell me he's okay."

"Honey . . ." She paused again, the sadness in her voice evident. "He's in pretty bad shape."

Please, God. No! Tears filled my eyes as fear wracked through my body, my hands suddenly shaking. *Don't take him from me.*

"Kenzie?"

What if Tanner didn't make it? I never got to tell him I was sorry. I never got to say that I—

"Kenzie! Are you okay, honey?"

"No." My voice cracked, my breath coming in gasps. "I can't—" I tried to swallow back a shuddering sob. This was so unfair! Why? Why did it have to be Tanner? *I* messed everything up. Why couldn't it be me who had to suffer this way?

I had to go back. Tonight. I didn't care how late into the night I would have to drive.

I finally got my emotions under control enough to say, "I'm coming home."

32

TANNER

Annie squeezed my hand—the one not all bandaged up. "I know you're upset you're stuck in this hospital bed, but maybe try being happy you're alive, okay? Your broken bones will heal eventually, then you can go after your flaky girlfriend."

I closed my eyes and inhaled—slowly—my cracked ribs and collapsed lung made breathing pretty miserable. How could I be happy? Every day in this bed was another day Mac believed the worst about me. And I was utterly helpless to fix it. All my plans to go to California and convince her of the truth were snatched away the moment that car collided with my body, making me about as useful as a paperweight. I didn't want to wait months. I *couldn't*. The week and a half we'd been apart already felt like an eternity. But a man in my condition didn't exactly have a choice—not when I couldn't even stand on my own two feet. "She's not flaky," I rasped, annoyance flaring inside me.

"Then where is she? If she cared, she'd be here."

I didn't respond. There was no use trying to explain things when Annie was so bent on disliking a woman she hadn't even met. And likely never would.

But what if there was a shred of truth to Annie's words? Maybe

Mac didn't care about me as much as I cared for her. It didn't matter how hard I tried, I couldn't force Mac to love me just as Sydney couldn't force me to love her. The worst feeling in the world had to be knowing you weren't worth the risk.

A knock sounded at the door. I let out a groan. Probably another doctor or nurse coming to tell me another thing they found wrong with my body, like an old jalopy at the mechanic's shop.

"Pretend you're asleep," Annie instructed quickly. "I'll make them go away." She dropped my hand and left my side to meet them.

I kept my eyes shut and forced my face to relax when the door opened.

"He's sleeping," Annie said quietly. "Could you come back later?"

"Please, I just need a few minutes," came the hushed reply. "I've been driving all night. I need to know he's okay."

Mac? I held my breath, straining to hear over the sudden pounding of my heart, afraid to hope.

"So you're the heartbreaker," Annie said, her voice edging toward derision.

"I'm guessing you're Annie?" Mac replied—I was sure of it now, though I didn't dare open my eyes, for fear she'd turn out to be a figment of my imagination. I mean, I was on a cocktail of drugs for the pain . . . so yeah, it was possible I was losing my sense of reality. But at this point, an imaginary Mac was better than no Mac at all.

"Yep."

"Nice to meet you. I'm—"

"Tanner's girlfriend," Annie stated, cutting her off with that sharp tongue of hers.

This exchange had to be real; unless I'd imagined Annie, too—which would be pretty impressive—considering she'd been here for over an hour talking my ear off. *Please be real.*

There was a moment of hesitation before Mac said, "Yeah. Can I come in?"

Annie didn't answer right away, probably glaring daggers at her while deciding whether or not to let her in. "Go ahead. I was leaving anyway."

Thank you, Annie.

The door clicked closed, and I held perfectly still, staring at the back of my eyelids, concentrating on my breathing. It wasn't easy lying in bed, emotionless, waiting for proof that I wasn't completely out of my mind. What if I opened my eyes and found it was just the nurse coming to check my blood pressure?

I couldn't think of a more depressing thought.

Footsteps drew nearer. I waited for Mac to speak, my insides twisting in knots at the thought of her actually being here with me. She sat in the chair beside my bed, then her soft warm hand slid down my arm, distracting me from the pain of my bruised and beaten body, sending a shock of electricity rippling through me—not unlike her little pink taser when we first met, only this was infinitely better.

Definitely not the nurse.

"I'm so sorry," she whispered, taking her hand away. I missed her touch instantly but said nothing. "I came as soon as I could." Her voice wavered as she continued. "I should've been here for you. I was so stupid. If it weren't for that dang video . . ." She sighed, sounding about as exhausted as I felt. "I never should've doubted you. And now this." She sniffed as if her eyes were suddenly filled with tears. "I can't believe I almost lost you."

I wanted to reach out, to open my eyes and comfort her in what little way I could in my current state. But I held back, letting her share what was in her heart without fear of judgment. Part of me needed a little reassurance from her as well. A week and a half of silence wasn't something I could ignore and pretend never happened. It hurt that she hadn't trusted me or at least tried communicating. Would she run away every time things got hard? I wanted to believe she wouldn't.

"I suppose now I truly understand why Emily gave you up."

Oh no. Maybe this wasn't such a good idea. My jaw clenched with anxiety. I didn't think I wanted to hear the rest.

"She was afraid to commit because she knew that someday she might lose you." A small sob escaped her lips. "I can't lose you, Tanner."

No! Not again. Mac was supposed to be different—strong enough to accept the risks. *Please, Mac. Have faith in us.*

"I can't," she repeated brokenly, as if she knew the thoughts swirling in my head.

Despair filled my soul, adding to the depth of my physical pain. For all my wanting, I couldn't make her love me any more than I could get out of this bed and walk on broken l—

"I love you."

Wait. She loves me?

"I'm sorry I left you." She exhaled slowly, her breath shuddering, though her voice gained in strength. "I promise I won't make that mistake again."

She's not leaving me. Heat spread through my body like wildfire. Unable to stop my lips from smiling, I opened my eyes. Mac's head was down, her left hand resting next to mine on the bed.

Yeah. This was real.

"Loving you makes me so happy it hurts," she continued, still speaking to her lap, unaware that I'd awoken from my fake nap. "Before I learned the truth, I tried to convince myself that I didn't need you in my life—that I didn't care. All that did was make me more miserable." She wiped her eyes and chuckled. "I didn't even read your messages until yesterday. That's how dang stubborn I am."

"But you read them," I replied, my voice annoyingly dry and scratchy. "That's the important thin—"

"Tanner!" Mac bolted from her chair, one hand instantly holding mine and the other covering her mouth. "I knew it! I knew you were pretending to sleep, you big jerk face!" she said, squeezing my hand.

I grinned and laced my fingers through hers, loving the feel of her hand in mine—it had been way too long. "What gave me away?"

Mac lifted a brow, then uncovered her smiling lips and pointed to the screen hanging up behind my bed. "Your heart monitor." She leaned forward with sparkling eyes and lowered her voice. "Apparently, my touch has an effect on you."

The tips of my ears grew hot. *Guilty as charged.* I started to chuckle, then groaned instead from the sudden stabbing pain in my chest.

"Hey . . ." Mac frowned and reclaimed her seat, covering our entwined hands with her other hand. "How bad is it?"

I exhaled slowly to try to ease the discomfort and regain my ability to deal with the breakthrough pain. "So far? A collapsed lung, a couple cracked ribs, broken collarbone, and fractures in both legs." Mac's jaw dropped. "The good news," I continued, slightly raising my other arm in a sling, my hand wrapped in an ace bandage, "my wrist is only sprained." The scrapes and bruises marring a good portion of my skin weren't even worth mentioning by comparison.

Mac shook her head, her eyes full of compassion. "Are you in a lot of pain?"

"Yeah . . . just about everything hurts. But it's manageable with pain meds."

She gently ran her fingertips over my knuckles, leaned forward, and kissed the back of my hand. "Does this hurt?"

My chest warmed, and for a moment, the aches and pains dulled as I focused on the beautiful woman at my side. *Not anymore.* "Mmm. All better. You seem to have the magic touch," I rasped, giving her the power to heal more than my battered heart. "Come here. My lips could use some of that too."

She chuckled softly, her warm brown eyes fixed on mine as she closed the distance.

Her kiss was slow and hesitant at first, like she was worried about injuring me further. I lifted my good hand and slid my fingers through her hair and behind her neck, grounding her in the moment and urging her closer. She responded, caressing my stubbled jaw and melting into the heat of the kiss. I loved the way she set my skin on fire, numbing the pain of all I'd endured. There wasn't anywhere I'd rather be than here with her—even if it had to be in a hospital with my body broken. Anything was better than living without her. My heart pumped harder, reveling in the joy of feeling whole again, like all was finally right in the world.

An alarm went off, beeping repeatedly from the monitor above us. Mac broke the kiss. "What's that?"

I didn't care. I pulled her back in for more, murmuring, "Just ignore it."

She agreed, returning to my lips with equal fervor. Nothing would stop me from drinking in the sweetness of her love.

A minute later, the door swung open and fast moving footsteps pattered into the room. "Oh," a feminine voice said.

Mac and I broke apart and faced the blushing nurse hovering a few feet away from my bed.

"Your heart rate was spiking . . ." She stepped forward to silence the alarm on the monitor above. "I'll just bump up the parameters a tiny bit for you." After pushing a few buttons on the screen, she cleared her throat and turned to leave, saying over her shoulder, "Carry on."

Mac bit her lip, holding back her rolling laughter until the door clicked shut. "Told you my touch has an effect on you," she teased, her perfect smiling lips drawing me back in.

I'd never get enough of this woman. Never. "I'd be worried if it didn't. I love you, Mac."

"I know," she said, leaning in, her mouth a mere breath away from mine.

She believed me. "Oh yeah?" My eyes flicked between her sparkling eyes and her devilish smile. "How do you know?"

She rested her palm on my cheek, tracing her thumb back and forth across my lower lip. "You mean, besides the half a dozen times you told me in those voicemails?"

Oh yeah. I'd forgotten about those embarrassingly sappy messages I'd left when she wouldn't answer my calls or texts. Was it getting warmer in here? "Finally got around to listening to those, did you?"

"I did." She kissed my cheek and whispered, "I may have played them a few times on the drive over." Her lips slowly trailed along my jaw from my ear to my chin.

A thrilling shiver rushed through me. Maybe I should make a habit of pouring out my heart to this woman. She seemed to like it. A lot. Finally her lips found mine once again, every kiss a promise of love—from now until forever.

33

MACKENZIE

I backed my Ranger into the Hansens' driveway next to Tanner's Silverado, then circled around to drop my tailgate before heading to the front door. Tanner stepped outside and wrapped me in his arms as I reached the welcome mat. He stood there, drinking me in, and sighed like he hadn't held me in weeks when it had only been a matter of hours.

"Good morning, beautiful."

I grinned and tipped my head back to claim his soft lips, savoring every moment. It didn't matter how many times we'd kissed over the last four months—he rocked my world every time. I loved that he was finally strong enough to do something as simple as wrap both arms around me without pain or walk to the door to greet me. Words couldn't express how grateful I was that he was well again. "Mmm. Good morning to you too," I said, watching his silvery blue eyes crinkle at the corners. "How's packing going?"

I studied the attractive curve of his mouth as he stepped back and slid his hands down to my wrists, tugging me softly towards the door. "Why don't you come and see?"

I smiled and followed him inside; a glimpse of the Freeman house caught my notice before Tanner closed the door behind us. I was positive I had seen the edge of the curtain swish through the window. Someone had been watching us. A familiar pang of regret dropped to the pit of my stomach, casting a shadow over the joy of the moment.

Sydney still refused to speak to me, though not for lack of trying on my part. She ignored every visit, every text, and every voicemail. I knew from my own experience that healing took time, so I was determined to be patient with her. It may take months or even years, but I wasn't giving up hope.

I turned, facing the living room. Stacks of boxes lined the wall near the music room. "Wow." My eyes widened in surprise. "And here I thought you'd need my help," I teased, bumping into his side playfully.

"What? And let you fold my underwear and thumb through my old yearbook photos?" He shook his head, cracking that crooked smile I loved. "I couldn't do that. Not until you marry me, anyway."

I lifted a brow, my lips forming a smirk. He'd been doing that a lot lately—hinting that I wanted to be his wife. *He's not wrong.* "Oh really?"

"Really." His eyes gleamed with a secret, the kind he was dying to share.

"What?" I asked, fighting a smile.

"Nothing. I just love making you blush."

I bumped into his side again, feeling as giddy as a six-year-old who'd just held hands with her first crush.

"Well hello, Mackenzie!"

I turned to give Tanner's dad a smile. "Hello, Mr. Hansen."

"It's good to see you," he said, setting down a laundry basket of folded clothes next to the boxes. "How's school going?"

I caught Tanner's wink as he squeezed my hand, then disappeared down the hall, leaving me to chat with his dad. "It's great," I said, returning my gaze to Mr. Hansen's friendly gray-blue eyes. "I'm loving all my classes so far." It was the truth. Even music theory was better than I expected it to be.

"That's good." He smiled encouragingly. "We're sure glad you're putting that gift of yours to good use. It's going to bless a lot of lives."

I smiled, my heart warming at his kind words. "Thank you." I looked around and saw my second favorite guy missing from the corner of the room. "Is Hunter still asleep?"

The light in Mr. Hansen's eyes seemed to dim. "Yeah. He had a rough night with pain. Maggie had to get up to calm him a few times."

Oh, sweet boy. "After the move, I'll come play for him for a while."

His friendly smile returned. "Thank you. He'll love that."

"Ready to start loading up?" Tanner reappeared, holding a pillow under one arm and his lanyard of keys in the other. Happiness radiated from his handsome face. How I loved that man. I wanted to wrap my arms around him and never let go.

I nodded and lifted a box from the top of the stack. "Let's get it done."

Just over an hour later, we were driving our truckloads to Tanner's place—which, until recently, had been occupied by Annie and a few others. They had agreed to rent his house for six months while he helped his parents out with Hunter. The timing of everything had turned out perfectly. Mr. Hansen was all healed up, back to lifting Hunter when his nurse had time off. Annie got married last week, and no longer needed a place to stay. And Tanner was back on his feet, ready to live on his own again.

My phone started ringing. I dug it out of my pocket and quickly glanced at the screen. *Thea.* I answered the call, put it on speaker, and then placed the phone in the cup holder, all while keeping Tanner's blue Silverado in my sights. "Hey, Thea! How's it going?" I loved that the distance hadn't kept us from checking up on each other every few days, like old friends do.

"Hey, Kenzie! I'm sooooo tired. Rosie was up all night again, crying her little face off like there's no tomorrow."

"That must be so hard." I had absolutely zero experience pacing the floors at night with an inconsolable little one, but I could imagine it gave her that tired in the bones, foggy brain feeling. "How are you holding up?"

"Declan was such an easy baby. I don't know why Rose is so

unhappy," she lamented. "Ugh. Colic really sucks. But I'm surviving. I just feel so bad that I can't do anything to help her, you know?"

If it was anything like watching Tanner cry out in pain when he first started physical therapy, I could relate. *Not fun.* "I'm sorry you guys are having such a rough time. Just two more months until Thanksgiving, then I can come cuddle your sweet baby while you take a nap."

"You're the best. Hey! When's Tanner going to pop the question? Didn't you guys look at rings the other day?"

"Yeah," I confirmed, chuckling. "I'm not expecting anything for a while, though. He just barely went back to work this week, so he needs a little time to save up."

"Okay, girl. Keep me posted!"

"I will," I promised.

"Alright. I've got to go take Declan to preschool. I'll talk to you later!"

"Sounds good. Bye!"

I ended the call and followed Tanner down a quiet residential street with irrigated lawns and mature shade trees. I let off the gas and soaked up the peaceful feel of the neighborhood as if it were tucked away in the mountains—not in the bustling City of Tempe. He'd never told me how close his house was to ASU. When we finally got married, my drive to school would be down to ten minutes. I could get used to that.

Tanner pulled into the driveway of an old red brick house with a tire swing hanging from a big cottonwood tree in the front yard. I smiled and rolled in behind him. It was so homey and quaint. I could see us starting a family here someday. *Don't get ahead of yourself. Marriage first. Graduate second. Babies third.*

Tanner walked over as I stepped out of my truck. "What do you think?" His expression said it all. His searching eyes, the hesitant lift of his brows. He wanted my approval.

I snaked my arms around his neck and smiled up at him. "I love it."

"Good." He slid his arms around my waist and leaned in for a kiss, my heart instantly fluttering, my knees growing weak. He tightened his hold on me, lifting me off the ground just enough to spin us around.

I laughed and kissed him again as my feet touched the ground. "I love you," I said when we broke apart. The feeling grew a little stronger each and every day.

"I love you too." He smiled and gestured toward the house with a tip of his head. "Come on. I'll give you a tour before we unload."

I squeezed his hand and followed him through the garage entrance. He opened the interior door and pulled me over the threshold into the dark house.

"Wait here while I turn on the lights." He kissed my hand, then disappeared somewhere into the house.

It was odd that he had to go so far to find a light switch.

A few seconds later, a soft glow of light poured down the hall, illuminating a trail of rose petals on the tiled floor. My breath caught. Was he proposing? *But he didn't have the ring yet, right?* Now I wasn't so sure. My heart started beating fast, my body buzzing with anticipation. I commanded my feet to move, following the path of flowers to—

Tanner.

He stood in the center of the room, surrounded by petals and tea lights, his guitar in his hands, waiting for me to find him. I grinned and covered my mouth, my feet slowing to a stop two arm lengths away as he began strumming a song. After a few measures, he sang:

> *It started one night when you called for a ride.*
> *Your fight and spark burned like hope in the dark.*
> *You said that you needed space and kept us apart.*
> *It took time to find a will to trust in your heart.*
> *Your kindness meant more than the world.*
> *I couldn't believe the feelings inside.*
>
> *Oh, carry me away to my greatest dream;*
> *Two hands to hold and a love that grows;*

Deeper than all the hurt and pain.
I'll never lose my future again.
Because I have faith in us.

I tried to follow that light in your eyes.
It wasn't the end when you pushed me away.
My head and my heart were all yours from the start.
I couldn't stop missing you each time we were apart.
Your kindness meant more than the world.
Our love is destined to last, you'll see.

Oh, carry me away to my greatest dream;
I got two hands to hold and a love that grows;
Deeper than all the hurt and pain.
Our future is here to stay.
Because I have faith in us.
I have faith in us.

When the music stopped, I wiped away the tears running down my cheeks, my heart bursting at the seams with love for this man.

Tanner leaned his guitar against the wall, dug a velvety red box out of his pocket, and got down on one knee. "Mackenzie Elise Parker, you are the thief of my heart and my best friend." He revealed a gorgeous three stone diamond ring. "I love you more than anything. From the moment we met, you've given me a reason to hope, to laugh, and to love. I can't imagine spending the rest of my life with anyone but you. Will you marry me?"

So many emotions flooded through me at once—joy, relief, amazement, disbelief. I was the luckiest woman in the world.

"Yes!" I cradled his face and leaned down, sealing my promise with one heart stopping kiss. His familiar, mountainy scent enveloped me like a thousand hugs; his warm breath on my cheek, sending a thrill up my back.

I lifted my head and paused to come up for air. He grinned and grabbed my left hand, sliding his ring on my finger. *A perfect fit.*

I laughed and stretched out my hand, admiring the glittering ring and all it stood for. I was *his,* and he was *mine.* Was it really just six months ago when I'd stolen his truck and nearly died from embarrassment? Never in a million years would I have thought I'd end up here with him.

Tanner stood and wrapped his arms around me tightly; our lips met once more, dancing like two souls made to collide.

All my dreams and secret hopes—everything I ever truly wanted had become my reality—only a thousand times better than I ever imagined.

Tanner said I'd stolen his heart when we met, but the truth about that day was, he had stolen mine.

EPILOGUE
TANNER

Orange and pink saturated the sky as we reached the long tables set up on the lush winter lawn. The groomsmen and bridesmaids took the seats beside us while Mac's parents settled in at one end and my parents at the other. The rest of the guests filled in the tables lining the perimeter of the dance floor. Friends old and new, my entire squad, neighbors, aunts and uncles, cousins, my sister Jen and her family, Mac's brother Justin—they all came to support us. My heart was overcome with joy, gratitude, and relief. Things couldn't have been more perfect.

Mac squeezed my hand under the table, then leaned in and whispered, "We did it."

I squeezed back and kissed her on the cheek. She was my everything. Just the sight of her put a stupid grin on my face. "This has been the longest six months of my life. I'm so glad I finally get to refer to you as my smokin' hot wife. How did I get so lucky?"

She grinned and shook her head. "You're ridiculous. And I'm definitely the lucky one."

"That was the most beautiful ceremony," Thea said, drawing Mac's attention away just as a server set a plate of chicken tacos in front of me.

Mmm. I wasted no time digging in. It had been a long day. Amazing. But long.

"Wow." Seth chuckled and tilted his head to speak over Hunter at my side. "This mango salsa makes me want to sing." He took another bite and hummed in appreciation.

Apparently, I wasn't the only one dying to eat. My lips curved up as I finished swallowing my own mouthful of deliciousness. Street tacos may be a bit messy and unusual for a wedding reception, but I had no regrets. "My wife can get you the recipe." The word 'wife' still felt strange on my lips, but I sure liked saying it.

My smokin' hot wife.

Seth lowered his taco, staring back in disbelief. "Don't tell me she made this."

I chuckled while I took a second to straighten Hunter's tie that had gone askew. Even though Seth was my best man, squad mate, and married to my favorite cousin, he had yet to discover how talented Mac was in the kitchen. Married life kept him all sorts of busy. But in a good way. "No, but she would've if she had the time. She bribed the caterer to use her recipe."

"Asking nicely is not a bribe," Mac chimed in from my left.

I turned and watched my beautiful wife lift her glass to her lips, thinking about how lucky I was to have her in my life for the hundredth time that day. "It is if you bring them brownies to sweeten the deal."

Mac's teasing eyes sparkled over her glass. "It's called a thank you gift."

"Oh yeah?" I'd do just about anything for her homemade brownies. *If that's not bribery, I don't know what is.* "Did you give the gift before or after you asked?"

She bit back a smile as she set down her glass. "No comment."

"Hmm . . ." I snatched her hand and pulled it to my lips. "It sounds like you knew exactly what you were doing, Mrs. Hansen."

She shrugged as her mouth stretched into a mischievous grin. "Still not a bribe."

I chuckled and kissed her hand again. "Then what do you call it?"

She leaned in and kissed my jaw before whispering, "Persuasion."

"I love you," I whispered back, before claiming her delicious lips. With every glance and every touch I knew—life with this woman was going to be amazing. She made me so happy.

Seth laughed, cutting through the moment and reminding me yet again how many eyes were watching our every move.

"What's so funny?" Annie asked, pushing her wild red hair out of her face.

Seth kissed her on the cheek and picked up his glass. "I've never seen Tanner blush before. Looks like he didn't need our help finding the right woman after all."

Annie turned her blue eyes on me, her expression light and free from the heaviness that so often weighed her down in the past. "You're right. He did good." Her focus shifted to Mac. "Thank you for making my cousin so happy."

"It helps that he's so easy to please." Mac grinned, finding my gaze, her eyes shining with warmth and love. "He makes me happy too."

Butcher's voice blared through the sound system the second I swallowed my last bite of food. "Ladies and gentleman, can I have your attention, please?" It was weird seeing my squad mate in action as a deejay, but he was surprisingly good at it. "It's time for the happy couple to have their first dance."

I stood and took Mac's hand in mine, leading her towards the makeshift dance floor. Our progress stopped when she paused to speak to Hunter. She touched his shoulder and leaned down to kiss his cheek before whispering, "save me a dance" in his ear. How I loved the way she loved my brother. I couldn't have picked a better wife. She was all I'd ever wanted—more than I'd imagined—and everything I'd needed.

In a few strides, we were standing in the center of the dance floor, the first strains of music filling the air. The sea of smiling faces watching us from the sidelines faded away when Mac slipped her arms around my neck, tipping her head back to meet my gaze as I pulled her close and swayed to the rhythm of our song—the one I'd written for her all those months ago.

Mac had never looked more beautiful, and it had nothing to do with the elegant way she'd styled her hair or the fancy dress hugging her curves in all the right places. It was the way she looked at me, like I'd given her the world. "You're glowing, Mrs. Hansen."

Her lips curved in that devilish way I loved; her brown eyes twinkling with mischief. "You don't look so bad yourself. In fact"—she brushed the corner of my mouth with her tantalizing lips, then met my gaze once more—"I can't seem to take my eyes off you."

"Oh, really?" I grinned and leaned in to whisper. "Careful now. You are flirting with a married man."

"Oh, I'm fully aware." Her laughing eyes and seductive smile drew me toward her lips. "And he's all mine."

Our lips met, and my heart blazed with fire. She had me body and soul. In this woman's arms—in the taste of her kiss—I'd found forever. And I was never letting go.

ACKNOWLEDGMENTS

First and foremost, this book never would have seen the light of day without my husband, Shawn—my best friend and biggest supporter. Thank you for the countless hours spent taking care of our children, reading my chapters, being my sounding board and cheerleader when I got discouraged, and sending me out of state to a writer's conference to chase my dreams. And thank you for being my number one fan, telling everyone about what I've been working on when I was too scared to bring attention to myself.

To my children who have been my hype-team from the start, thank you for your patience while I typed away, living in my fictional world part-time. Someday you will understand the measure of the gift you have given me.

Kiri, thank you for your invaluable feedback and friendship. You've been an excellent critique partner from day one and I'm so proud of what we've accomplished together.

Carisa, your honest impressions of those early drafts were just what I needed to level up my game. Stuart, I really appreciated you taking the time to read my manuscript and keep my male point of view authentic.

To my beta readers, Kaylia, Emily, Jen, Debbie, Sarah, Mary, and Steve, thank you for loving this story and being my cheering section through this publishing journey.

Sam Millburn, thank you for your kind words and encouragement when I needed it most. Knowing that someone in the publishing world enjoyed what I was writing gave me just the spark I needed to get it done.

Isaac Lundgren, thank you for the hours spent on the gorgeous cover you designed for me. Rachel Garber and Sharon Coleman, my fabulous editors, I couldn't have done this without your keen eyes.

And last, but certainly not least, my parents, who instilled in me a love of reading. Mom, thank you for letting me borrow all your books and giving me the courage to take that first leap to write my own. It's been one of the biggest blessings of my life.

RADIO CODES

Confused by all the cop lingo used in the book? Here's a list for your reference.

1856: TANNER'S CALL SIGN

10-4: OKAY

1019: EN ROUTE

CODE 7: MEAL BREAK

1042: PLACE OF RESIDENCE

926: TOW TRUCK

UNIT: TROOPER ON PATROL

CODE 34: DISABLED VEHICLE WITH OCCUPANTS

IN THE GREEN: AVAILABLE

ABOUT THE AUTHOR

Melody J. Williams is a clean romance novel enthusiast, lover of ice cream and the great outdoors. When she's not reading or writing about happily ever afters, you'll find her at the piano composing songs, in the kitchen perfecting recipes, or running around with her supermom cape. Melody resides in Arizona with her husband and five children.

To stay up to date on Melody's latest books, you can follow her on social media.

Made in United States
Troutdale, OR
02/23/2024